The Guns Of Antwerp

NYPD takes Boston

John Monaghan

ISBN: 978-0-578-56413-5

For Maura, the love of my life.

*Human history becomes more and more a race
between education and catastrophe.*

— H. G. Wells

1

They arrived at the edge of the building and peered around the corner. Without turning his head, Jimmy motioned to Frank. "Get Jack on the air." The Chief of Detectives could wait. The entire shift in counter terrorism tactics in New York City could wait. Jimmy knew where all that was headed but he couldn't give up on this; not today. He was sure of what he saw down the block —even though he didn't want to believe it, he was sure.

Frank sighed and pulled his portable radio out from under his suit jacket. They were dressed for headquarters. The meeting with the Chiefs of Intelligence, Counterterrorism, and the Chief of Detectives was scheduled in lower Manhattan in less than an hour. At One Police Plaza. And they were in the ass end of Brooklyn. No way they make it. Frank keyed the mic and spoke: "Sergeant Donohue, on the air?"

From his surveillance perch two blocks down, three flights up; an empty apartment loaded with high-tech gear, Jack answered. "I'm here Frank, what's up?"

"Stand by for the Captain." Frank shook his head and handed the radio to Jimmy.

Without taking his eyes off the mosque at the end of the street, Jimmy took the radio and spoke: "Jack, hold off on breaking it down. Give it another few minutes, here."

Jimmy didn't wait for an answer; he handed the radio back to Frank.

He would not ignore his instincts. Nearly 42 years old and just past his twentieth year with the department, Jimmy was never good at making career-type decisions. And this wouldn't be the first time he was right but not correct. Jimmy Gallagher had a history of sensing trouble on the street where no one else did —but was tone deaf when it came to sensing trouble in his career.

His Organized Crime Terrorist Unit had been set up on this mosque for three days now and whatever was brewing over there was coming to a head right now.

"Get the car." Jimmy turned the corner. Downtown could wait.

Siban knew that if the trust he had just placed in these men were to be betrayed, he would be dead by the end of this day. In fact, if they joined him in his plan, and it were to be found out, they would all be dead within hours.

He had made the proffer. Now he spread his hands out to his cohorts, for their response. The men whispered around the conference table on the ground floor office of the mosque.

Siban patiently brought his hands together, interlocked his fingers, and placed them on the table before him. He had laid out every detail. Made it all very clear. This was to be the dawn of a new era, and Siban would lead it. The war on terror, the war on the west; everything would change now. Today.

The murmurs died down. Siban looked around the table and then stared each man in the eye, one at a time. Each man, in turn, nodded and glanced to the next. They agreed. Siban stood. He signaled to his assistant, who had been standing with his back to the conference room entrance, arms akimbo, watching. The man turned around, opened both of the double doors, and motioned for the three youngsters who had been waiting in the hall to join them.

The three teenagers were clean-shaven. Their hooded sweatshirts were oversized but not bulky. The assembly eyed them closely. No one spoke. There was a single sheet of paper on the table. One man picked it up, perused it one more time, and nodded. He tossed it back onto the table. The gathered Islamic leaders all watched the single sheet waft to a landing on the smooth, sheer table. Then their eyes all came together and, almost in unison, they stood and bowed to the three teens.

Siban circled around from the head of the table and stood before the young men. "You must exercise the utmost of caution as you travel to your destinations." He paused for an acknowledgment from each of their faces. "Come then." He led them out of the conference room and toward the front door of the mosque. Siban opened the entrance door and stepped outside. His assistant blocked the teens and stayed just inside the door with them. Siban said over his shoulder, "I will signal for them."

Frank pulled up in the unmarked car, Jimmy jumped in. He grabbed Frank's radio off the dash. "Jack, any further chatter?"

"Negative, Captain."

"So all attendees are present at this meeting?"

"It would seem so, sir."

Though this particular mosque was not exactly a hotbed of terrorism, the way its leaders went about setting up today's meeting —messengers, hand written notes, no cell phones, etc. —Jimmy knew they were hiding something.

And these community leaders (storeowners, youth soccer coaches, teachers of Islam and the like) had invited terrorist supporters to attend —not actual terrorists, but supporters. Mostly financial supporters; but still. It bothered Jimmy that these ordinary, every-day Muslims would get involved with terror supporters at all. And where were the heavy hitters? —the zealots?

Jimmy knew the Imam of this mosque. He and Siban had crossed paths a few years back during the Queen Mary incident. It did seem that, especially since being installed as Imam, Siban had distanced himself from the extremists in his midst.

But then Jack and the IT division in OCTU intercepted one errant communication. The attendees at this meeting were on high alert. They were nervous about whatever it was they were doing in there. Siban was heard saying it was a matter of extreme importance. And now the meeting was about to break —just as the Department was about to pull back on its counterterrorist surveillance efforts.

Frank rolled the unmarked car slowly down the block. The front door of the mosque opened and a man in a long, flowing robe stepped out. "Pull over." Jimmy pointed Frank to a hydrant at the curb. He spoke into the radio again. "Jack, is that Siban coming out?"

"I believe it is Captain." Sergeant Donohue paused. "The meeting might even be over; I see other movement just inside the door."

Jimmy watched as Siban scanned the street, scrutinizing passing pedestrians. After a moment, Siban turned back to the front door of the mosque and nodded to a man standing in the doorway. The man then stepped inside, but pulled the door in with him and opened it wide. Then three clean-shaven teenagers stepped out onto the sidewalk. In oversized hoodies.

"Jack," Jimmy spoke into the radio, "cameras rolling?"

"That's affirmative, Captain."

The three young men crossed the sidewalk and apprehensively did not look at Siban. They stared off into space, like wind-up toys waiting for a push. Siban walked past them one-by-one without looking directly at them, though he appeared to whisper something to each one. Then, all at once, the three youngsters walked off in different directions. Siban turned away and hurried back into the mosque.

Frank put the car in gear. One of the teens wore a blue hoodie and walked in their direction —on the opposite side of the street. Frank made a U-turn. The kid made a right. Jimmy barked orders over the radio for the backup teams to pick up on the other two. Frank rolled along about twenty feet behind the kid in the hoodie and turned to Jimmy.

"How do you want to play it, boss? And please don't say 'Head On;' this kid could have a fucking bomb under his shirt —again."

Jimmy nodded slowly without taking his eyes off the kid. "Okay." He loosed his grip on the door handle. "Let's get him as isolated as we can." Jimmy peered up ahead.

Just before the next corner stood an old stone church. Abandoned. Jimmy pulled on his door handle.

"Let me out here."

Jimmy pointed up the block. "Pull into that church driveway ahead of him. Leave the car across the sidewalk and bail out. I'll grab him from behind; you come at him from the front."

Frank stopped the car. Jimmy opened the door. He looked right at Frank." We'll let instinct take us from there." He got out.

Jimmy didn't draw his gun. He walked behind the mark and waited for Frank to obstruct the sidewalk. Once the radio car was in his way and the kid stopped to change direction, Jimmy slipped his hands under the kid's elbows. He forced the teen's arms up over his head. He locked his own hands together on the back of the kids' head, holding the teen's arms away from his body.

Frank rushed up and gingerly lifted the kid's sweatshirt. Suddenly, hundreds of pieces of paper fluttered out from the kid's body. Frank flinched. Jimmy held tight. Flyers. The kid had nothing under his shirt but a stack of flyers.

Frank patted him down anyway, just to be sure. Jimmy loosened his grip.

"Please?" the young man quivered. "What have I done?" He was worried, and very sincere.

Jimmy frowned. "Sorry, kid." He picked up one of the flyers and read it. "But what's with all the secrecy?" Jimmy finished reading the flyer. It called for a last-minute rally to be held tomorrow morning outside the United Nations Building on First Avenue in Manhattan. "Why are you guys hiding all this?"

The kid answered; "It is not you from whom we hide, sir."

2

The Manhattan skyline shimmered in the pale blue façade of the United Nations. Below, on First Avenue, an uneasy murmur rumbled through the crowd as it anticipated its next speaker. Across the street, Zafir stood on a park bench to command a better view. He watched his fellow Muslims huddle toward the makeshift stage on the opposite sidewalk. He wondered which of them would receive the bullet he was about to have delivered.

It mattered not to Zafir who would die this morning; it was the show of force and determination that mattered. He was here to win minds; he cared not about bodies.

From his perch, Zafir watched a calm, professional chaos send the microphone from unsure hand to unsure hand —each high-minded idiot working up the nerve to be the face of this movement. Little did they know that whomever they chose as the next speaker would soon breathe his last.

Zafir climbed down off the bench and filtered his way in from the back of the crowd. Some people recognized him and stepped back as he passed. Others smiled at his presence and nodded, unsure. He remained stoic and continued toward the stage. As he neared the far sidewalk, the crowd grew thick. He approached the barricades and two uniformed policemen glanced at him. Zafir nodded politely. He had no reason to fear them. He was unarmed. From behind his dark sunglasses, Zafir scanned the crowd without turning his head. He smiled at that tactic. Wearing sunglasses to scan a crowd with one's point of interest obscured —he'd gleaned that from the U.S. Secret Service. —They were never without their dark glasses on such assignments.

He found his mark. Malik noticed him and ran his fingers through his hair, signaling his readiness. Zafir glanced down at Malik's waist and saw that the gun he'd given to Malik this morning created no bulge. He thought of the specific weapon secreted beneath the shirt of Malik and frowned. He was short on guns. Whether it be the crazed 'stop and frisk' efforts of the NYPD lately or the mistrust that even criminal gun dealers had for Zafir and his fellow Muslims, it had become increasingly difficult for him to procure handguns in New York City. Maybe he should look elsewhere.

Without proper armaments, he was not quite ready to launch his campaign. But this unanticipated event before him forced his hand. He could not allow this nonsense to continue. He had to throw caution to the wind and begin right now. He would find the guns later, somehow.

Amazingly, the intellects made a decision. A speaker took the stage. Zafir shouldered through to the front. Some of the gathering stepped back at the sight of the American Khalifa of Jihad. Zafir smiled and shrugged, to appear ambiguous, but kept his sunglasses in place.

The speaker gained the crowd's attention. Zafir brazenly climbed up onto the improvised stage and joined him. The American correspondent for Al Shorouk, Cairo's daily newspaper, barely noticed Zafir and prattled on into the microphone; "The West will respect us when we take part in civilization and turn away from the murder and hatred of terrorism."

Zafir braced for the moment. He remembered, as a

child, receiving inoculations from doctors who visited their village, on occasion. He remembered the heart-thumping fear as he looked away, waiting for the needle to pierce his skin. The next time that doctor visited, he had decided to look directly at him and at the needle as it impaled him. Less fear. But now, he had to look away. It was part of the plan.

He put his arm around the speaker. Holding the journalist close, Zafir turned to the crowd and waved. The signal. His heart pounded but he didn't cringe. He steeled himself and waited to hear the bullet whiz toward him —but nothing happened. There was no shot.

Without lowering his head, he looked down through his sunglasses and found Malik struggling with the mechanism of the gun. Damn it, Zafir thought in an instant. *The garbage that passed for weapons in this city.* Zafir stood firm and prayed Malik would follow through with the final step.

On cue, two uniformed officers of the NYPD burst through the crowd. One yelled, "Gun!" Malik turned and squarely pointed the useless gun at the approaching policeman. The speaker dropped the microphone. Two shots rang out. Malik fell dead. The crowd burst out across the avenue. The leaders of the rally dove back onto the sidewalk and Zafir joined them, appearing also to be a victim of an assassination attempt.

3

From the front passenger seat of the unmarked car, Jimmy could see the crime scene tape fluttering at the end of the block. Forty-Second Street was packed with motorists trying to make U-turns, having been turned away from the crime scene at First Avenue.

After eighteen years in uniform, numerous shootouts, a few sets of disciplinary charges, and a total of over twenty stitches across his face –though Jessica said he still looked good –Jimmy couldn't fathom telling these cops they should've set up on Second Avenue and diverted the traffic from there. Wasn't his bag anymore. Ever since they put him in command of the Organized Crime Terrorist Unit, such uniform concerns just weren't his to deal with it.

He stuffed his half-empty coffee cup into the holder in the dash and pushed open his door. He looked over at Frank and grabbed his forearm. "Partner," –they weren't really partners. Jimmy was Frank's Commanding Officer, but that was one of the reasons he'd taken Frank with him into plainclothes. Frank never mistook Jimmy's casual ways as an invitation to disrespect the rank. That, and other reasons.

"Spin it around and go park up on Tudor City Place." Jimmy pointed up to the overpass above them. "Then find the team and meet me in there." He jumped out and slammed the door.

Jimmy made his way toward the crowd. He was disappointed that his team wasn't in place when this shooting occurred –though they were on their way now.

After arriving late for yesterday's meeting at Headquarters, Jimmy was told the Department was changing direction. He knew it was coming; everyone had heard the rumors. Jimmy and the other counterterror and intelligence field commanders were told to conduct less surveillance of certain groups.

But then Jimmy told the Chiefs about the kid and his flyers. Didn't matter. Decision made. The bosses told him to stand down from the advertised rally. "Like we said, less surveillance." Now he really, really hoped at least one of those Chiefs would be here at the crime scene so he could say 'I told you so.' But his career already hung by a thread, so he probably wouldn't. But still.

He waded through the understandably upset motorists and pedestrians who found themselves dead-ended at Forty-Second Street and First Avenue.

Just ahead of him, two suits, obviously from the department, approached the yellow tape. Jimmy recognized them as Internal Affairs. Assistant Chief Burgos and one of his minions. They approached the cops on the line with swagger and arrogance, obviously far removed from any real police work.

Jimmy watched as the two uniforms on the perimeter recognized Chief Burgos, but held their ground. The uniforms played dumb and made the suits pull out their shields and IDs before pulling up the tape to let them through.

Jimmy wore a suit, too. Had to. His position called for 'proper business attire.' But when he approached the tape, the cops' eyes widened and they lifted it up right away.

One of them nodded slowly. "Captain Gallagher, how you doin'." It wasn't a question. Jimmy clapped the uniform on the shoulder and ducked under. "Thanks, pal."

Between the size of the crime scene and the frenzied media response, First Avenue was completely shut down. Jimmy waded in through the crowd of witnesses and uniforms to a vantage point on the outskirts. He needed to find his team but he also wanted to talk to the Shooting Team Leader.

Jimmy stood with his back to the outer crime scene tape. It extended from 42nd Street all the way up to 44th Street and detained at least a thousand people waiting to be questioned. And this was no ordinary shooting. Not only was the UN General Assembly due to begin its annual meetings later this week, but these shots were fired by 'Members of the Service.'

Jimmy stepped away from the outer tape and made his way toward the inner crime scene —a double line of yellow tape encompassing the stage and immediate vicinity of the actual shooting. The familiar smell of gunfire surfed up through his nose and into his mind. A host of memories wafted through. Some good, some not. He breathed deep and expelled them.

Amidst the Chief of Internal Affairs and other top echelons ringing the inner tape, Jimmy spotted the Shooting Team Leader, Captain Joe Rosado, scribbling furiously in a small notepad on the outskirts of the inner perimeter. Normally, the Shooting Team Captain would lead and direct the investigation. But until it was decided by the Chiefs and leaders from Internal Affairs that the shooting was justified, the Shooting Team Captain ended up being just a recording secretary.

"Hey, Joe."

Rosado looked up from his notes. "Jimmy. Hey."

"How's it looking?"

"It's a fucking nightmare, Jimmy. Internal Affairs has the lead, and they won't let the precinct detectives talk to any witnesses, yet. Same shit, different shooting. You know how it goes: once a cop is involved as the shooter, IAB forgets an actual crime occurred. They could give a fuck if it ever gets solved; they're more interested in hanging the cop on the slightest technicality. Politics, you know?"

"Yeah, politics." Jimmy nodded in agreement and they both looked out over the crowd for a moment. "But what do you know so far, Joe? Motive? Anything?"

Rosado dropped his shoulders and tilted his head at Jimmy. He looked defeated. He really wasn't supposed to be discussing the investigation with anyone outside of Internal Affairs just yet. But most cops hated to say no to Jimmy Gallagher.

Rosado glanced over his shoulder at the Chiefs surrounding the immediate crime scene. Then he stepped in closer to Jimmy. "Looks like a lone psycho; Jihadist, maybe. These people were here calling for peace. They're like some new group of moderate Muslims or something; and shithead, here," Rosado motioned to the dead body at the curb, "tried to pop the speaker. Looks like the gun jammed, but our guys say they couldn't have known that, so when they stepped up and shithead pointed his gun at them, our guys let go with two rounds each, center mass, and dropped him."

"Who was the speaker?"

Rosado stepped back from Jimmy. He looked over his shoulder at the Chiefs and then turned back and shook his head. "Sorry, Jim, I gotta go." He walked off.

Jimmy turned back to the crowd and found his team

approaching: Detective Dhakir and Sergeant Donohue. Hatim Dhakir, formerly the department's leading Arabic interpreter, joined Jimmy's unit shortly after the Queen Mary investigation a few years back. Jack Donohue had been with OCTU from the start and Jimmy found him to be the most studious young investigator he'd ever worked with. Plus, he was good with computers. You always need one of those guys.

"Where's Clark?"

"The Lieutenant took his own car, Captain. Said he'd meet us here."

"Alright, Jack, let's not waste any time. Find the precinct detectives and see what they're up to. If I know the 17th Precinct Squad, they're not out here twiddling their thumbs just because IAB has the lead. Find them and see what they got." He patted Sergeant Donohue on the upper arm.

"Hatim," he turned to Detective Dhakir, "circulate. Listen in on the witnesses." Jimmy glanced over at the crowd of Internal Affairs Chiefs and Inspectors at the center of the crime scene. "Don't question anyone outright." He turned back to Dhakir. "Just see what you can hear." Hatim walked off and Jimmy turned to scan the crowd again. Frank approached.

"Saturday Night Special."

Jimmy raised an eyebrow and glanced back at the shooting scene. "Really." He looked back at Ramirez. "How'd you get that?"

"An old friend in Ballistics. You know these IAB guys aren't actually detectives, right? They rely on the real police for every bit of information. They don't know shit but how to prosecute a cop."

Jimmy shook his head from one side to the other,

ambivalent about agreeing with his subordinate. "So, Saturday Night Special. Was he more specific?"

"Yeah." Frank pulled out his notepad. "Raven Arms, 25 caliber. Rickety old piece of shit, probably like twenty years old."

Jimmy nodded. "Okay." He turned back to surveying the crowd of witnesses. He realized they were broken into two distinct groups; one much larger than the other. After a minute or so, Lieutenant Clark made his way through the crowd.

"Hey, Kevin."

"Captain." Clark pulled out his detective-sized notebook. Kevin Clark was one of the few remaining forty-year veterans in the NYPD. A third generation African-American cop, Clark was one of the most respected homicide lieutenants in the entire department. But after working with Jimmy on the Queen Mary incident, he felt he needed a change. Clark left the Homicide Unit and joined Jimmy's OCTU shortly after that caper. Clark glanced down at his notes. "Looks like IAB is approaching the witnesses from two angles: people attending the event…" Clark looked out over the larger of the two crowds, "and the organizers." He motioned over his shoulder at the smaller group, cordoned up onto the sidewalk behind him.

"Captain." Sergeant Donohue hurried in and interrupted. "IAB is not letting the precinct detectives interrogate the witnesses. They-"

Jack stopped talking when he noticed that Jimmy didn't turn to him but, rather, stayed focused on Lieutenant Clark. Jack turned to Clark and was met with the now department-wide famous Kevin Clark deadpan.

The forty-year veteran just stared at Jack with his

notepad held out in front of him, frozen from the moment of interruption. Jack dropped his shoulders and sighed, realizing he may have disrespected his lieutenant. Clark finally spoke: "And you found all that out without using a computer?" Clark turned back to Jimmy. "He's getting better, Captain; there might be hope for him yet."

Jimmy laughed. Just then, he noticed a familiar face in the crowd. Colin Kelly was a man Jimmy knew of, but didn't know personally. But he knew Clark had a connection to him. "Kevin, isn't that Lieutenant Kelly over there, the Commander of the 17th Detective Squad?" Clark turned to look. "Sure is."

Clark stared at Lieutenant Kelly and waited for eye contact. Like every cop in a crowd, Kelly's eyes would eventually land on everyone in his vicinity. Kevin waited. Kelly finally noticed him. Kevin smiled and beckoned him over with a tilt of the head.

"Hey, Kevin."

"Colin, how've you been? How's the family?" Clark said out loud. After the handshake, Kevin pulled Kelly in a little closer. "Colin, this is Jimmy Gallagher, my Captain in OCTU."

"Oh, no fooling." Kelly stuck out his hand. "Pleasure to meet you Captain. I've heard a lot about you; great to finally meet you, sir."

"Good to meet to you, too, Lou." They shook hands.

"So." Jimmy got right down to business. "What do you think we have here?"

Kelly sighed. "We'll see. I'm on the sidelines until they tell me otherwise; you know how this goes."

Jimmy squinted. "But what do you hear so far? Was this guy just a lone psycho, or was he part of something organized? Where'd he get the gun? All that?"

Lieutenant Kelly didn't smile. He was one of those experienced middle managers who dealt with pressure every day, but never felt the pressure. "Those are my questions exactly, Captain, and I'll ask them when I get the chance." Colin Kelly glanced over Jimmy's shoulder at the group of Internal Investigators surrounding the crime scene.

"Look, Captain, we've all been down this road before. By the time I get to these witnesses, their heads will be spinning from all the questions IAB will have asked. As far as the job is concerned, the shooter is not at large. My criminal investigation takes second place here; you know that."

Jimmy shook his head. A fresh witness was a good witness: getting first shot at them meant everything. "Where's the Chief of Detectives?" he asked Kelly. "Isn't Chief Shea responding to this?"

"He might, but don't hold out any hope, Captain. When Jim Shea first got appointed to the position of Chief of Detectives, he'd tried to step in front of IAB on a cop shooting —and nearly got re-assigned for it." Kelly put his hands in his pockets. "Don't worry, I'll pick up the crumbs when they're done and get as much as I can out of the witnesses. There may not be much left by the time I get to them, but you're welcome to whatever I find, boss." Kelly stuck out his hand. "I'll keep in touch." Kelly went to leave, but Jimmy thought of one more thing. He shook Kelly's hand but didn't let it go.

"Colin, what about the cameras?" Jimmy motioned up to the United Nations building. Kelly laughed. "Captain, you think you're pissed off at IAB? How do you think the feds feel right now? The cameras belong to them. I might get the footage in my office in a week or so, you know?" Kelly shrugged and left.

"That's fucking ridiculous." Jimmy said. "We gotta get started on something, here. What if this guy represents something? What if he's not just some insane suicide gunman?"

Hatim ambled back and reported that the witnesses were keeping quiet; very little small talk, even. And the detectives from Internal Affairs had begun working their way through the two pens, taking down people's names and phone numbers.

The groups were fairly large, but the chaos began to dwindle. Then Jimmy saw another familiar face. He locked his eyes directly on the features and called to his lieutenant without averting his gaze: "Kevin." Jimmy didn't point, but waited for Clark to look at him and then follow his gaze into the crowd. Then Jimmy said, "Isn't that our old friend Siban, right there?"

Clark squinted. "Well, what do you know."

"Hatim." Again, Jimmy didn't avert his gaze from Siban. Detective Dhakir stepped up to Jimmy and eventually followed his eyes to the man in the crowd of organizers. "I need to talk to that man." Jimmy finally looked at Hatim.

"Slip in there; be very cool. Speak to him, tell him to follow you out of that group." Jimmy turned his back to the crowd and looked directly in at Hatim. "He'll remember me from the Queen Mary job. I wasn't too hard on him; I questioned him with respect. Tell him you work for me and that I need to speak to him." Jimmy turned sideways. "Go ahead."

Jimmy watched Hatim enter the dwindling crowd and approach Siban. The detective subtlety greeted his mark like an old friend. Lieutenant Clark then stepped into the arena and started arguing with an IAB Captain about priorities. Cover. Jimmy watched Siban closely.

The Imam seemed wary at first, but after listening to Hatim for a moment, he finally raised his eyes and looked over at Jimmy. Their eyes met across the crowd and Siban nodded slowly. Hatim began to walk off. Siban fell in behind him and together they casually strolled off the sidewalk.

Jimmy led them across First Avenue, occasionally glancing over his shoulder. When he reached the barricade on the West side of the street, Jimmy peeled Hatim away. "Walk him through. Say you're from IAB if you have to, but just get him out of here. I'll meet you up on top, by Forty-Third Street." Jimmy turned back to the chaos.

4

Zafir opted for the windbreaker and dropped the heavier jacket on the bed. Realizing he would need to spend the night in the next city, he stuffed a pair of clean socks into the pocket. But he would return shortly. Hopefully fulfilled.

He picked up the two baseball hats Nagreb had laid out for him and examined them. One had a New York symbol on it; the other, Boston. Both baseball. He smiled at his own genius. When the speakers back at the UN had dived for cover from the police bullets that killed Malik, he joined them. As expected, the police had turned their backs to the group of moderate leaders and prowled the crowd for other possible assassins.

When Zafir had gotten to his feet and helped up the man next to him, the man embraced Zafir in gratitude and began to speak. Zafir had not listened to the man's words but stared into his eyes, trying to remember where he had seen this European before. Zafir never forgot a face.

The man prattled on and Zafir remembered. This was The Irishman from Boston —a loud and demonstrative supporter of this newly-formed MMOA —Moderate Muslims Of America. Zafir had heard The Irishman speak before, through moderate Islamic media outlets in this country. The Irishman had been going around the Muslim community insisting that peace would come, as it did in his country, from the unity of the moderates over the violence of the radicals.

Zafir had barely restrained himself from ripping the man's tongue from his throat right there on First Avenue.

But of course he had maintained the persona of fellow victim, lest he be connected to the actions of Malik.

Finally, he had zoned in on the words of The Irishman and heard him speak of how their people had worked together for generations through their similar struggles. It set Zafir to remembering how his father, a high-ranking member of the PLO decades ago, had worked closely with the IRA of the nineteen seventies, and of the free flow of weapons between Europe and Boston back in those days. And of the legend of The Guns of Antwerp. And then he knew where he would get his guns.

He had immediately released himself from The Irishman's embrace. He avoided the scuffling police and headed for the subway, trying not to run.

He chose the Boston hat, squared it on his head, and dropped the New York one on the bed. His calls to the homeland were answered promptly and the meeting was set.

He had twenty-four hours to get to his destination. It would be dinner time on Saturday. He glanced at his watch; there was no clock on the wall in the apartment of Nagreb. The living space was established years before Zafir's arrival on these shores. Effective missions were prepared well in advance. Nagreb had maintained residence here for the past two years.

When Zafir arrived a few months ago his first priority was to direct Nagreb to gain employment in a particular neighborhood in lower Manhattan.

Nagreb's apartment was just a short subway ride to the target. The target. It could be years before that mission ever became a reality, if at all. The chances of Zafir actually coming into possession of one of the suitcase-sized nuclear devices that supposedly were planted in various places throughout this country by the Russians years ago were slim. He understood that. But still, teams of patriots scoured the country every weekend with radiation detectors, posing as tourists with cameras. One day, with the help of Allah, they would find one.

But Zafir also knew that if one were to be found, then, for the proper target to be hit, Nagreb would have to be properly positioned in its immediate vicinity. Effective missions were prepared well in advance.

There were a number of employment possibilities that would get Nagreb where Zafir needed him to be. Any manner of service or utility position would have worked. But those jobs, it turned out, were considered to be careers; employment that workers expected to maintain for a professional lifetime. There were unions and civil service protections and such, making these positions highly sought after and, so, difficult to attain. 'Deliveryman' was found to be lower on the chain in this culture; people did not have such employment protections in those positions, and so there was a high turnover. It was easy for Nagreb to find such employment.

At first, Zafir directed him to take up with a dry cleaners on Chambers Street in lower Manhattan. That went well for a month, but the volume of visits to the target was not sufficient. So Zafir watched the target building himself for one month straight. There was a Starbucks coffee shop on the corner that facilitated his effort nicely.

Once his data was collected and a great number of delivery persons had been followed back from the target to their various places of employment, Zafir chose the one with highest volume of visits –the Amish Market on West Broadway.

After just six months, Nagreb became a model employee there and a fixture in and out of the lobby of the target. His presence was welcome by all thereat. Without disclosing the reason for such a specific location, Zafir was even able to direct Nagreb to especially ingratiate himself to the family in a particular apartment. The Zimmermans on the eighteenth floor had come to appreciate Nagreb's work. Nagreb would continue to deliver their groceries for years to come, if need be —even if a nuclear weapon was never found. Such was the patience of the soldiers of Fateh.

Zafir drew a deep breath and prayed that one day he could actually acquire such a spectacular weapon. And then he would reveal to the whole world just how Satanic America has been throughout its history.

Zafir watched as Nagreb leaned from his computer over to the printer. Nagreb retrieved the freshly printed Amtrak ticket and handed it up to Zafir.

"Well done." Zafir examined the ticket. New York to Boston, tomorrow afternoon, one o'clock. Though he hoped to one day find a portable nuclear weapon and fulfill his true mission, today he would settle for starting a ground war in New York City. And now, after this trip, he would have the necessary resources to begin. He folded the ticket into his pocket.

5

Once Detective Dhakir and Siban were out of sight, Jimmy turned away from the pens of witnesses on First Avenue and followed. At the top of the stairs, Forty-Third Street ended at Tudor City Place and became a small, pocket-sized park. Jimmy found them sitting on a park bench. As Jimmy approached, Dhakir strolled off to the edge of the park and casually leaned against a tree. Jimmy sat down on the bench next to Siban.

"We meet again." Jimmy smiled.

Siban nodded. "We do, Captain; and again, under terrible circumstances."

Jimmy raised an eyebrow. "The kid with the gun, the dead guy —he's a friend of yours?"

Siban shook his head. "Captain, there is much more at stake here today than the death of some poor manipulated youth. This was to be the beginning of a worldwide movement toward peace. Peace and acceptance. Principles held dear by both the religions of your Western culture and of the Islamic world." Siban hesitated. He looked Jimmy up and down. "Regardless of what you might think, Islam is not the religion of hatred and war."

Jimmy nodded. He needed to cajole this witness, but felt the need to make a point. "No argument here, Siban. It's just, well, some of the verses I've heard from your Koran lend themselves to some pretty violent interpretations."

Siban clenched his jaw. "Have you not read your Judeo-Christian Bible?" He turned sideways on the bench, facing Jimmy directly. "There is more violence and immorality in your Bible than in any text I have ever studied. Brother killing brother, women raping their fathers." He looked away in disgust. "Examine your own house before you condemn mine, Captain."

Siban looked out over the finely-trimmed park and continued. "It is ignorance and deprivation that must be overcome. That is what leads to the misguided, literal following of religious texts —no matter the source." He looked at Jimmy. "It has taken generations in your culture, I know. And we must begin now, in ours. We had hoped that today would be a start." He looked back over his shoulder at the UN Building. "But now I am not as confident."

Siban's cellphone rang. He didn't remove it from his belt, but twisted it upward to read the caller ID. He dropped his shoulders and tilted his head. He looked up at Jimmy as he pulled the phone out of its holder. "I am sorry." He held up the phone. "I must take this." He pushed the green button and brought the phone to his ear,

"Yes, Aamira." He listened. "Yes, I heard of that. I don't know that I would call it an attack, but–" He paused. "No, no, you're right, I don't mean to belittle the complaint made by the girls. Those three boys need to learn respect for women. You are right. I will counsel them. Arrange a meeting with all three at my office sometime later this week." He smiled kindly into the park. "Okay, Aamira, very well. I must go now. Goodbye."

He put the phone away and glanced back toward the UN. Then he turned to Jimmy and shook his head.

Jimmy said, "Look, maybe I can help."

Siban shot a quick glance at him and then looked away with a smirk.

Jimmy wasn't put off. "One thing you can believe, Siban, is that I do want to help."

Siban looked back at him. Jimmy continued, "You know you can believe that. I'm not promising anything, but you can trust me."

Siban blinked slowly and said, "That young boy with the gun today was no one of consequence. His kind is for you to concern yourself with, but, as an individual, his identity is meaningless. His leader…" he looked squarely at Jimmy, "…that is who you must find."

"Who is he?"

Siban turned away and again surveyed the park. He shook his head and said, "There are legions of young men like this one today. They are willing to follow a strong leader. They are malleable. I counsel them myself as their Imam – as you just heard." He motioned to his phone. "But it is difficult to align the tenets of religion in the modern culture. I am constantly settling disputes: sexual, financial. I conduct counseling with these young men on a regular basis, but it is not easy. We must reach them –before he does."

"Who?" Jimmy asked again.

Siban finally turned back to Jimmy. "His name is Zafir. He was here today. He is Khalifa –leader of jihad. He stood on the podium as the speaker was to be shot. He is not just a danger to you; he is a danger to us –we who would turn these young men away from the violent answer of jihad that he supplies. You must stop him, Captain. His plan is most devastating. He is low-minded, but intelligent, at the same time. He wants blood to run through the streets of New York as it did once in Beirut. He wants Americans to feel the pain they have caused around the world, and to feel it at home. He will stop at nothing."

Siban dropped his gaze to the ground, but continued. "He approached and lobbied us, the Muslim support network in New York, to help him acquire many firearms. He has an army of young, impressionable men; but he needs to supply them with guns. If he can do this, it would be a great show of strength and ability, and they will follow him. You will have a war on your hands like you have never seen before in this city. We rebuffed him but his vision was a turning point for us. We are Americans now, too. We don't want this city turned into a war zone any more than you do. We finally decided to speak the truth of what we see as the solution —peace." Siban glanced again, back at the U.N. Building. "And you see the results of that."

Siban stood up. "You must stop him, Captain. He will get the funding from his people overseas. And he will buy guns; many guns."

"Who will fund it? Where will he get the guns?" Jimmy stood with Siban.

"I have said too much." Siban looked down at the ground. "I don't know from whom, exactly, but he will get the funding. He is well known and respected in the circles of jihad in Pakistan and Jordan. His father was a Libyan; a high-ranking member of the PLO a generation ago. Zafir will get the funding, and then he will get the guns. You need to stop him, Captain."

6

Father O'Leary needed to prioritize. The lesser of his two tasks had to be done first. And the real priority had to remain secret. So he would perform the first task with all the grace and patience expected of a Jesuit priest.

He strolled along the winding footpath and enjoyed a bright New England morning. Luckily, both assignments would take place in the same building, Gasson Hall, so he needn't hurry. A few early-autumn leaves fluttered around him as he wound through the still mostly green oak and birch trees, perfectly placed along the pathways of the sprawling Boston College campus.

Father O'Leary followed the path around the library and Gasson Hall came into view.

He had turned that corner a thousand times, but the spectacle of the Cathedral still gave him pause.

One of the most renowned Gothic structures in all of Boston, the great Gasson Hall was less a construct of man than a bulwark of the earth itself; the foundation was not man-made but rather was the base of the quarry from which the building's stones were cut.

The first building erected on the Chestnut Hill campus at the turn of the century, Gasson Hall stood today as a monument to what the Jesuit priesthood had accomplished in America. *And not just how we brought about the evolution of the underclass,* he mused, *but how it all led to the defeat of terrorism.*

The first meeting would be in five minutes, so he continued walking. And continued thinking. Gazing up at the spires that towered closer with each step, he pondered how the American dream was not a mirage; but neither did it deliver to post-civil war Catholics what they were led to believe it would.

Hard work, maintenance of the nuclear family, and self-discipline were not actually enough to elevate the immigrant Catholics of the time. Despite those efforts, they were still seen as a permeating horde clinging to a barbaric religion.

But the Jesuits of 1800s America understood what was necessary. They knew what it would take for Catholics to assimilate into the new world and yet maintain their faith: education.

By the 1860s, poverty, ignorance, and hatred ran rampant throughout the Boston-Irish immigrant community, but the Jesuits set about changing that.

For half a century they remained dedicated to educating and enlightening the Irish Catholics in Boston, and guided them through bigotry, civil unrest, and war. But it was not an easy task. It took nearly a lifetime just to obtain a charter for their new school from the staunchly anti-Catholic Massachusetts State Legislature of the day. And when it came time to build their institutions, permits and other necessary resources were surreptitiously denied and the struggles continued. But the Jesuits persevered —and eventually prevailed. And the result was Boston College. And the monument to all that was Gasson Hall.

Father O'Leary stepped through the doors of Gasson and ambled across the inspiring rotunda. The circular granite walls swept fifty feet up around him as he passed the white marble statue of Michael the Archangel, posed in violent defeat of Satan.

A small group of administrators awaited him outside Room 101. They appeared anxious. The coach of the

Division One women's track and field team frowned. "They're not here." She put her hands on her hips. "I spoke to their coach: they're coming, but they're going to be late." She pushed her hands off her hips. "Morning practice ran late." She turned on her heel and pushed past the others and into the office.

Father O'Leary frowned and shook his head. An allegation of possible sexual abuse had been lodged against members of the Boston College Division One football team. Nationally ranked again this year. The aggrieved ladies from the track team weren't letting it go. A counseling session was called. The religious leader nodded to the remaining women outside the counseling office. "So be it." He clasped his hands in front of his waist. "I'll deal with them when they arrive." He glanced around the lobby and then turned back to the group of women. "I'll go for a short walk and return presently." He bowed and stepped away.

The priest retrieved a small ring of keys from his pocket and continued to a back corner of the Rotunda. He turned down a hallway just inside the rear entrance of the building and, after a short walk, began his descent of the basement stairs. *This works out just fine,* he thought. *I can take care of this business first and return to my pastoral duties after.* Priorities.

He held the railing as he descended the granite steps. He didn't worry about falling but knew he couldn't afford to, at this age. He had broken his leg once as a young man and had recovered quickly, but at seventy-two, he knew it would never be same if he fell now.

He jangled the keys and thought of his heritage as an Irish Jesuit in Boston. Though the ignorance of the nineteenth century had been overcome, by the end of the twentieth century, terrorism had taken its place. Peace didn't seem possible until the cease-fire of 1998 —but the IRA would still not lay down their arms. Then Omagh happened.

Though the IRA was not completely disbanded, their tactics of violence and terrorism had finally been renounced by their own community. The very people whose freedom they claimed to fight for had had enough. Extremism, unsupported, had died.

Father O'Leary had forgiven his brethren their violence, but like absolution after confession, secrets of the penitents still had to be preserved.

For generations, the Irish in Boston —cops and criminals, priests and terrorists —all were committed to one another's subsistence. And from the very beginning, they were in conflict. But no moral divergence ever pierced the powerful bond of mutual survival.

Father O'Leary reached the bottom of the stairs and looked again at the ring in his hand. He had been handed this particular set of keys by his predecessor some twenty years ago and had sworn an oath that he would maintain the privacy of those at risk of discovery.

Though it was widely known that Boston College was the secure repository for a set of audiotapes that the British Government would literally kill to get their hands on, their exact whereabouts was known only to Father O'Leary. These were the keys he held. Though there was another set, a set he did not possess.

The tapes were recordings of candid interviews of older members of the Irish Republican Army and snippets of undercover recordings made at times of great uncertainty and paranoia. Great Britain was currently suing in the U.S. Supreme Court for release of The Belfast Tapes. And it wasn't just the old terrorists whose identities would be revealed. Some of their supporters and sympathizers from across the generations were now highly-placed world leaders. And many of them were not only indicted on those recordings, but could actually be heard.

The priest arrived at the last door at the end of the basement hall and singled out one of the two keys on his ring.

When construction of Gasson Hall neared completion, the Irish uprising of 1916 in Dublin was already a whispered hope. The Irish were involved in strife both in Boston and back in Ireland, and there was a need at the time to hide certain resources. So when the Irish masons built the cathedral they put in a secret passage that, to this day, is known of by only a handful of trusted servants. And Father O'Leary, literally, held that key.

The priest unlocked the door and entered a musty room. He flipped on the light and found the area just as he had left it. This room was no secret; though it was kept off-limits to unauthorized personnel.

Half the size of a typical classroom, the rough-hewn natural stone walls were covered with large framed portraits of old Jesuits and other Irish patriots. In the center of the room sat a lone desk. The priest walked over to the desk, pulled out the chair, and sat. With the second key on his ring, he unlocked the center desk drawer. Pulling it open he nodded at the sight of four sets of old reel-to-reel audiotapes. He closed and relocked the drawer.

Then he went back to the entrance door, pulled it open, and peered out into the hall. Seeing no one, he stepped back in the room and locked the door behind him. This time he went past the desk to the far corner. He lifted one of the huge oil paintings off the wall and gently placed it on the swept earthen floor.

He stared at the wall for a moment and marveled at the masonry. Every time he observed this, it amazed him that the cracks were completely imperceptible. He put his hands in just the right spots and pushed hard. A large section of the wall slid straight back. It made hardly a sound and felt as if it had no weight. The huge block of granite stood back now, and the darkness of a secret chamber beckoned.

There was no light switch inside. The priest closed his eyes to adjust them to the darkness and felt around to his right, where he maintained a flashlight on a small table just inside the heavy stone passage. He turned on the flashlight and stepped inside.

First, he admired the ropes and pulleys that led away from the back of the large slab. The apparatus connected up to the ceiling and then down to a set of granite blocks used as counterweights that allowed the 'door' to be opened and closed easily. The chamber itself was only eight feet wide and ten feet deep, with the counterweights dangling in the center of the room. The priest sidled past the lightly-swinging boulders and to the back wall.

Fully half of the rear wall was an iron gate built into the stone. Again he marveled at the craftsmanship from the turn of the century. Not so much as a sheet of paper could be slipped between the stone and the iron. The gate itself had two thick iron arms extending past the frame and onto the stone on the right. These clasped onto embedded eyehooks, each secured with modern solid steel, short-shank padlocks.

He got down on one knee and shined the flashlight up into the keyholes of the oversized padlocks. The tiny pieces of tape he had inserted there some years ago remained untouched. Satisfied, he stood, but did not turn away. He fingered the locks and wondered if the myth were true.

The priest released the padlock from his fingers and sighed. He had never actually seen this gate opened. This was the key he did not have. He went back out to the anteroom and hoped that the legend of The Guns of Antwerp was only a myth.

7

Jimmy Gallagher glanced down again at the calf of his pant leg. Tough to do while driving, but he wanted to be sure Jessie couldn't see the bulge caused by the little box he had hidden in his sock. *Today is the day,* he thought, and tried not to burst into a silly grin. He would ask Jessica to marry him. They'd been dating for a number of years now, and it was their second-go-round. They had dated briefly once when they were younger and then stayed generally single, but after their experience together during the Queen Mary incident, they had become inseparable.

He was pretty sure she'd say yes, she'd been dropping hints all over the place —for years. So he'd bought a ring. A nice ring. He glanced down at his pant leg again. *I'm not nervous,* he tried to tell himself, and again tried not to grin.

The FDR became the Harlem River Drive and the ramp to the George Washington Bridge rose up ahead in the near distance. Even though they lived together over on the West Side in Jessie's place off Hudson Street, there was a bakery on the East Side that Jessie wanted to visit. She was thoughtful that way. Jimmy smiled: she wouldn't arrive as a guest without bringing something nice for the host.

They topped out on the ramp and turned hard left onto Interstate 95 —The Cross Bronx Expressway. The short lead-up to the George Washington Bridge was less than a mile long, and Jimmy felt like holding his breath.

The roadway went underground, and a total of twelve lanes of some of the world's gnarliest traffic came together in a huff. Trucks, buses, trailers, and vehicles of every sort conspired to blacken the walls of the tunnels, which were covered with a man-made maze of some of the ugliest conduits and piping Jimmy had ever seen. The guts of New York City. This stretch of road always reminded him of some kind of bad, futuristic horror movie.

But then they rolled out onto the bridge and the big blue sky opened up before them. The bridge itself was also less than a mile long, but the panorama of green-brown cliffs on the far side and the wide-open river below made it beautiful; particularly on a sunny day like this.

Jimmy got over into the right lane. Just as the bridge touched down on the Jersey side, the lane swept them off the Interstate and onto the Palisades Parkway, northbound.

Jimmy took one hand off the wheel and relaxed a bit. They needed this —a day off. A real Saturday. They'd both been swamped lately; Jessica with cases out at the department's Psych Services Division where she was now the Supervising Chief Psychologist, and Jimmy had his hands full with the UN shooting.

The remainder of yesterday at the UN had been filled with bureaucratic wrangling at high levels between Internal Affairs and the Detective Bureau. Jimmy liked to stay out those fights. Plus, there were interagency communications, too, which Jimmy was never good at.

But this morning his team was back in the office and, through a connection with a friend in the NYPD's Joint Terrorist Task Force, the cops that worked shoulder to shoulder with the FBI, they got their hands on the UN surveillance tapes —quicker than they thought they would. Quicker than Internal Affairs. So now, at least, they could find out what this Zafir guy looked like. Jimmy had Lieutenant Clark and Sergeant Donohue going over the tapes today to see what they could come up with.

Jessie had shut off her cell phone, but grudgingly agreed to let Jimmy keep his on vibrate. Jimmy slid his hand down off the center armrest and caressed Jessica's forearm. Like he knew she would, Jessie responded by slipping her soft, dainty hand into his. There would be nothing but a canopy of lush, green landscape for the next ten miles and they were determined to let the real world slide off their shoulders and enjoy the time away. Even Van Morrison played along.

They were heading up to Rocket's place. The occasion was Joseph Gallagher's sixty-eighth birthday. Jimmy loved 'heading up to Rocket's place' and was happy to finally share it with Jessica. It's something he'd been doing with his Dad for as long as he could remember.

Joseph Gallagher and Rocket John Fahey had returned from the war in Vietnam back in 1969 when Jimmy was just a toddler. And the two combat veterans had been as close as brothers ever since. Jimmy thought of The Rocket as an uncle, but didn't call him that. No one called John Fahey anything but Rocket.

"So," Jessie gazed absent-mindedly out the window, "why do they call him Rocket, anyway?"

Jimmy smiled out through the windshield. "You know, I'm not sure. Something to do with his assignment over in Vietnam, but I've never gotten a direct answer to that question myself. Rocket John is a man of few words."

Jessie looked over at Jimmy. "Did he fire rockets over there or something?"

"I guess. That would make the most sense. But I heard he was one of those guys that crawled through tunnels, too. Then I heard other things, but never anything specific. They did a number of tours over there together. He and Dad were gone for two years.

After a pleasant fifteen minutes of driving up the Parkway, they passed the last exit in New Jersey and the canopy of tall, undulating trees gave way to a distant vista of hills rolling onto the horizon.

"Jimmy." Jessica nuzzled sideways into her seat and held Jimmy's hand with both of hers. "Have you thought any more about getting out?"

Jimmy raised his eyebrows, but didn't look at Jessie right away. He took a deep breath and absorbed the pastoral beauty enveloping them. "I have," he nodded. "Nothing specific, but," he glanced down at his pant leg and then turned to her and smiled, "…it'd be nice to raise a family in a place like this."

Jessie brought both legs up underneath herself and nestled further into the seat, "You could always work for your dad; his firm is doing great. He's got all those new executive protection contracts with visiting dignitaries, and the expansion into Boston seems to be going well." She glanced out the windows wistfully. "We could live anywhere."

They eventually got off at Exit 6 and headed west. Veteran's Memorial Parkway swept wide through a sleepy suburb, and the view of distant hills continued. After a mile or so, Veteran's Parkway settled down onto a flat with two beautifully trimmed, sixty-acre parks on either side.

At the end of Veteran's Park, on the left, a submerged fountain sent a gentle geyser up into the middle of a quaint pond, keeping the surface clear. Jimmy turned left around the pond. After a few stonewalls and white picket fences, a small sign on the right, opposite the park entrance, announced the entrance to the Pearl River Little League

Baseball complex. Jimmy turned in. Jessica mused; "The Rocket lives on a little league field?"

"Ha. Yeah, almost. You'll see." After a few yards, the blacktop gave way to a narrow dirt road. After a hundred feet of brush that nearly swiped the car, they pulled out into a clearing. Jimmy stopped the car for a second and pointed off to the far left at a covered picnic area with its own little parking lot. "See that?"

Jessica strained to see over Jimmy's shoulder. "That little shack with the… -what is that, like a long carport with picnic tables under it?"

"Right," Jimmy answered. "That's the American Legion Post." He turned back. "Rocket's the Commander of the Post. '–Caretaker' is what that really means, though. People rent the space out for picnics and such."

"The American Legion. I've heard of that." Jessica said. "It's a fraternal organization for military veterans, isn't that right?"

"Yes, but…" Jimmy paused for effect. "Not just any veteran can join. The Legion is only open to combat veterans. It's only for guys who actually faced enemy fire or received certain combat medals and such."

"Oh. Interesting."

"Yeah. Rocket's the commander of that post."

Jessica smiled. "You mentioned that."

Jimmy caught himself and smiled back. "I guess I'm proud of him. I've known him since I was, like, three."

Jessica patted his shoulder. "I know. I felt that way about my dad and some of his friends, too."

Jimmy rolled the car slowly past The Legion Post and out into a larger clearing. Fences of baseball fields ran off in every direction. At least two hundred people milled throughout the complex and distant cheers mixed with the occasional cloink of an aluminum bat. A little-league Saturday.

At the foot of it all, immediately on their left, stood an old clubhouse complete with a concession stand selling hot dogs and ice cream. Picnic tables with young families surrounded the two-story converted barn, and an old wooden corral fence penned it all in. Jessica smiled as they rolled by. "Ain't that America."

Jimmy smiled broadly and nodded slowly. "Yeah, ain't it." Jimmy rolled the car across the long grass parking field. At the far end, a huge mound of sandy dirt used to replenish the playing fields blocked their path.

A couple of younger children played on the little mountain, and Jimmy stopped the car. "Just gotta check in real quick, hon." He pulled his cell phone out from the center console and dialed into the office.

"Okay, sure." Jessica looked all around, out all four windows. There was nothing beyond the maintenance mound but thickets of tall, almost ancient trees. "But where are we? Why did you pull into this dead end?"

With his cell up to his ear Jimmy shook his head and smiled. Then he turned to the phone. "Kevin? Hey, yeah, it's Jimmy; what's goin' on with those surveillance tapes?" He paused and listened. "Good, good. Okay, you guys spend some time reviewing them and see what you come up with. Supposedly Zafir is the guy on the podium with his arm around the reporter –the guy with the microphone."

Jimmy switched the phone to his other ear. "Okay, yeah. I'm up here at Rocket's place, I'll…" –He was interrupted. "Rock- never mind. I'll keep calling in, you guys keep at it, we'll talk soon." He hung up.

"Sorry." He turned to Jessie and slipped the phone in his pants pocket.

"No, no, that's fine. —I understand." She looked all around again at the dead end of the parking field, and again saw nothing but tall trees. "But where are we?"

Jimmy laughed. "Welcome to Rocket's Place." He put the car in gear and slowly, ever so slowly, edged around the back of the mound.

8

Father O'Leary emerged from the basement of Gasson Hall just in time to find three smirking young men arrive outside the counseling office. The priest walked over and stood between the three young men and the office door. He opened his two hands before him and asked, "Follow me?" He waited for a response. The three smirking young men finished glancing at one another and eventually nodded to the priest. Father O'Leary turned and led them through the door.

The day had grown warm and the blast of air conditioning in the counseling hallway was a welcome touch. The track coach and two other women stood conversing in the hall, blocking their path. The cleric gestured politely for them to make room and then escorted the boys down the newly carpeted hall.

The case of sexual harassment bordered on abuse. Some members of the football team had hosted a party in their dorm and some of the women's track team had attended. Things almost got out of hand when 'no' wasn't understood to mean 'no.' But when a few of the women's shot-putters heard panicked voices from a back room and took decisive action, the full meaning of 'no' became clear.

No one got hurt, but there were bad feelings all around. Everyone was referred to counseling and Father O'Leary was asked to speak to the boys. He led them to the end of the hall and stopped outside a small private office. Though Gasson Hall itself was well over a hundred years old, the interior spaces were nicely maintained and beautifully modern.

The religious leader held open the conference room door and nodded the three smirking young men into the nicely appointed room. He smiled inwardly, thinking of how his work in bringing about civil behavior in violence-prone young men was never really done. The Jesuits had made great progress in the last one hundred and fifty years, he mused, but the evolution continued. The cleric stepped into the room and closed the door behind him.

9

Jimmy guided the car between the mound of baseball sand and the trunk of a giant oak tree. Just past the tree, a path peeked out and disappeared into the woods.

"Gee," Jessica said, "is there a troll going to pop out and ask us to pay a toll, now?"

"Actually…" Jimmy peered out the windshield and guided the car slowly onto the hidden path. "Yup, there he is."

Just around the bend, a giant Harley Davidson motorcycle leaned on its kickstand alongside the path. A large, gnarly old veteran reclined his feet up on the handlebars and pillowed his hands behind his head, leaning on the sissy bar. Jimmy pulled up alongside. "Hey, ya old fart."

"Well, well." The man with the big-black boots and black leather vest didn't move. "If it ain't Captain Kid. How are ya, young fella?"

Jessica leaned over to Jimmy and whispered, "Captain Kid?" Jimmy turned to her. "Not like the pirate. He's one of Rocket's guys; they've all known me since I was a kid. What can I say?" Jimmy turned back out the window. "My dad here?"

"Yes he is, Captain," The man swung his feet down off the bike and stood up. "We're all in, now." He walked around behind Jimmy's car. He reached into the brush and grabbed at something, then called over his shoulder: "Go ahead, kid, pull up."

"Got it." Jimmy answered, and pulled the car forward

slowly. He continued his way down the path and watched Jessica turn around to look out the rear windshield. Jimmy looked in the rearview mirror and watched the gnarly old vet swing a hidden iron gate out of the woods and across the path. The old timer let it go, and it clanged into place against a sheared boulder on the opposite side of the path.

"Wow," Jessica said. "What is this, like, the Batcave?"

"Ha, ha." Jimmy really laughed. "Like I said, welcome to Rocket's Place."

At the end of the path, they rolled out into another clearing, and the view took their breath away. It was like a scene from the Adirondack Mountains in a place just 15 miles outside of Manhattan. Jimmy parked at the end of a long line of cars, right behind an Orangetown Police cruiser.

They got out and walked around to the back of the one-story brick caretaker's cottage. The land behind the house was flat and clear for about fifty feet until a stand of trees swept down to the shore of Lake Tappan in the near distance.

The grass was cut but not trimmed. A few plastic tables dotted the yard and a barbeque grill smoked just off the back porch to their left. Fifty or so people milled about in small clusters. Jessica took a moment to notice. "Eclectic group."

Bearded biker types in leather vests, some with 'Nam Knights' printed in bright block letters across their shoulders and others flying the colors of the 'Blue Knights' mixed with couples in business casual slacks, button downs, and dresses.

"You're observant." Jimmy pointed to a wooden plaque on a tree next to them. "Check out their Motto."

Jessica read the calligraphy.

WE ARE LAWYERS, WE ARE LABORERS.

WE COME FROM YALE, WE COME FROM JAIL.

WE COME FROM PARK AVENUE,

WE COME FROM PARK BENCHES.

BUT WE ALL DEFENDED OUR COUNTRY IN THE GODDAMN TRENCHES.

–AMERICAN LEGION

POST 1199

A large, intense-looking German Shepard trotted up. Jimmy bent down to greet him. The dog hesitated and sniffed, but then nuzzled up to Jimmy. "Hey, Sarge." Jimmy petted the dog. Sarge licked his face.

"Jesse-James." A large, barrel-chested, red haired man in casual clothes blustered toward them.

"Do you think he'll ever stop calling us that?" Jessica frowned to Jimmy.

Jimmy looked at Jessie and shook his head. "I doubt it, Hon; -he's a twelve-year-old boy in an old man's body."

"Old man?" Murry Elfman, Joseph Gallagher's old partner and now Director of Operations for his private investigation firm —and a close friend of the family —pushed out his enormous chest. "Did you just say 'old man'?"

Murray put a paw on Jimmy and playfully separated him from Jessica.

"Miss Shore." He bowed, took one of her hands, held it up gently, and kissed it. "It's always a pleasure to see you, my dear."

Jessica giggled like she always did when Murray greeted her that way. Murray and Jessica shared a certain bond. Among other fraternal organizations, Murray ran the NYPD's Shomrim Society. There were plenty of Jewish doctors, like Jessica, but there weren't that many Jewish cops, Murray would often say. Murray made up for that with his presence. The man filled every room he walked in to.

Someone approached from off to their left and growled, "How do you take your burgers?"

"Rocket." Jimmy smiled and put his arms out to hug the old timer.

"Well?" Rocket didn't put his arms out. He just stood there, all five foot seven of him, with a very serious look on his face, waving a spatula. "How do you take them? Medium? What? Come on, I got work to do."

"That's a fine 'how do you do' Rocket," Murray teased him. "Why can't you Marines say hello like gentlemen?"

Rocket pointed his spatula at Murray. "Don't start with me, Squid."

"Hey, Rocket, why don't you tell us what it said on your paycheck when you were in the Marines. Did it say 'Marine Corp' on there?"

Rocket turned away from Murray and looked at Jessica, stoically. "It's a pleasure to finally meet you, Ma'am. Now, what about you. How do you take your burger?"

"It said Department of The Navy on your paycheck, didn't it?"

Rocket completely turned his back to Murray and bent his elbow out for Jessica to put her arm in. She did, and Rocket spoke softly to her: "Come with me, Miss. Let us ignore the unmannered riff-raff."

Murray called over to Jessica, "Hey, did you know that,

Jess? That the Marines are a department of the Navy?"

Rocket growled over his shoulder, "Yeah, the men's department." And Rocket John Fahey escorted Jessica into the party like gentry in his scuffed old boots and torn jeans.

Jimmy glanced back out across the yard. "So, where's the man of the hour?"

Murray pointed with his chin to a table on the far side of the barbecue where Jimmy's father sat with three other men, all in slacks.

Jimmy took a moment to observe them. Then he turned to Murray. "Kelly? Mike Kelly's here?"

Murray tilted his head. "Jim, you know how deep those bonds are. They've been friends and neighbors since they were born." He shook Jimmy's shoulder. "When are you gonna get over it?"

Jimmy frowned. "Murray, I get it, but the guy's a freakin arch-criminal, I might have to investigate him someday."

"Not in a terrorist unit, you won't"

"Yeah, maybe not anymore, but…"

"Jim, the war in Northern Ireland is pretty much over. Plus, Kelly's guys aren't strong-arming people these days; they're not that kind of organization anymore."

Mike Kelly and Joseph Gallagher came from Manhattan's West Side. What, today, is called Chelsea; in their day was called Hell's Kitchen. Kelly and his organization used to run the numbers game and other street crimes in that part of Manhattan. But they'd evolved into controlling much of the construction and labor unions on the West Side.

Jimmy didn't dislike Mike Kelly personally —he'd known him all his life —but Jimmy was just such a cop that it bothered him to socialize with anyone associated with shady activities.

"Jim." Murray put his hand on Jimmy's back and ushered him forward. "Mike Kelly may be a lot things, but one thing for sure: he's a good friend to your father. Try and remember that."

"Fine." They walked together over to the barbecue where Rocket was busy explaining to Jessica the best way to grill a burger.

"Hey, Jess." Jimmy stepped in between them. "I'll understand if you lose your appetite."

Rocket stopped what he was doing and turned and stared hard at Jimmy. He waved the spatula and growled, "It's gonna be pretty hard to explain to your cops how a sixty-eight-year-old man kicked your ass." Then he abruptly turned back to the grill and ignored Jimmy. Jessica laughed and Jimmy patted her on the shoulder.

A man walked up holding an empty plate. "Hey, Jim, still just 'hangin' around' for a living?" The man turned to Jessica. "'cause you know, that's all cops do: just 'hang around.'"

"Oh, for God's sake." Jimmy turned to Rocket. "Who invited the smoke eater?"

Rocket waved the spatula without looking up. "Fireman are people, too."

The man put the plate down. Jimmy smiled and walked around the grill. They hugged.

"You're looking well, John." Jimmy said to his oldest friend. At one time, they were inseparable. But as the years passed, they saw less and less of each other. Life got crowded. And even though John Wilson worked out of Ladder 1 on Duane Street, just around the corner from Jimmy's Chambers Street office, they still only ran into each other the rare once in a while.

But they always seemed to pick up right where they left off. They released one another and John Wilson looked himself up and down. "Yeah, just a few bumps and bruises over the years." He looked back up at Jimmy and Jessica. "But still in one piece."

Jimmy just nodded for a moment. John Wilson had been with FDNY on September 11, 2001.

When the first tower fell, Wilson and his team survived, but their twenty-ton rig overturned and trapped their lieutenant. So they got out the Hurst tool and in the swirling dust and mayhem of the collapse, started lifting the wreckage off their boss.

As firemen do, they joked with the L-T about maybe having to leave him there in case the other tower fell. Then it did. John landed some hundred or so feet away. The lieutenant's body was never recovered. No other member of the team survived. John Wilson came out without a scratch.

"Yeah," Jimmy said, "still in one piece." He patted Wilson on the upper arm. "Thank God, John." The two men just stared at each other for a moment. Jessica broke the spell.

"Hi, I'm Jessica. I don't believe we've met."

Jimmy introduced them, and a crush of partygoers descended on the grill with Rocket's announcement that the burgers were ready. Rocket enlisted Jessica as his new assistant and so Jimmy and Murray went around the grill and approached the far table.

Mister Gallagher and his friends saw Jimmy coming and all pushed back their chairs to stand and say hello. Jimmy's cell phone vibrated in his pocket. He pulled it out and looked at the number –Lieutenant Clark was calling in from the office. Jimmy put one finger up to the table and hit the 'answer' button with his other hand. "One sec, Pops, gotta take this."

Mister Gallagher nodded and Jimmy stepped back about two feet. "Hey, Kevin."

Lieutenant Clark started in with an update about the surveillance footage from the UN. He explained that they were able to freeze frame a shot of Zafir and pull it out to make a mug shot. What to do next was getting complicated. And tedious.

Clark explained:

"Boss, we got a picture, but there's nearly a million people we have to show it to if we're going to find anything out about this guy. So far, we have the system running to find matches with arrested persons using that new facial recognition software, but it's popping up every dark-haired male in the database."

"What's Donohue up to?"

Jimmy could hear Clark turning in his chair, probably glancing across the room at Jack who, Jimmy expected, was hunched over his keyboard, like he often was.

Clark spoke:

"That boy's got smoke coming out the top of his big head. He's been buried in that computer for hours." Jimmy could practically hear Clark frown over the phone line. Clark continued, "I have no idea what the Eagle Scout is up to; he could be playing Pac-Man for all I know, but he's pretty intense about it."

"You're dating yourself Kevin. Pac-Man came and went years ago."

"What-ever," Clark drawled. Then Jimmy could hear

shouting in the background.

"What was that?"

"Hold on." In the background, Jimmy could hear Jack shouting. Jimmy held, and Clark said into the phone: "Boy Wonder seems to think he's got something. Let me see if I can interpret his new-wave nonsense. Hold on. I'll put you on speaker."

Jimmy smiled and listened to the background chatter. Donohue shouted again; this time Jimmy heard the words "Boston. He got on an Amtrak to Boston this morning."

"Explain yourself, son."

"Facial recognition. I've been running it all day on surveillance tapes I got from the Port Authority, Metro North, and Amtrak police. I had them pull tapes for me from all the transportation hubs in the tri-state area –in case this guy tried to leave town. Sure enough…" There was a pause; it sounded to Jimmy like Jack was spinning in his chair. "I got him. He boarded an Amtrak out of Penn Station bound for Boston an hour ago. Look."

Jimmy had heard enough. "Tell Ramirez to get the car ready, we're going to Boston. I'll be at the office in twenty-five minutes." He hung up and stepped over to the grill. "Hon," he tapped Jessica on the shoulder. "We gotta go." She drew back her head and asked why. "I'm sorry. I'll explain on the way. It's really important." Then he turned to Rocket. "I'm sorry. I have to go. I just got a lead on a case." He held up the phone. "I really have to go." Rocket responded with a stern nod and said, "Got it."

John Wilson grabbed Jimmy's arm. "Hey, no more hangin' around, huh? You gonna go do something for a living now?"

"That's rich, coming from a guy who's authorized to

sleep on duty. See ya later, Hose Jockey." They shook hands.

Jimmy stepped back to the table to say goodbye to his father, Murray, and their friends. He shook hands with everyone and Mike Kelly held onto his hand a moment longer. He nodded to Jimmy's cell phone.

"I couldn't help but overhear –you're going up to Boston. You know, Jimmy, we have friends up there. Whatever it is you're looking for, we have people that could put you in the right direction." Kelly stepped in closer. "You should stop into the Mayo Inn. A guy named Johnny Dineen owns the place, he's the big boy up there in that world. I know him, but we're not friends. One of his lieutenants is guy I know pretty well, though; Casey. Dermot Casey; ask for him."

Then Kelly let go of Jimmy's hand and stepped back. "Or, if you're looking for something more… -international…, -try the Saints and Scholars; we have friends there, too."

Jimmy stared at Kelly for a moment, reluctant to accept help from someone outside the law. Joseph Gallagher noticed and stepped over. "Jimmy, in Boston, people like that aren't as far removed from the police as you might think. And, they've been helpful to us in our efforts up there." He looked squarely at Kelly. "Nothing serious; there are no debts owed." He turned back to Jimmy. "But they might be of some assistance."

Jimmy nodded to his father. Then he turned to Kelly and patted him on the shoulder. "Okay, Mike, thanks. I'll try and remember that."

10

Zafir paced the red brick sidewalk of Beacon Street. After nearly five hours on the train, he welcomed the fresh air. As he paced, he stole the occasional glance through the plate glass window of the Saints and Scholars. He was told the restaurant was upscale but not entirely formal. Zafir dressed accordingly. Watching through the windows, he waited for the small table in the front to become free.

His people in the homeland had arranged this meeting. He was early. Though Zafir had been in this city once before as a child, he did not risk being recognized. These factions from the Irish Republican Army and the Boston underworld were expecting his father. But Zafir al Ayyad had died of cancer the prior year.

Zafir al Ayyad and these factions had run many successful missions together, in their time. But the young Zafir was not sure how they would respond to his leadership role today. So he explicitly instructed the homeland not to disclose the death of Zafir al Ayyad. Surprise was good. And Zafir enjoyed a vantage.

Finally, the couple at the bar-top table finished their meal and stood. Zafir peeled off his sunglasses and went in. A bus boy was just clearing the table, and Zafir stepped over to it and motioned to the maitre'd. The host, an older, petite Irishman, sighed but approached with a nod.

Zafir smiled shyly; "I'm a little early." he fidgeted. "It's a first date." He widened his eyes and held up crossed fingers. The host sigh-laughed and patted Zafir's arm. "She's all yours, fella." The host nodded to the table, "…just as soon as it's cleared."

"Thanks." Zafir flashed the thumbs-up, appearing as American as he could. He took his seat and turned his back to the window.

Normally when on a mission, one did not sit with their back to an access-egress point; but this was different. Zafir was undercover –for the moment. He patted his back pocket and felt for the outline of a small piece of heavy metal his father had given him before he died.

The object had the basic shape of a key, but instead of teeth, a hollow barrel extended out from the handle. His father told him it could be of some importance one day, and Zafir carried it as a talisman. He smoothed his hand over the bulge; not for reassurance, he just enjoyed having the token in his possession. Then he sat back and pretended to peruse the menu.

The bar emerged from the wall ten feet in front of him, and after two stools' worth, turned and ran directly away from him along the left wall, all the way to the back. On the right, forming an aisle with the bar, a hand-carved wooden partition obscured the dining room. The wood of the partition extended to bar height where panels of etched glass then rose to the ceiling, depicting various scenes of Irish history.

Within minutes, Zafir identified two men as IRA. Twice, now, they emerged from the doorway of a back room, dispersed suspicious glances about the establishment, and then returned to their roost. And they were young and well-dressed. Zafir smirked. Lately, the IRA considered themselves more politicians than freedom fighters, and endeavored to look the part. Zafir tried not to frown outwardly.

The host hurried up toward the entrance with menus in his arms and greeted two couples arriving in eveningwear. Zafir watched as the older, diminutive host waltzed the couples around the partition and into the dining room. A waiter approached. Zafir ordered only a club soda, saying, optimistically, that he would wait for his date.

The waiter smiled sadly and left. The meeting would begin soon, Zafir knew. From his intelligence reports and his elders, he knew there would be at least two, possibly three, cells coming together to resolve the request Zafir's people had made.

They must say yes, Zafir thought. *The guns of Antwerp were ours originally.* Although the guns existed only as whispers in his own circles, upon contacting the homeland today to fulfill his needs for this current mission, Zafir was finally told the entire truth. The key his father had given him was proof. Al Ayyad had been there in Antwerp in 1977.

The Russians initially supplied the weapons to the PLO compatriots in Libya. Then al Ayyad himself brokered the deal to sell them to the Irish. And so a cargo ship set out from Libya with three crates on board, bound for the Dublin shipyards. Al Ayyad was to meet the already famous leader of the IRA, Seamus O'Leary, and two of his men on the ship when it came in for a refueling stop in Antwerp, Belgium. But Israeli intelligence got word. And the Israelis gave the information to the British —as some sort of gift, so the Brits could seize the Irish. But the British did not have the manpower in place in Belgium, at the time. So the interdiction was left up to the local Gendarmes.

When they sailed into the trap set in Antwerp, al Ayyad and O'Leary quickly positioned one of three crates so it would be easily found. One Irish compatriot was arrested.

And he never talked. And since the fledging Irish Republic, barely sixty years removed from its own revolution, would not be so cavalier, the remaining two crates had to be rerouted. And so they were spirited onto a Boston-bound freighter. And al Ayyad and Seamus O'Leary became stowaways —and lifelong friends.

And for the last thirty-five years, the Irish in Boston had denied that the guns ever arrived here. But Zafir knew better. He knew that the guns of Antwerp had become a fable in these circles. He knew the Irish loved to whisper mysteriously about their existence as if they were some kind of Holy Grail.

These Irish, he laughed to himself: always shrouding facts with mysterious tales. Zafir didn't know much about the now-elder of this group, Seamus O'Leary, beyond the stories his father had told him. As when they'd parted on the Boston docks that day, the delivery complete, O'Leary had embraced al Ayyad and had given him this key.

Though neither of them ever saw the bill of lading prepared by the Russians, they both believed that the crate taken by the officials in Belgium was the one that held a new type of weapon which the key was meant to open or operate.

They believed handguns and attendant ammunition filled the remaining two crates, so the key was of no use beyond being a phylactery. And al Ayyad had described how O'Leary gave him the key with both hands as they embraced, like a ceremony of sorts, saying they were now bonded together forever in trust.

Such nonsense. Zafir shook his head. The Irish were such dreamers. And look where it took them. They had long ago given up their armed struggle and had surrendered, in

Zafir's mind, to the British occupation of Northern Ireland.

Peace, they called it. But in the circles of Fateh, it was clearly seen as surrender —something his people would never do. There'd be no 'Omagh moment' for his people, especially now, after Zafir's actions at the UN rally. Moderates were like a cancer: they eroded the strength of the movement. It appalled Zafir and his followers that the Irish had agreed to some kind of power sharing that allowed the Imperialistic British overlords to retain control of a part of their country. And all in the name of peace. Fools.

Zafir had to catch himself as he very nearly pounded the table. They don't know what peace is, he thought. *They think it is the lack of bloodshed but that is just allowing for defeat. Peace will come when these Western animals are defeated and Islam rules all cultures, worldwide.* He decided to put on his glasses —the time neared for him to make his presence known.

11

Jimmy hurried across the red bricks of the lower plaza. Frank would be picking him up in front of their Chambers Street office in about five minutes. After apologizing profusely to Jessie –and ensuring that that little box stayed firmly hidden in his sock, he had her drop him off at the back of One Police Plaza. It would be easier for her to loop around the Municipal Center from there, and over to her apartment on Hudson Street.

Hustling toward the employee entrance, Jimmy remembered how glad he was to move his office out of this building. A year ago, the Building Maintenance Section had declared office space inside One Police Plaza exhausted and that some units had to move. Jimmy had jumped at the chance.

He remembered his first day assigned to this building – walking across the upper plaza wearing a suit and carrying a briefcase. He had stopped and looked up at what was essentially an office building and remembered why he had dropped out of Manhattan College all those years ago.

The corporate world just wasn't for him. But being a cop wasn't supposed to be corporate. Or so he'd thought. Jimmy loved the first fifteen years he spent on patrol, chasing bad guys. But the last few years as a captain, mixed with the ambience of The Puzzle Palace, as his cohorts called it, just didn't fit him.

He made his way through the ID check and bypassed the bank of elevators. He was only going up one flight and so headed for the escalator. A soon as he stepped onto the up side, he noticed a couple of uniform cops riding the down escalator, looking completely out of place. Leery eyes and racks of medals. Street cops. Heading down to the back door.

Jimmy didn't recognize them personally, but smiled at them like a co-conspirator. They both recognized him right away. Jimmy had been involved in so many shootouts and other wild street incidents that he was somewhat well known outside the department, but very well known within —especially among street cops.

The cop closest to the up side stretched his arm across the steel divide and offered a fist. "Captain Gallagher, good to see you, sir." Jimmy reached across and fist bumped him. "Be careful out there," Jimmy offered. The cop nodded. Then, as an apparent afterthought, the cop smiled and said, "Yeah, and you be careful up there." The uniform tilted his head up at the whole of headquarters. Jimmy laughed. "Alright, pal, you take care."

The up escalator let Jimmy out right at the elevator bank behind the main Rotunda. A crowd shuffled between the six elevator doors. A car had just arrived and the exiting crowd jostled through the incoming. The whole thing spilled out nearly to the Rotunda.

A lieutenant in uniform emerged from the exiters and spotted Jimmy. Again, this was a man Jimmy had never met; but he could tell right away that the man recognized him. Jimmy was about to smile at the lieutenant and say 'hi' when the younger man cocked his head up, stared straight ahead, and walked directly past. Affected. Jimmy shook his head and remembered again why he'd volunteered to move his unit over to Chambers Street.

He went through the turnstile, crossed the soaring

Rotunda and went out the main doors onto The Plaza. His shortcut to Chambers Street. He traversed Police Plaza as it became a bridge over Park Row. He followed the red bricks till they ended at the Arch of the Great Municipal Building, the base of Manhattan's Civic Center.

Jimmy tried not to look to his left. But he couldn't help himself. In fact, he stopped walking for a moment and stared to his left.

That's where he'd stood. Right there. September eleventh was one of those moments when no one forgets where they stood. And that's where Jimmy stood. That morning, he had just come up out of the train. He never took the train. Normally, he'd have been driving by the foot of the towers when they fell. But he was teaching a class that night up at Fordham University, so he left the car on campus and caught the Metro North Train from Fordham down to Grand Central. Then he took the 6 train down to the Brooklyn Bridge stop.

At first, he wondered why everyone around him seemed so upset as he ascended the stairs to the street. Then he followed their eyes. And then he saw. The towers were in flames.

He choked up at the memory of that morning, and had to turn away. Before he could resume walking, though, he had to stand there with his eyes closed for a moment. He learned to take at least one piece of the memory at moments like this and process it out so he could get back to life.

Frustration: that was the main one lately. Today's image was of the line of empty stretchers standing at the ready and the hopeful, urgent looks of the medics. And then the heartache every time he and his guys crawled up out of the rubble empty-handed —again. He clenched his jaw and felt the burn. Then he slowly exhaled and opened his eyes. He drew a deep breath and kept walking. Just another day.

He walked through the Arch and stopped behind the crowd at the foot of Chambers Street. It would take at least a minute or two to cross Centre Street.

He thought about this kid; this Khalifa or whatever the hell he was called. *So it won't be one big splash this time, huh? You want a ground war? Woohoo,* Jimmy thought, *you got one, pal. Show yourself and I'll give you a fucking ground war alright.* With the memory of 9-11 so near, he had to close his eyes again to stay calm.

The light turned green and he resumed life's march, merging with the pack of pedestrians crossing Centre Street.

Having escaped the strain of bureaucracy inside The Palace, Jimmy found an appreciation for the neighborhood surrounding Chambers Street. It grew on him. He began to relish the area's history, old and new.

Foley Square began just to his right, and every time he passed it, he thought of his favorite TV detective, Lenny Briscoe, on Law and Order. Seemed like every episode had at least one scene on the sweeping courthouse steps of Foley Square.

Chambers Street began right there and ran straight out in front of him like it was born of the Arch. You could see almost all the way to the Hudson River from back here at the foot of the Brooklyn Bridge. Lower Manhattan was a target-rich environment. All the historic places around him made him grateful he wasn't tracking another large scale attack like September Eleventh.

Across Centre Street, a wide-open plaza swept up to the wrought iron gates of City Hall Park. Benches lined the enclosure and towering trees shaded the neighboring Boss

Tweed Courthouse, —one of the oldest and most stately structures in all of New York City.

It never made sense to Jimmy why they would leave that name on the building. Wasn't Boss Tweed supposedly like one of the most corrupt political leaders in the city's history? Jimmy smirked. Whatever. It was an awesome-looking building either way.

Just over the top of The Tweed Courthouse, the spires of The Woolworth Building peaked from the far side of the park. Now dwarfed by its neighbors, The Woolworth building at 233 Broadway had been the tallest skyscraper in the world back at the turn of the century.

The new digs at 51 Chambers stood directly across from Tweed and still bore the name of its original tenant, The Emigrant Savings Bank. 17 stories tall and well over a hundred years old, the elevators in here were hardly any faster than in The Palace. But at least it was out from under the eye. For the most part.

Jimmy spotted their unmarked right in front of 51 Chambers Street, with Frank behind the wheel. Jimmy felt bad for taking Frank's weekend away from him, maybe they could enjoy the ride. The department authorized an overnight stay up in Boston. *We'll make the best of it,* Jimmy thought, and whipped open the door and hopped in.

12

Down in South Boston, a man named Johnny Dineen sat behind a desk in the back room of the Mayo Inn. Johnny's family had come from County Mayo, Ireland, in the nineteen thirties, and Johnny named the place in their honor. Johnny's Dad was just a Boston City sanitation worker, but did okay for an immigrant —taught young Johnny right from wrong, and such.

Dineen slipped a lit cigar off a marble ashtray and took a long drag. He let it out slowly and admired the lazy, blue cloud. Johnny Dineen had been a loyal soldier in the Irish Mob of Boston most of his adult life. No emptying garbage cans for him. At sixty-seven, he'd recently retired his Mason's Union card but continued to run one of the largest construction companies in all of New England —a concrete outfit his grandfather had started in South Boston around the turn of the century —they were stonecutters.

With the disappearance of the mob's prior leader some years ago, all parties in the criminal network agreed on Johnny as the replacement. Sports gambling and loan sharking mostly covered the payroll of his small army; but construction and racketeering was where he made his millions.

That and the Members Only Credit Union. But his ownership interest in the Credit Union had to remain a secret of the highest order. The Members Only office was right next door to The Mayo but, especially after the Patriot Act was passed, no one could ever know he owned it.

The bar out front was a bit of a dump, but Johnny's

office in the back, though simple, was well-appointed and nicely furnished. Johnny sat with his back to the far wall where he could keep an eye on the door. Just in front of his desk he had two plush leather armchairs facing him. Beyond that, each of his two lieutenants had their smaller desks set up at the far corners, also facing the room —and Johnny.

Over on the right sat Peter Flynn, a fourth generation union organizer who had family ties all the way back to the Boston Police Riots of 1919. Flynn was a rough old gangster who, for some reason, always wore a bowtie.

In the left corner was Johnny's brother-in-law, Margie's brother. Margie was a great gal and had stood by Johnny no matter what, these thirty-seven years. Would he have made Dermot a lieutenant, otherwise? Maybe not. But Dermot was okay. Trustworthy, at the least. Not the brightest tough guy in Boston; but not overly ambitious, either. That was important. Dermot did what he was told.

Today Johnny had a visitor. One of his line-level managers; a thug really, but an effective thug —a leader of thugs. And, the kid was a legacy, too. Over the years, the IRA had played a big role in the Boston underworld. Not so much anymore. But this kid's granduncle just happened to be the grand old man of the IRA himself. Not really that active these days —that war had been lost long ago —but politically, still connected. And Johnny's people, of course, had close ties to the old IRA hierarchy. And Johnny himself was occasionally called upon to help them out when they needed it.

Dermot had ushered the visitor in and planted him in one of the plush chairs opposite the desk. Johnny had nodded for Dermot to head back to his workstation for now. But Dermot had been briefed. So when Johnny fingered his left ear, Dermot nodded. Dermot was to pay attention. Johnny had informed him earlier that he might be running with this ball, wherever it bounced.

"So." Dineen replaced his cigar in the ashtray and leaned back. "Your granduncle, huh?"

The visitor was known as Jimmy Junior, but his real name was Seamus O'Leary 'the third.' In the environs of Dineen's well-appointed office, young O'Leary looked out of place in his rumpled nylon sweat suit and filthy sneakers. But Dineen put up with it. Jimmy Junior was one of his top enforcers and, by far, his best killer.

Whenever Dineen looked into Junior's eyes, he could see the three bodies he himself had placed there. But when he looked real close, there was more back there; more than he cared to know. He reached for the cigar again.

"He's a good man, your granduncle. Very honored — revered, even. Boston will never see another like him. But this old stash of guns you're talking about; he tell you they exist? 'Cause I'm not saying, either way. Could be just local legend, you know?"

Jimmy Junior leaned back in the chair. "Right, right. Who knows, could be just an old fairy tale, right? But the old man is taking this meeting with this old A-rab friend of his. So that tells us something, right?" Junior leaned forward. "Besides," he smirked, "I've heard the old man speak of a key. Supposedly someone holds the key to this treasure?" Then Junior sat back and smiled.

Dineen didn't smile back. He stared at Jimmy Junior and decided to put some thought into his response. Along with being the grand old man of the IRA in this town, Seamus O'Leary 'the first' had been a close friend and associate of Johnny's grandfather. Obviously, the kid was talking about the Guns of Antwerp. Although Dineen did have a key that supposedly led to them, he didn't know exactly where they were.

All Dineen knew for sure was that back in 1977, as a thirty-year-old thug working for his grandfather, cutting stone and pouring concrete —and doing other things, the old man had given him a padlock key. He intimated something about Johnny now being one of the keepers of the mysterious Guns of Antwerp. But even Johnny's grandfather had never seen the crates, and wasn't entirely sure they existed. Johnny was just told to hold onto the key and, when the time came, do whatever old Seamus asked him to.

From what Dineen understood, the arsenal, if it existed, belonged to old Seamus, and not even he knew its exact location. Back in '77, old Seamus, as the story goes, had handed the shipment over to their great trusted servants and asked them to hide it.

And once the great trusted servants had them hidden under lock and key, they gave the key to Old Seamus —who gave the key to Johnny's grandfather. Who passed it on to Johnny.

Old man O'Leary had complete deniability: he didn't know exactly where the crates were and he didn't even hold the key. Johnny did. Old Seamus had complete deniability; and complete control.

Dineen definitely was loyal to his grandfather and all that history shit, but if these fucking guns did exist and he was found by the authorities to be holding the fucking key, it could mean life in prison. Enough thinking. Dineen put the cigar down.

"Fuck you smirking at? Someone tell you a fucking

joke?" Dineen stood. "Whether those guns exist or not is none of your goddamn business, got it?"

Junior smirked, unimpressed. Dineen never liked that smirk; in fact, it scared him. He decided to play on the kid's insecurity —everybody in the world's more insecure than they care to admit. Johnny picked up his cigar. "And don't ever mention that fucking key again." He stepped halfway around his desk. "Who do you work for? Huh? Who pays you, asshole?" Junior stood, still smirking, but said, "You do, Mister Dineen; you do."

"You're goddamn right. Now go out there and get the ball rolling for this meeting." Dineen pointed at the office door. He let Junior get across the room before he came all the way out from behind the desk.

"Dermot and I will be right out." Junior opened the door. "And pick two clowns to drive me and Dermot to the meeting," Dineen went nowhere without his muscle. Even though the meeting would be in friendly territory, it was all part of the show.

Dineen motioned to the bar. "We'll see what kind of judgment you have. Then you can go pick up Old Seamus; and me and Dermot will talk to him about the things we know. You understand? You're not privy on this."

Dermot stood up.

Junior frowned at him.

Dineen continued, "We think you need to know, we'll tell you; you don't guess. Got it?"

Junior stopped smirking and opened the door. "I got it, I got it."

Dineen followed him to the door. He half closed it and leaned back in to Dermot, "Go get that fucking key out of the safe, and get ready to handle this meeting." Dineen then followed Junior out into the bar.

The bar ran forward along the wall on their right. On the left, after a jukebox, a series of booths ran halfway up to the front. Most of the bar stools on the right and all of the booths on the left were occupied with up and coming tough guys, all hoping to become full-time members of Dineen's crew.

Some of them already had regular small-time assignments like taking bets at various storefronts, collecting from late payers, and so on. Dineen stood back and let Jimmy Junior wade down the aisle.

Junior quickly picked out two kids from the assembled thugs. "Alright, you two, stand up."

Dineen walked up to the two young guys chosen by Junior and looked them up and down. He frowned. Without turning away, he spoke to Jimmy Junior.

"Don't you know nothing?" Then he turned to Junior. "That place your uncle hangs out, The Saints and Scholars, that's a nice place. My kinda place." He turned back to the two hopefuls. "These two dirtbags will stand out like a couple of sore pricks." He looked each one of them in the eye. "Maybe next time, fellas. Have a seat."

Again, he turned to Jimmy Junior. "Use your fucking head." Dineen turned to the booths and quickly pointed out two others. They stood immediately.

One of them, slightly over six foot tall and wearing a black leather jacket and torn blue jeans, stood up in front of Johnny. His long, stringy black hair hung limply to his shoulders. His partner towered over him and puffed out his chest as he stood. A red ponytail ran down the length of his broad back, and Celtic design tattoos circled out from under his thick, red beard and disappeared into a torn tee shirt.

"You're a Coghlan, right?" Dineen pointed at the shorter of the two.

The guy in the leather jacket nodded. Dineen turned to the one with the red beard and ponytail. "And you're Pat Moroney's nephew. What's your name again?"

"Duffy. Brendan Duffy."

Dineen nodded. "Yeah, right." He stepped back and turned to Jimmy Junior.

"I'm taking these two."

Jimmy Junior pursed his brow at the two appointees. He looked them up and down and then turned and sneered at his boss. "There ain't no diff-"

Dineen cut him off. "Don't you have some place to be?" Dineen stepped in close. "Huh?" Dineen could see the fury building in Jimmy Junior's eyes. Dineen stared Junior down hard and seethed, almost whispering, "Step off, Junior. Go do your job."

Jimmy Junior turned away and headed for the door.

Old Seamus O'Leary sat in the back of the Town Car and peered across at the entrance to the Saints and Scholars. He knocked on the partition and signaled his driver to remain seated. Although he and Johnny Dineen were old friends and associates, Seamus didn't want to be seen arriving at his renowned meeting place at the same time as Dineen's people. He waited.

Meetings at the Saints and Scholars were just no longer what they used to be. Seamus' IRA had gone from freedom fighters, or what some had called terrorists, to political operatives –The Sinn Fein political party. He remembered the day the transformation began.

It was a week after the Omagh bombing in 1998. The

people had had enough. Too many innocents were killed. They'd filled Boston's Kenmore Square by the tens of thousands, demanding the peace process be given a chance. They'd demanded an end to the violence —our own supporters, Seamus thought, turned on us. On us. Not the cause, he knew. The people still wanted a united Ireland, they just wouldn't support the violence anymore.

He'd tried to take to the podium but was booed down. Then his own brother, the symbol of peace in his official garb, stepped up. And the crowd cheered. His own brother. Afterwards, they spoke. And Seamus agreed —they would lay down their arms. And, as his brother suggested, join the civilized and find a lasting solution.

So the IRA was no longer the power of the Irish underworld in Boston. But Seamus still commanded a network of highly placed and loyal constituents. Since Omagh, most of the actual fighting in Northern Ireland was over, but the political battle raged on. And the leaders in the North still counted on him for support —both financial and political.

Once Dineen's brother-in-law and his two thugs disappeared through the front door, Seamus knocked on the partition and signaled his driver to get out and open the door for him. Protocol. As a man of tradition, Seamus insisted those around him adhere to proper etiquette. Also, at the age of eighty-four, Seamus didn't get around easily. He needed a trusted operative to drive him and handle any minor skirmishes that could arise.

Internally, many of his people questioned his demand that his last living relative be his attendant, but the boy carried his name, and that meant more to him than appearances. Seamus the third opened the car door.

Frank worked the wheel and Jimmy worked the phone. Heading up to Boston. One of Jimmy's favorite things.

It had taken over an hour just to get out of the city and up onto the I-95 corridor. Jimmy stared out the window for a second, trying to remember something. Then he nodded to himself and typed into the navigation app on his iPhone. He mindlessly spoke as he typed: "The -Mayo -Inn. Boston." He watched the little wheel spin at the center of the screen until a tiny red pin dropped on the spot. "Cool. Okay, now, let's try The -Saints -and -Scholars."

The small pinwheel took longer this time. Jimmy dropped the phone on the center console. They had crossed the city line out of The Bronx just fifteen minutes ago. Now, as they crossed the state line into Connecticut, The Hutchinson River Parkway became The Merritt Parkway. Just less than two-hundred miles to go. Jimmy relaxed back into the seat. The narrow blacktop unfolded like a garden path through the well-manicured greenery of the parkway. Little rest stops for gas and such appeared directly on the shoulder every so often.

The road trip to Boston always filled Jimmy with a comfortable excitement. On random weekends when life had nothing scheduled, his Mom and Dad would load the car and head up to Boston. The trip, and the town, became a mystical place for Jimmy. A place you went to unwind, to get away from it all. He thought of his Mom and how she'd died much too young. And then, how his Dad had plunged himself into his work.

Jimmy stretched as best he could in the front passenger's seat of the unmarked car and remembered he still hadn't found the moment to propose to Jessie yet. He still had that ring, stuffed in a desk drawer back at the office. He tried leaning sideways into the seat and his Glock 9mm pistol dug into his side. He sighed and thought again about getting out. With Jessie. Maybe move to Boston?

Jimmy gazed at the passing landscape and smiled at the idea that, after taking this escape route with him a few times, Jessica had come to appreciate the look and feel of his personal little retreat; the red brick streets and townhouses, the upscale colleges, the seafood. Jimmy couldn't put his finger on it: was it the town itself, or was it the easy ride up through New England, or just the idea of getting away that made the trip to Boston special to him?

He glanced over at Frank, who was lost in the monotony of the white lines. Then he rolled his head back to the greenery. He decided just to enjoy the aura of the trip rather than trying to define it.

The department cell phone rang through the car speakers. Frank answered it with the Bluetooth button on the steering wheel. Leaning in from the front passenger's seat, Jimmy checked the caller ID on the dashboard and called out, "What's up, Jack?"

Sergeant Donohue's voice came over the car's speakers. "Hello, Captain, how is the trip going?"

Jimmy and Frank exchanged glances. Still looking at Frank, Jimmy answered, "Well, Ramirez is starting to stink a little. He hit a Taco Bell a while back, but other than that, we're good." Frank smiled and checked the side mirror outside his driver's window, shaking his head. Jimmy pulled himself up in the seat and sat forward with his forearms on his thighs. "All right, Jack, what do you have? What's up?"

"Captain, the FBI figured out we received a copy of the surveillance footage from the UN. They want to know if we found anything out from our review. I just came back from a sit down with them."

"Yeah, and?"

"I must say, Captain, you were right and I was disappointed. They had nothing but questions for me and wouldn't tell me a single thing they found from their review."

"Yeah," Jimmy laughed. "Welcome to the world of joint-federal task force work. The FBI treats local law enforcement like mushrooms."

After a pause Donohue asked, "Mushrooms sir?"

Again, Jimmy and Frank exchanged glances. "Mushrooms, Jack: they keep us in the dark and feed us nothing but shit."

"Oh," Donohue answered. "Humor. I see; forgive me." Jack cleared his throat. "Anyway, Captain, what I did glean from the meeting is that there are a number of people in the footage that they are interested in speaking to, but can't locate. In the chaos of the immediate aftermath of the shooting, apparently not all witnesses were detained."

Ramirez threw in, "They never are, kid: another fact of life the feds don't seem to understand. It's a city of eight million; it's not perfect."

Donohue cleared his throat again. "Yes, well, they have a handful of photographs of those they are actively seeking for questioning, and Zafir and Siban are amongst them. I told the FBI nothing about Zafir, but didn't feel I could reasonably say I didn't recognize Siban —I mean, we have an entire folder on him from the Queen Mary incident."

"That's fine," Jimmy interrupted Jack. "They have a folder on Siban, too. And you were right to identify him; they already know that you know who he is."

"Yes. Thank you, Captain," Jack continued. "So, even though they had no answers for me —only questions, I was able to slip some information out of them that may be useful." Jack paused and Jimmy could hear paper shuffling through the car speakers. Jack continued the briefing. "After the shots were fired, the last man that Zafir was seen with is an ex-terrorist from the IRA."

"*Ex*-terrorist?" Ramirez said into the windshield. "Is there such a thing?"

Jack answered, "The feds didn't pay much attention to his presence. In fact, they thought very little of it and so I was able get some information about him. Apparently he was on their terrorist watch lists for years, but that was a decade ago. They say he saw the light when a peaceful, political solution was reached in Northern Ireland, and now he's working with the moderates in the Arab community to try and work out something similar with them.

"Anyway, they wouldn't give me the folder on him. I don't even have his name, but that's all I got out of the meeting. Zafir was last seen talking with some Irishman."

"Okay," Jimmy said. "And you didn't tell them that we found Zafir getting on an Amtrak to Boston?"

"No, sir. But that left me wondering, Captain. Why didn't they look as hard as we did, and find that themselves?"

"They haven't interviewed Siban, yet. They don't know Zafir is the bad guy. Or that he's looking to score a load of guns."

"Oh, right," Jack said.

"All right, Jack, good work. Now tell me: from what you saw in the footage, what did it look like? Is this Irish guy in on it with Zafir, or did they just happen to cross paths? Like, did they talk in close, were they whispering, or just talking? What?"

"Ahh, it's hard to say, of course, without audio; but from what I saw, I don't think they were previously connected. They happened to climb out of the pile together, but, -I don't know… -something in Zafir's manner when they parted… -it's hard to describe Captain, it looked almost like an idea came to him while he was looking at the guy. If that makes any sense."

Jimmy and Frank looked at each other again, but this time they both nodded slowly and smiled. "You know what, Jack?" Jimmy spoke. "It sounds like you might just become an actual detective someday. That's good work, my friend. At the very least, you may have given us a starting point in a city of two million. Anything else?"

"No sir, but I'll keep at it."

"Great; tell Clark we said hey. We'll be in Boston in a few hours."

Frank hit the Bluetooth button on the steering wheel again, terminating the call. Jimmy glanced down at his iPhone and noticed that the other pin had dropped. On the Saints and Scholars.

14

Johnny Dineen stopped in the vestibule of The Saints and Scholars and let the inner door close behind his two men. This was no Mayo Inn. He took a moment to check his suit jacket –again. There was no more cigar ash there, but he brushed his lapels anyway, just to be sure. He let another minute go by. While he waited, he checked his shoes. They were fine, really, but he stood on one foot and brushed the tops against the back of each calf again anyway, just to be sure.

Finally he looked up. He took a deep breath, nodded for Dermot to open the inner door, and Johnny Dineen stepped in to The Saints and Scholars.

His two thugs, Coghlan and Duffy, had done their job. The whole place was on notice. Even Gaughan, the little host, stood back and only shyly offered a menu to Johnny. Johnny waved him off.

He scanned the dining room first, and basked in the attention. He nodded slowly and tossed out a few conspiratorial winks and nods. Everyone wanted to be a player. Not for real, Johnny knew, but in spirit. Which was enough.

He turned to the bar. He stepped between his two thugs and led them and Dermot down the aisle.

Suits and ties, dresses and pearls; all turned for a glance. Johnny kept his smile on and nodded at each face. He stopped at one vaguely familiar couple and patted the man's shoulder. "How've you been?" The man blathered something and Johnny ran the back of his hand down the man's upper arm. "Is that Brooks Brothers?" He ignored the man's response and smiled at his companion. "Nice. Very nice." He turned away and said over his shoulder, "You two behave yourselves tonight, alright?"

A few stools down, a pair of Boston PD detectives turned their backs to the bar and faced the aisle. Homicide guys. They were known to show up at places like this, Johnny knew, trying to class themselves up. Johnny nodded at them. They nodded back. No smiles.

Johnny continued on and stopped at an open spot. The bartender hurried over. Johnny stepped in and tossed a hundred dollar bill on the mahogany. He leaned in, "Take care of my guys." Then he nodded up towards the detectives. "And give the guardians of the peace a round on me, got it?" The bartender nodded. Johnny stepped back and his two thugs took their places. Johnny tried not to smirk when the lovely people on either side skootched away from the leather jacket and pony tail taking up residence in their polite little world.

Johnny left his men at the bar and continued along with Dermot in tow. Past the end of the bar, the two young IRA guards in suits didn't move and didn't smile; they just stood there with their hands crossed in front.

Johnny didn't like that they stood their ground before him. This was a century-old standoff, he knew. There was them, and there was us, and then there were the cops and city hall and all that, too. There was no pecking order, just some kind of mutual respect. The whole thing was bigger than him or anyone in the place. He just nodded at the two of them and spoke: "Mister O'Leary here yet?"

He was met with two shakes of the heads and one verbal 'no, sir.' At least he said 'sir'. Johnny turned his back to them and looked up to the front. He stuffed his hands in his pants pockets and waited.

Didn't take long. The front door opened and the little host hurried forward, hugging his menus to his chest. Johnny watched the little man turn away abruptly at the sight of Jimmy Junior and stuff the menus back into the little rack he had up there.

Amidst the soft clatter of linen, crystal, and china, the host stepped to one side and guarded his lovely dining room. He stretched out his arm, signaling Junior into the bar area.

Junior glanced over the host and into the dining room. Then he scanned the whole place and met Johnny's eye. Junior nodded at Johnny, but then abruptly lurched at the host, as if he would hit him. "Back off," Junior growled, and everyone in the place heard him. The startled little man nearly fell down. The two homicide detectives noticed.

Johnny wasn't too worried about that, but did hope Junior knew not to antagonize the cops. Cops didn't like bullies; that was one thing they wouldn't tolerate in public, though they had to let a whole lot of other shit slide with Jimmy Junior —that was part of the territory.

Sure, Junior had been arrested a few times over the years, Johnny knew; but always by some dumb rookie that caught him in the act and didn't know any better. Detectives wouldn't come looking for Jimmy Junior no matter what was reported. It was just that way in Boston. He was Seamus O'Leary —The Third.

Jimmy Junior reached back and held open the front door. Old Seamus O'Leary himself entered the Saints and Scholars and stepped out in front of his grandnephew.

The old man and his ever-present shillelagh ambled past

Junior. "Behave yourself; this is a nice place."

Junior lead the old man down the aisle. The two homicide dicks still had their backs to the bar and did a slow nod to Mister O'Leary, who winked at them. Junior sauntered past them with his ever-present boxing glove pendant dangling from a gold rope chain around his neck. It was part of his shtick, Johnny knew; Junior wanted everyone to remember he was once Boston's Golden Gloves welterweight champ.

Junior stood only about five-ten, but when he walked past Dineen's thugs, they both leaned back just a bit. Junior always kept people on edge. That was part of what Johnny liked about him —as long as he stayed on the leash.

Junior stopped next to Coghlan and Duffy, then turned back to the detectives. He said to them all: "Nice to see you boys getting along." The detectives snorted and turned back around to the bar.

The two IRA men stepped up from the back door to greet Mister O'Leary. They ignored Junior.

Gaughan, the host, appeared from around the back of the partition and approached Seamus with a menu. Seamus was known to dine at the Saints and Scholars at least three times a week and used the back room as his temporary headquarters. The old man politely waved off the host, saying that he and Mister Dineen would be out to sit for dinner after the meeting.

Gaughan bowed and disappeared. Johnny put his hand on Old Seamus' shoulder. "How are you, old friend?"

"I'm well, John, thank you." Old Seamus glanced around the room. "Any sign of our old Libyan friend, yet?"

"I don't know if I'd recognize him, Seamus; it's been a while."

Junior stepped in. "Ain't gonna be too many towel heads in here."

Both Johnny and Mister O'Leary stared at Junior until he lost the smirk and looked away.

"Yes, John, it's been some time for myself, too. We were close associates over the years, but when they decided to bring their fight to American soil, we cut all ties. But I never remove anyone from my Rolodex."

Then Seamus turned to Junior and motioned to the dining room. "Go take a look —and be polite."

Jimmy Junior strolled off into the well-appointed dining room, his sweat suit and filthy sneakers raising a few eyebrows. Junior took his time and looked at every face in the room. The old Arab wasn't in the house. Junior got up to the front and stepped around the top of the partition by the front door. He'd already seen everyone at the bar, and so turned to check the cocktail tables by the front window.

To his surprise, he recognized Zafir immediately. He hadn't seen him since they were kids, some twenty years ago, but their fathers were friends back in the day and they had spent some childhood time together.

Zafir stared at Junior and nodded once.

Junior barely smiled in return. He stepped over to the small, round table. "Your old man here?" Zafir only shook his head. Junior continued, "You're runnin' this operation?" Zafir nodded.

Junior thought about that for a moment and glanced back at his old granduncle and the others. Then he frowned and stepped away from the table. "Alright, come on." He waved for Zafir to follow him.

They arrived at the back and Junior announced the guest to old Seamus, "Zafir Junior, here."

Seamus stared hard at the young Arab. He pursed his lips and squinted his disapproval.

"I recognize him, boss," Junior offered. "I met him when we were kids. Ain't that right, Zafir?" Zafir partly bowed.

"Where's your father?" Seamus asked.

Zafir bowed again. "He is no longer with us, Sayed. Cancer took his life a year ago."

The elder O'Leary raised his shillelagh and said, "Toss him." Junior turned on Zafir and grabbed him by the elbows. In one swift move, he threw Zafir's arms up over his head and stepped into him. "This'll only take a sec; hold still." Junior patted Zafir down and turned back to his granduncle. "Clean."

"Alright. Let's get started." Old Seamus turned for the back room and all the players followed.

Along the opposite wall of the rectangular room, a set of empty sterno trays misted on a buffet table. At the moment, a conference table filled the center of the room, with three chairs on either side. Johnny went around and took his place along the far side with his back to the sternos. Dermot sat to his left. Their usual spots.

Jimmy Junior stepped to the end nearest the door and pulled out the seat for his granduncle to take his place at the head of the table.

The two young IRA men in suits directed Zafir to the seat opposite Old Seamus at the foot of the table –furthest from the door. The IRA men then came around and took positions just inside the door. Then Junior walked around the room and stood behind Zafir, just over his shoulder.

They all settled in and Old Seamus started the meeting: "Gentlemen. Obviously, I keep in touch with every connection I have ever made." He looked directly at Zafir. "But I was expecting to see your father. He and I had conducted business together. But that was many years ago. I'm not sure what it is you're here for."

The young Arab looked directly at Old Seamus and got right to the point: "The Guns of Antwerp."

Old Seamus hesitated. "I'm not sure I know what you mean. Your father and I did business in Antwerp once, but —"

"Please, Sayed," Zafir interrupted Old Seamus. "Do not pretend." He leaned over and reached into his back pocket. In the blink of an eye, a revolver was pointed at his temple. Zafir looked up at Jimmy Junior.

"Please, my friend," Zafir said to Junior without moving his hands. "Observe me closely." The young Arab deftly stuck just his thumb and forefinger into his pocket. Junior kept the gun right where it was and stepped back. He cocked the revolver with a loud 'clack' and told him, "Go ahead, Raghead; do what you gotta do."

Zafir ignored the insult and slowly slid what looked like some sort of barrel-like key out of his pocket. Junior withdrew the revolver and gently dropped the hammer back in place.

"For you," Zafir said, and slid the heavy metal object across the table. It made it only a few feet and they all stared at it. Johnny shot Seamus a quizzical look. Old Seamus ignored him and said to Zafir, "I had forgotten about that. That belonged to your father, didn't it?"

"Yes," Zafir said softly. "And to you before him, Sayed. It is the key to The Guns of Antwerp."

All eyes were on the table. Johnny didn't understand. He'd thought he had the key to wherever these mysterious fuckin guns were hidden. He noticed Dermot lean back and reach into his pants pocket saying, "If that's the key, then what —"

Johnny grabbed Dermot hard and whispered, "Shut the fuck up and put that away." Then he turned to Seamus. "We need a minute, here." He motioned to the door.

Old Seamus nodded to Johnny. Then he looked over at his two young IRA men and motioned for them to take Zafir out of the room. The young Arab perceived the message and stood as the IRA men approached.

Inside of a minute, they had the room. Johnny turned to Mister O'Leary. "Seamus, what the fuck?" He spread his hands open. "These things exist?" Johnny half-stood and reached across the table. He picked up the barrel-like key. "And if this is the key for them, then what's up with the key I have?" He rolled a thumb toward Dermot.

Old Seamus nodded slowly, then spoke. "There were three crates all together. We lost one in Antwerp and escaped with the other two." He tilted his head toward the door. "Me and his father. The Russians said we'd need that thing," he pointed to the barrel-key in Johnny's hand, "to operate the weapon in one of the crates. But we believe that weapon, whatever it was, got taken by the Belgians, rendering that thing useless to us. So I gave it to al-Ayyad. Decent man, actually. I liked him. We were stowaways for quite a trip across the Atlantic. Anyway, that thing means nothing."

Johnny still had questions. "So what's in the two crates you kept? And where are they?"

Seamus looked down at the table and shook his head. "Not unless World War Three breaks out right here in Boston, John."

"Alright, but what's in them; what are they worth?"

Seamus looked up. "A few hundred handguns and thousands of rounds of ammunition."

"That's it?"

"They're untraceable John. Not even the Feds could track them from any crime scene. All Russian made, like magic bullets."

"You counted them?"

Seamus shook his head again, but smiled. "Even though we owned Boston at the time, John, with that kind of weight, the heat was on. We had to move. I never opened the crates. I just assumed the bill of lading the Russians described was correct."

"But you didn't get a copy. You never opened the crates?"

"We didn't have time. I gave them over to our sacred protectors and that was that. Once they secured them, they gave me the key to the padlock," he pointed at Dermot, "which you now have. And that was it."

"So you don't know where they are."

"No, but I know who does. And no one could ever make those men talk. Not in two thousand years."

Johnny just nodded at that.

Jimmy Junior spoke up from the far side of the room. "I bet he offers a pretty penny for them, though. Those A-rabs got plenty of cash, ya know?"

Again Johnny and Mister O'Leary stared at Junior until he lost the smirk and looked away. Johnny found himself disappointed that Junior was even privy to the conversation at all. He didn't trust the kid like that.

Seamus nodded for his two IRA men to bring the Arab back in. Again inside of a minute, Jimmy Junior pulled out the chair at the foot of the table for Zafir to sit.

Johnny watched and waited. Mister O'Leary spread his two gnarled hands out on the table in front of him and looked at Zafir. Then he spoke.

"Young man, your people told me you had an offer to make. Make it."

"Two million," was all Zafir said.

Johnny sat up straight.

Old Seamus blinked slowly. "What will you do with them?"

"I will bring them back to the place of their origin. We need them today in Libya. I will use them there," Zafir said.

Johnny didn't believe one bit of that. "For two million dollars, you could buy a whole lot of guns anywhere in the world. Why these? Why here?"

Zafir turned to Johnny. "These cannot be traced. No one in your government even believes that they exist; that they ever made it to America. Their mystery is my asset."

"Hold on." Johnny had some more questions. "Why do you give a fuck if they can't be traced? I don't get that. You say you're going to send them back to Libya, so what does it matter to you if they can be traced or not?"

"They were my father's guns. I want them back." He leaned forward onto the table. "When you needed us, we gave you our assistance; we helped you procure these weapons. But Belfast is no longer burning. You no longer have need for them. But Libya, the origin of these weapons, my Libya…" the young Arab pointed to his own chest, "…is on fire."

Johnny stared hard at Zafir. "I don't like it." He turned to Old Seamus. "His people want to kill all of us —Irish, British, Americans —all of us. I don't agree. I'm not even sure what the fuck is going on here, but I'm not getting involved. Not even for two million dollars." Johnny pursed his lips and watched for a response from old Seamus.

The elder IRA leader leaned back and searched the ceiling. Johnny waited and after a moment, Seamus returned his gaze to the table and spoke, "You pay up front and we'll ship them. Just let us know what port and we'll handle the transport."

Zafir frowned. "I'm sorry Sayed, that is unacceptable. We must take possession immediately. We can –"

"No fuckin' way." Johnny turned to Seamus. "I don't trust this guy one fuckin' bit Seamus, if we can't –"

Seamus held up a hand and silenced the room. He looked long and hard at Zafir before he spoke. "Either we ship them out of the country, or no deal."

Zafir closed his eyes and drew in a deep breath. Then he looked up at Seamus. "Sayed, we have the resources in place necessary to move the weapons. I thank you for your offer of transport but, we need to take possession immediately. We can –"

Again, Seamus held up a hand and this time, he shook his head.

Jimmy Junior pushed Zafir's shoulder. "Get up; you're done. No deal."

Old Seamus stood. "The truth of the matter is, these guns don't actually exist anyway." He paused and stared at the young Arab. "Understand?"

Zafir shook his head as he stood and protested softly. "Sayed, my father was there. He told me of two crates that he personally gave to you in Boston Harbor."

Old Seamus just smiled. "Did you ever see the bill of lading?" he asked, knowing that the Russians never supplied the official list of contents.

"No, Sayed, my father said it did not exist."

"Oh, it existed, young man; we just never got it from the Russians. Do you know what those crates were marked as?"

Zafir thought for a moment. "Yes; yes I do." He stopped his walk around the table and closed his eyes to concentrate. "In fact, they were marked as luggage." He opened his eyes. "–Suitcases manufactured in Moscow, I believe."

"That's right. And that's exactly what was in those crates. The whole thing was a scam. The guns never existed. You Libyans ripped us off." Old Seamus pushed his chair in under the table. "So, really, you and your Libyan friends have come full circle now, haven't ye?" He bowed. "Good day."

"Alright, c'mon." Junior pushed Zafir toward the door but kept an eye on his bosses. He made a show of pulling his windbreaker out over the gun in his waistband –and slipped a business card out of his pocket.

He put his hands on Zafir again. "Meeting's over, Raghead, let's go." As the two IRA men at the top of the room turned to open the door, Junior slipped the card into Zafir's hand.

Junior hoped this A-rab would have some fucking clue. Zafir did not react outwardly. *Good boy,* Junior thought. Zafir deftly slid the card into his own pocket and turned to the door.

Junior took hold of the door from one of the IRA men and held it open. "Let's go pal, you're out." Zafir stepped through. Jimmy didn't look Zafir in the eye. Instead, he stared at the pocket into which Zafir had put the business card. He kept staring until Zafir finally tapped that pocket.

Then Junior looked him in the eye and almost imperceptibly, Zafir nodded and left. Junior closed the door behind him.

Junior took up his place next to his uncle. He listened as Dineen prattled on with some objection or another. *Stupid son of a bitch,* Junior thought. *Two million fucking dollars; what's the matter with these people?*

"Now is not the time, John," Old Seamus said. "You just keep that key safe for the present. This is a matter of legacy and loyalty." Seamus took out his cell phone and sat down.

Junior watched Dineen motion for Dermot to go out to the bar and collect their two goons. Dineen said, "Take the guys with you and head back to The Mayo. I'm staying for dinner with Mister O'Leary."

Junior watched Dermot put the padlock key back in his pocket. Seamus leaned back in his chair and held up a finger for Dermot to wait until he was off the phone. He spoke to Dineen: "Especially since I don't know exactly where these guns are, right now I feel the need to check on them; make sure they can't possibly be found. I don't trust that the Arabs will give up that easily. If they think the guns exist, who knows how far they'll go to get them." The old man selected a number from his cell phone directory and dialed.

Junior stared intently at the phone. But Old Seamus turned to him. "Junior, have the host get a table ready for Mister Dineen and me."

Junior nodded at his granduncle and purposely turned very slowly to the door. He needed to hear this. Needed to know who was hiding those fucking guns.

As he turned, Dermot held out a hand to him. "And tell my two guys to saddle up. I'll be out in a few minutes." Junior restrained himself from bristling at having to take instructions from a middle manager like Dermot but he sucked it up, happy for another few seconds to remain in the room. He stood still to nod his compliance to Dermot.

Then a ringing emanated from Old Seamus' earpiece. Junior turned to the door as slowly as he could. He knew his granduncle's hearing wasn't what it used to be. He knew the old man always kept the volume high —and others could hear, if they were close enough. An unintended consequence. Junior opened the door —slowly.

Finally, the call was answered. Junior suppressed a smirk as he heard Old Seamus' brother's voice come over the line: "Boston College. Father O'Leary, how can I help you?"

15

Junior closed the door behind himself and walked straight up to Dineen's two bodyguards. For his plan to work, he had to move fast, real fast. But for two million…

"Take a hike." The two thugs furrowed their brows at him. Junior stepped in between them and up to the bar. He grabbed the money Dineen had thrown down for them to drink with and put it in his pocket. Then he stepped back.

"Are you two fucking deaf? You got a new assignment. Follow the A-rab." Junior pointed to the front door. He knew too much time had passed for them to actually put a tail on Zafir with such short notice but it was better than trying to deck the both of them and drag them out to the gutter. Not that he didn't think he could. He just didn't have time to roll around with them. Dermot would be out of the back room in another minute. The two goons panicked. One of them asked, "What's he driving?"

"Who said he's driving?" Junior stepped all the way back to the partition. "You two assholes better a get a move on. And you report to me on this. Mister Dineen just put me in charge of this operation, and –" he poked his forefinger into the chest of the larger one, "don't fuck this up, understand? I want a call from you every hour until you find him, got it?"

Dineen's thugs hurried for the front door. Just in time – Dermot emerged from the back room. Junior hustled to the front of the crowded bar and grabbed the host –physically.

"Get a table for Mister Dineen and my uncle." He looked over his shoulder and saw Dermot searching up and down the bar. "And tell the old man I'll be back for him."

He shoved the host. "Go."

Junior turned back into the bar aisle. Dermot spotted him and shrugged in question.

Junior frowned with an agreeing nod. "Yeah, right? The boss has got some bad taste in personnel, huh?"

Dermot looked him up and down. "What the fuck are you talking about?"

Junior tried to appear sheepish, not prideful. "Sorry, Dermot, but those two assholes you brought took off with a couple of horny housewives." Junior pointed to the busy bartender. "Guy tells me the broads were slumming, ya know? Like a couple of cougars or something." Junior shrugged. "I guess the boys couldn't help themselves; took off from here, like, ten minutes ago."

Dermot fumed. Junior continued: "C'mon, I'll drive you." He put his hand on Dermot's upper arm. "And I promise I won't say 'I told you so'." He laughed.

Junior watched Dermot's pride well up. Junior tried not to laugh when Dermot snarled and glanced back at the empty bar stools. "I want them bloodied up, Junior. Not dead, you understand? But I want their fucking noses broken and I want them brought before my desk, bleeding; ya got it?"

Junior put his best good boy face on and played along. "Yes sir; I'll do that, sir, and I'll make sure they know it came from you, too." Junior escorted Dermot to the door.

Once they got in the car, that awesome excitement kicked in that Jimmy Junior always felt before a killing. He loved it. It was like the ultimate powerful secret. *You're about to die; I know it and you don't, ha, ha.* He loved it. "So, boss: home, or back to The Mayo Inn?"

"The Mayo," Dermot said.

"So." Junior started driving. "This deal with the A-rab. I want to do it. I want the two million. I want that padlock key you got in your pocket."

Dermot stared at him for a moment and then said, "What the fuck do you think you're talking about? Did you not hear Mister O'Leary say 'no' in there?"

Junior laughed. "Ha, yeah, I'm just kidding, Dermot. I just figured I'd give you a chance to live tonight."

Dermot turned sideways in the seat toward him. "Who the fuck—"

And Junior shot him. With his right hand on the steering wheel and the revolver cradled in his lap with his left, he didn't even have to look over. He put a bullet directly into Dermot's heart. He stuffed the revolver under the seat and reached over and turned the heavily bleeding man to face forward. "Now sit up straight and die like a man so I can get through the toll booth, alright?"

16

Just outside of New Haven, Connecticut, the unmarked car sped out of the Wilbur Cross Tunnel and a sharp sunset burst through the windshield. Frank adjusted his visor. Then he looked over at Jimmy doing research on his iPhone and asked, "What do you got? What's up with these places? What the hell are Saints and Scholars?"

Jimmy smiled up at Frank. "What. You don't know what Saints and Scholars means?" The phone beeped answers. Jimmy tapped a link as he spoke. "An old friend of my dad's said something about stopping in to these places when he heard we were going to Boston. Said he's got friends there that could give us the lay of the land as far as where guys like Zafir might go to get connected. You know, the underworld."

Jimmy laid the phone down in the center arm rest, waiting for it to load. "Ever since my father expanded his PI firm into Boston, he's been feeling his way around up there."

"Yeah," Frank said, "how's that going? They getting any business up there? I mean, they practically cornered the market in New York, bro, what with all those executive protection contracts for visiting dignitaries and such."

"Yeah, New York is good. But Boston's been slow going."

"Is he going to be up here? Your father?"

"No, he's busy down in New York. The UN General Assembly is meeting next week and he's working on signing contracts with a few diplomats and such. Not all of those people get government protection. And even the ones that do, like to sneak off the leash now and then; so they like to get private protection, you know?"

"Yeah." Frank glanced down at the iPhone on the center console. "So Beacon Street, huh?" He brought his eyes back to the road. "I've heard of that. I think I know where it is." He glanced down again. "We still have to GPS it, though."

"No problem, we got time." Jimmy sat back and stared out the window again. After a few miles he lolled his head over toward the driver's side. "So, Frank, you know why they call Ireland the Land of Saints and Scholars?"

Frank looked like he didn't hear him. He kept driving but then glanced about half way over and said, "Do I care?" He smirked. Then he looked at Jimmy and smiled. "If you want to know why we call Puerto Rico, Boricua; then sure, Jimbo, tell me all about the Land of Saints and Scholars."

"Ohh. Okay." Jimmy looked directly at Frank, searching for a response. Then he said, "That's Captain Jimbo to you, Bub." Then he leaned back on the headrest and relaxed. There was always plenty of time for the flow of conversation on a road trip. Finally Frank said, "It's what we were called before all you Europeans came in. You and all those poor Africans you kidnapped."

Jimmy turned to Frank and pulled his head back into his shoulders with a 'what?' look.

"Boricua." Frank took his gaze off the road for just a moment. "Boriquenos. It's what the people of Puerto Rico were called 'pre-Columbus,' bro."

Jimmy put his head back down again. "Oh." He gazed out the window and nodded. "Cool." After a few more miles he said, "The Enlightenment." He got no response and so let it sit there for a minute. Road trip timing. Then

Frank turned to him and raised his eyebrows. Jimmy smiled. "During the Middle Ages when the rest of Europe fell into the Dark Ages and lots of writings and scholarly works and such were being destroyed, Ireland was kind of like the ends of the earth, at the time. So a lot of that stuff was, well, safeguarded there. A lot of historians say the Enlightenment came out of Ireland –The Land of Saints and Scholars."

The pastoral Wilbur Cross Parkway ended and Frank merged onto Interstate 91, heading eventually for the Massachusetts Turnpike. Then he turned to Jimmy. "So this friend of your father's, what is he: a gangster, a gunrunner? What?"

"Gunrunner?" Jimmy looked at Frank for a moment before responding. "So you know a little about the Irish in Boston, then, huh?"

Frank smiled but kept his eyes on the road. "Boriquenos can read too, bro."

Jimmy smiled and nodded slowly. "Cool." Then he looked back at the map on his phone. "First we'll go to The Mayo Inn." He looked up. "We're looking to talk to a guy named Dermot Casey. The place is run by a Johnny Dineen but Casey is his right-hand man and is a friend of a friend."

Frank nodded but asked, "We gonna treat him like a friend? Like, how do you want to make the approach?"

Jimmy thought for a moment and then said, "We'll let the atmosphere in the place dictate."

Hours later, the dinner hour long past, it was full dark in Boston. After taking the Mass Pike to the very end and heading south on I-93 along the shore of Boston Harbor, Jimmy and Frank looked for an exit. Frank threw his hands up at the second exit ramp which led only to a broadened shoulder of the road but with no actual exit. "What the hell. I guess they don't want outsiders coming into this neighborhood, huh?"

Jimmy laughed and checked the map on his phone again. "Yeah, you can't get off this highway in Dorchester. To get into the neighborhood, we have to go down to Exit 12, a little south of it."

Jimmy studied the map and they eventually wheeled off the interstate. "We're in luck." Jimmy looked up. "The map says the Mayo Inn is just a couple of blocks from here." After a few turns they went across Gallivan Boulevard and found Adams Street. "Make a right, here."

They made the turn and a red brick island curved them onto Adams Street. The tiny triangle park was replete with an old-style street lamp and ornate clock tower.

"There it is, right there." Jimmy pointed across the street. Two young guys, one in an army surplus jacket, the other in a hoodie, hung around outside the door of the Mayo Inn, smoking. Frank made a U-turn and pulled up right in front.

Jimmy and Frank got out and approached. The kid in the hoodie took one look at them and slipped inside. The other guy stayed out front, blocking the door.

"Pretty far from home officer," he said looking at the license plate. Jimmy stepped up to him and smiled. "Are we that obvious?" Jimmy stepped back and turned to his partner. "Frank, the guy made us already, imagine?" Frank ignored Jimmy's comment and brushed right into the kid as if he wasn't there. Then he pulled open the door, looked the kid in the eye and said, "After you, Captain." They went in.

The bar began on their left and ran straight to the back. A row of booths ran down the right side wall. The bartender did not approach. He leaned on the back wall of the bar, about midway to the front, watching.

Half the booths were filled with young guys in jeans, boots, and raggedy jackets. One older guy in a rumpled shirt and bowtie stood in the back, past the run of booths, with a small group of young toughs surrounding him. Jimmy waded in.

He walked slowly down the aisle, studying the faces and the body language, looking for something in particular; something he would recognize immediately.

After a silent minute of navigating the sea of menacing glares, he stopped and turned in a circle. He canvassed the room one more time. He paused his eyes for a moment on the guy in the bow tie. Rough-looking fella with big, gnarled hands; but not what Jimmy was looking for.

"So." Jimmy didn't shout, but spoke loud enough for everyone to hear. "Boss ain't around, huh?"

"Who's asking?" a voice came from one of the booths.

Jimmy turned, but couldn't identify which guy said it. "Captain Gallagher," he answered. "NYPD. Is this Johnny Dineen's place or what?" He put his arms out at his sides.

"What's it to you, Copper?" A twenty-something stepped up from the crew surrounding the older guy in the bowtie. "Johnny Dineen ain't got no business wit you or your kind." The kid waved at the door. "Whyn't chu and your boy over there take a fucking hike back down the pike —fore you get yourself kilt." He smirked. The kid talked with his hands mimicking something between a mobster and a rapper. A few in the room laughed.

Jimmy stepped toward him and smiled. "Do yourself a favor kid, save that 'Bada-Bing bullshit' for someone who's impressed by it."

He turned his back to the kid. He opened his jacket and put his hands on his hips, revealing the Glock 19 strapped to his belt. "Look." He glanced past the bartender and addressed the entire place again. "I didn't come here looking for trouble, but I am looking for Dermot Casey —need to have a word with that man."

A rumble ran across the room. A few guys stood up from the booths. The man in the bow tie stayed in the back, but shook his head. Finally, the bartender came off the back wall. "Captain." He walked up the barwell towards the front, away from the crowd, and motioned for Jimmy to join him. "Can I have a word?" He leaned in on the front end of the bar and waited. Jimmy walked up toward the front but kept his eye on the crews. Then he sat down and turned to the bartender. "What's up?"

"Some advice?" the bartender asked, and waited for a response.

Jimmy nodded his head. "Sure."

"You check in with Boston PD before you come in here?"

Jimmy just stared at him.

"I'm just saying." The bartender wiped down the bar, even though it was already clean. "Half these kids," he motioned with his head toward the booths, "their fathers are on the job up here. And the ones that don't end up with felony convictions by the time they turn twenty-one." The bartender shrugged. "Might end up on the job, too; know what I mean?"

"Okay, got that." Jimmy looked back over the crew. "But what's up with the reaction to asking for Casey? That seemed to rile them up."

"Yeah." The bartender looked out the front window.

"He's not missing or anything; we just haven't heard from him tonight. Was supposed to be here like an hour ago. Not like him. If he don't show, he usually calls, you know?"

"But he's not missing," Jimmy deadpanned at the bartender. The barman shrugged. "He's taken a hiatus before." He looked back at the crowd and then out the front window again, where his voice would trail away. "Left here with Mr. Dineen earlier tonight to go to dinner and hasn't been heard from since."

Jimmy stared at the bartender and waited. Getting no response, he raised his eyebrows and nodded his head forward. The bartender sighed. "Saints and Scholars. Up in downtown. Beacon Street."

Fifteen minutes later the unmarked car rolled slowly down a narrow one-way street in downtown Boston. Jimmy and Frank sat forward, turning their heads from side to side checking addresses and street signs. The narrow street turned sharply and two other narrow streets ran off in either direction at different angles.

"Man, I appreciate history as much as the next guy," Frank remarked, "but they had to follow the hoof-prints of the Pony Express up here? They couldn't straighten this shit out before they built all these buildings?"

Jimmy laughed and kept looking. "Here we go." He pointed up at a street sign.

Frank looked up. "This is Beacon Street? I thought it would be wider."

"There it is." Jimmy pointed to the right sidewalk. Frank kept driving, looking for a spot to pull in. They passed the restaurant and Jimmy looked over his shoulder. "Good timing. Looks like the dinner hour is over."

They parked the car half a block down and walked up to the Saints and Scholars. Frank remarked, "No thugs out front here, huh?" They walked in and were immediately approached by a diminutive host. Jimmy greeted him politely. "Kitchen still open?" The host nodded and held out two menus.

"Great." But Jimmy held up a hand. "We don't need menus, though." Jimmy looked around and pointed to the small tables on his left, between the front window and the bar. "Can we just grab some burgers over here?" The host nodded again and ushered them toward the front alcove.

Jimmy quickly took stock of the place and tapped the host lightly on the elbow. "Listen, after we order," Jimmy pulled his shield case out, "can you come back over?" Jimmy showed the host his NYPD Captains' shield and ID. "I have a few questions maybe you can help me with." The host frowned and hesitated, but then nodded and walked away with his menus.

Jimmy and Frank settled in, and when they were half way through with their meal, the host came back and pulled up a chair. "What can I help you with, gentlemen?"

Jimmy wiped his mouth with a linen napkin. "I'm Captain Gallagher," he said; then he motioned to Frank, "and this is Detective Ramirez."

"Francis Gaughan. I've been Maitre'd here for twenty-seven years," the host said proudly. Jimmy took note of that and smiled. "Then you're just the man I'm looking for. I'm trying to get the lay of the land up here." He glanced over at Frank. "We were just in a place called the Mayo Inn?"

Gaughan sniffed. "Dive."

"Tell me about it," Frank sneered.

"But this is a different place." Jimmy glanced around. "A

nicer place."

"Oh yes, yes," Gaughan said. "And we do a good business here."

"I can imagine," Jimmy appreciated. "But do any of those guys ever come in here?"

"In here? People from The Mayo Inn?" The host frowned. "We're upscale; this is downtown Boston, my dear Captain. No, those Southies don't frequent our establishment."

Jimmy kept smiling and nodded. "Oh yes, yes, I can see that." He took another appreciative look around the place. "But what about earlier tonight?" Jimmy leaned in over the table. "Do you know who Johnny Dineen is?"

"Oh." The host perked up and looked at the ceiling. "No, you're right, yes. It's been a busy night but, you're right, Mister Dineen was in here earlier." Gaughan leaned back. "That man I don't mind; he's usually a gentleman – good tipper, too." The host smiled. "But the riff-raff he carries on with, ugh. Those people should stay in their own part of town."

"So Dineen was here. And he brought some people with him?" Jimmy looked over at Frank, who already had his notepad out. "Can you describe them?"

"Acch." The host waved his hand. "Two unsightly ombathans." The host turned over his shoulder and pointed at the bar behind him. "Mister Dineen left them there at the bar and went into his meeting with his –uh, -Casey. Dermot Casey, another of his associates. An upper classman, if you will."

"So they were a party of four?"

"Well, I didn't seat them, as I said. But yes, there were four: Mister Dineen and Mister Casey and the two street people." Gaughan pointed again at the mid-point of the bar.

Jimmy looked at Frank to make sure he was getting this down. From behind his notepad, Frank looked at Jimmy and mouthed the word 'om-ba-than?' Jimmy shook his head and kept on with the host. "Okay, so there was a meeting? Tell me about that."

"Oh, yes." The host looked down the bar again. "In the back room there, just past the end of the bar. Mister O'Leary utilizes the back room often for his meetings."

"Mister O'Leary? Who is that? Tell me about him." "Oh yes, Mister O'Leary is a regular here. He –" The host hesitated and turned slowly to Jimmy. Then he looked down at Jimmy's pocket, where he had put his shield case. "Tell me again why you're asking all this? You're from New York, you said?"

"Yeah. No, I'm just the curious type, Mister Gaughan. You've been a great help. I really just wanted to know if Mister Dineen or Mister Casey was in here tonight. I know all about who Mister O'Leary is," Jimmy lied and sat back and reached for his burger. "I just wanted to see how much you knew about the people who come in to your restaurant." He took a bite and ignored the host.

"Ha." The host sat up straight. "I know everything about my customers. I've been here twenty-seven years."

Jimmy just lifted an eyebrow and nodded, but showed more interest in his cheeseburger than in anything Mister Gaughan had to say.

"Mister O'Leary is a civic leader here in Boston," the host boasted. "He's well known to everyone in City Hall and the State House. He is an international gentleman." The host huffed.

Jimmy finished chewing. "So he's IRA." Jimmy reached

for his napkin. The host demurely glanced away. Jimmy continued, feigning disinterest. "I know all about that," Jimmy lied again, and wiped his mouth with his napkin. "Doesn't make him a bad guy, though, right?" he chuckled, and tossed the napkin on the table. "Anyway, that's not what we're here for. So, continue: who else was here for the meeting? Show me how much you remember." Jimmy leaned in over the table.

"Well…" Gaughan searched the ceiling again. "The O'Leary's came in together and –"

"The O'Learys, plural," Jimmy interrupted him.

The host looked at Jimmy like he should have known this, "Yes, of course. Old Seamus needs help getting around, these days. He had his grandnephew with him, Seamus the third. Though he goes by some other name. Another ruffian. Not the sort we normally entertain here at the Saints and Scholars."

"More a Mayo Inn type?"

"Well, of course." The host shrugged again, as if this was common knowledge. "That's where he's from. He works for Mister Dineen."

"That's the younger O'Leary, he works for Dineen." Jimmy opened his eyes just a bit wider, looking for confirmation.

"Yes, that's right."

"But he didn't come in with Dineen, he came in with his uncle."

"Granduncle, yes. He escorts Old Seamus about town. After all, the man is well into his eighties."

"Right, no, of course." Jimmy glanced over at Frank, making sure he was getting all this down. He reached for his Diet Coke. "Go ahead, continue. What else about the meeting?"

The host went on to detail the interactions, including the indignity he suffered at the hands of young Seamus O'Leary —the third. "Okay, excellent." Jimmy continued coaching Gaughan. "Thanks for all that; you're a very observant man. So the older O'Leary is a respectable sort, but his nephew is one of Dineen's thugs; do I have that right?"

"Yes, yes, that's right, you understand it correctly." Gaughan looked away. The restaurant was quiet now, but Gaughan glanced around towards his dining room. Jimmy sensed the man's interest winding down.

"Okay." Jimmy turned to Frank and motioned to Frank's jacket pocket as he continued talking to Gaughan. "Just one more thing, Mister Gaughan: have you ever seen this guy in here?" Frank pulled a folded pieced of paper from his jacket and handed it to Jimmy. It was a copy of a photo he had received from Jack Donohue before they left the New York office. Jimmy unfolded it and showed Zafir's picture to the host.

"Oh yes." Gaughan closed his eyes. "He does look familiar." He opened his eyes and looked at the picture again. "Earlier tonight. That's right." He looked at Jimmy and smiled. "In fact, he sat right here at this very table." Jimmy tried not to show excitement. "Okay, great. Do you remember who he was with?"

"Oh no, he was alone. Poor fellow was waiting for a date that never showed."

"His date never showed? You're sure? What time did he leave? Did he eat? Did he order a drink?" The host's head looked like it was about to start spinning. They were already towards the end of the interview now and you could only squeeze but so much out of any given witness before they got confused and frustrated.

Frank tapped Jimmy under the table. Jimmy responded to Frank without turning to him. He took a deep breath and realized his shoulders were all hunched up. He relaxed. "So, okay, he left alone this guy?" Jimmy still held out the picture.

"Ahh, you know, I'm not sure." The host gazed off toward the entrance door, then to the back of the restaurant and back to the table. "I don't remember him leaving, but I do remember him arriving alone."

"Okay." Jimmy leaned in again, but remained patient. "Now think slowly." Jimmy looked to the back of the restaurant. "Where are your restrooms?" The host motioned to a short hallway beyond the back room. "Okay, now think," Jimmy continued. "Did this guy use the restroom at all? Take your time and visualize: did he get up from this table at all? Did he interact with anyone?"

The host stared down the length of the bar. "Oh, you're right again. Yes, yes, he did get up. In fact," he turned squarely to Jimmy, "he went in the back room. That's right, he did; he was in the meeting with them." The host looked around again. "How do you like that? I didn't even realize that until now."

Jimmy placed his hand on the man's forearm and spoke softly. "Could you close your eyes again for me?" Gaughan hesitated, but then smiled and closed his eyes. Jimmy continued. "You said 'they' went in the back room. Visualize it again: who did he go in the backroom with?"

Gaughan stayed silent for a moment and then responded with his eyes closed. "He came down the bar with the younger O'Leary and then…," he paused. "Oh yes, O'Leary patted him down and then they all went in together."

"Excellent. Mister Gaughan, thank you; you make a

good witness. So tell me, if you remember: what time did the meeting end? Did you see them leave?"

"No." The host thought for a moment. "Messrs O'Leary and Dineen stayed for dinner and the nephew came back later to pick him up but, no, that's all I remember."

"So what about Casey and the nephew and the two, uh, ombathans. And the man in this picture. Did they all leave together? Did you notice?"

"Ahh." The host stood and peeked around the partition into the dining room. "I'm sorry, that's all I can remember."

"But they didn't stay for dinner, Casey and the others."

The host drew a deep breath. "The dining room was quieting down by then and the bar was crowded." He put his hands on his hips. "No, they didn't stay for dinner, but I didn't see them leave. I'm sorry, gentlemen, that's really all I remember." He threw his hands up.

Jimmy stood. "Thank you again for all your knowledge, Mister Gaughan; you've been a great help." Jimmy pulled out a business card. "If you think of anything else, would you give me a call?" He handed Gaughan his card. The host took it and slipped it into his breast pocket. Jimmy continued, "Do you have a number where we can reach you in case we come up with any more questions?" Jimmy smiled.

"Sure." The host rattled off a cell phone number and Frank jotted it down.

Jimmy and Frank paid the bill and stepped outside to the car. They got in and Frank slumped behind the wheel. "We've got to get a place to crash. I'm going to fall asleep soon."

"No problem, I got that covered. We have a room

booked." Jimmy took out his phone. "Let's just check in with the office real quick." Frank started the car and Jimmy used the controls on the console to dial the number. After a moment, Sergeant Donohue's voice came over the car speakers.

"Hey, Jack, what are you working on? You got anything?"

"You sound like the FBI Captain."

Jimmy and Frank looked at each other and shook their heads. Ramirez said, "Kids today."

"Don't break my balls, Sergeant," Jimmy said into the windshield. "But I'll start anyway. We got Zafir spotted hanging out with some Irish gangsters and IRA types, okay?"

"Wow," Donohue responded. "That was fast. Good work, Captain, how did –"

Jimmy spoke over him. "What have you got down there, Donohue? What have you been doing while we're up here doing police work? Playing video games with Clark?"

Donohue didn't answer right away. They heard tapping on a keyboard in the background. Then Jack spoke. "I've been researching relevant topics, Captain. I've Googled PLO, IRA, Boston and keywords of that nature, and found a few stories linking those three together." Jimmy heard a few more keyboard sounds come over the phone line as Donohue continued.

"In 1986 the FBI caught the IRA trying to fly guns out of Boston on a private jet bound for Ireland. In 1990 a group of IRA supporters were jailed in Boston for trying to smuggle a homemade missile system into Ireland." There was a pause and Jimmy and Frank could hear the scratching of Jack's scroll wheel.

"There are some other potentially relevant cases connecting the IRA to Arab terrorists, specifically the PLO back in the seventies, but not much that connects them in Boston."

"When you say 'not much,' that means there was something?" Jimmy said.

"It's tenuous, at best." Jack said. "In 1977 the PLO sold an arms shipment to the IRA. There were three crates in all; 2 supposedly filled with handguns and the third had handguns, too, but also contained some kind of super-secret weapon. No one seems to know exactly what.

"Anyway, the cargo ship stopped in Antwerp, Belgium and the Brits were onto them. But they let the Belgium authorities do the actual intercept. Turns out, only one crate was recovered. No one knows where the other two ended up.

"Rumors abound, though. Some bloggers say they made it in to Northern Ireland after all, but they never surfaced there. Others say they were put on another ship bound for Boston. It's all rumors, but it's become somewhat of a legend up there, apparently. The Irish in Boston like to whisper about 'The Guns of Antwerp' being hidden amongst them. But, like I said, nothing but rumors."

Another scratch of the scroll wheel could be heard and then Jack continued. "Although there is this other story, a more modern one —in fact, it's happening right now in Boston —that may be of interest. There's this set of audio recordings made by a reporter. They call it The Belfast Project. Interviews of IRA people apparently incriminating themselves over the years and many, many others; some of whom are now highly placed in governments around the world.

"Anyway, the British Government is in Supreme Court up there in Massachusetts, trying to get custody of the tapes, but they're being denied. Interesting stuff; but nothing useful that I can see."

Jimmy stared out the windshield and thought about that for a long minute.

Then he asked Jack, "Where are they now?"

"Who?" Jack answered.

"The tapes, Jack; where are the tapes?"

"Oh, uh, hold on." A few more keyboard taps and then, "Boston College."

17

From the front passenger seat of the rented van, Zafir glanced over at young Seamus O'Leary. Zafir knew O'Leary carried a handgun in his waistband, in the front, slightly to the left. Zafir had been trained to notice such things. As long as they remained within arm's length of each other, Zafir felt confident he could disarm the criminal if it came to that. *Keep your enemies close.*

O'Leary sniffled and wiped his sleeve across his face. Zafir smirked inwardly at O'Leary's manner of dress today. He was still a filthy pig, but in finer silks.

Zafir grinned at the Irishman's attempt at appearing mature by wearing slacks and shoes. *Something must have changed recently,* he thought. *This low-level criminal thinks he's moving up in the world.*

Zafir looked out the passenger side window and watched the streets of Boston roll by. The difference between Dorchester where he met O'Leary this morning and Roxbury Crossing where Zafir had spent the night at his cousin's place was not clear to him. It all looked the same. No different, really, than the Brooklyn neighborhood he grew up in. Five or six story apartment buildings with the occasional row of two and three level frame houses, all mixed in with big, brown boxes of public housing.

Boston, Brooklyn –it made no difference; it was cold and it was America. And he hated every bit of it.

He began recognizing some of the scenery and realized they were headed back toward Roxbury Crossing. The van turned left through a wide, park-like intersection filled with lush trees and trimmed bushes onto Malcolm X Boulevard. Americans, Zafir grimaced. They sat atop the green earth as if they owned it; actually believed they owned it. He gritted his teeth. He would show them. He would now rise up above all the others of Fateh and show the world what a real soldier looked like.

After a few blocks, they passed a giant mosque on their left: The Islamic Society of Boston Cultural Center; the place his cousin encouraged him to visit last night. Fools, Zafir thought as he watched the tall brick Minaret rise up to the sky before him. He knew all about the ISBCC and the foolishness they put forth.

The poverty, ignorance, and hatred that ran rampant through the Arab community couldn't be fixed by religious leaders. It could only be harnessed and put to good use in the fight for freedom –by people like himself.

Besides, this mosque had been standing for two years now, and what effect has it had? None. But his efforts; they would have an immediate effect. He leaned his head onto the window to catch a glimpse of himself in the van's side view mirror. He smiled at his own reflection and thought of how the elders in New York had rebuffed him. But he was Zafir, a born leader. He had the attention of hundreds of young soldiers in Brooklyn who would follow him. The war on the West was about to take a turn, and he would lead it.

They drove on for a while and the van eventually crossed a narrow set of train tracks. Zafir sat up straight and relished the idea that he knew the path to victory for his people. Guns, bombs and blood –that was the only way. And now this filthy Irishman was about to deliver the guns.

The van turned left off Commonwealth Avenue and onto the campus of Boston College.

18

The three smirking young men sat across from their religious leader. They finally dropped their grins. The cleric believed he was getting through to them.

The table was large, but old and worn, chipped and scarred in many places. The three smirking young men sat next to each other on one side and no longer exchanged furtive smiles. They shifted in their seats. The chairs were uncomfortable and old. They were padded on the backs and seats but were stained and flattened; somewhat bent. The room was stuffy with no windows but the atmosphere was just right. The cleric didn't want the boys too comfortable.

Not that he was so comfortable himself. Being a religious leader trying to integrate modern human experience with the principles of their faith was a difficult position. He knew the world these boys lived in. He was entirely aware of the prevalence of outright pornography and its lesser, more subtle forms of misogyny in the current culture. And their religion was slow to moderate –if at all.

A faith based on two-thousand-year-old tenets didn't translate easily into the modern vernacular. Though he needed to try, for the sake of their religion, for the boys, and also for sake of their parents, the older generation. He worked for them, too.

Many of the boys in his charge came from families of stout believers: people who joined with the upper echelons of the religion in taking a hard line on sexual topics like birth control, abortion, marriage, and the like.

As a man of the cloth, he had to proceed cautiously with

a mix of what the boys were inundated with every day and what their ancient and respected religion required of them.

Earlier in the meeting, one of the administrators out in the hallway had stuck her head in to inform the religious leader that a group of professionals required his attention. He had told her he would be out in ten minutes. Fifteen had gone by. They were just about done. He stood.

"Gentlemen." He spread his two arms out at his sides. "We shall live up to the standards of our forefathers, yes?" The three no-longer-smirking young men stood and nodded in agreement.

"Good. You must stand as examples to those around you and, indeed, to the whole of America; that we can and will become an asset to this society." He motioned to the door and three young men filed out. He continued standing and wondered how long it would take. How many generations would have to prove themselves until Western civilization put aside its bigotry toward their religion and accepted them as faithful, hard-working people. Siban pushed his bent, filthy chair in under the old, worn table just as the secretary re-entered. He looked up at her and smiled. "Who is here?"

She opened her eyes wide and whispered, "The FBI."

19

No guard booth. That was the first thing Zafir noticed about the side entrance to the campus. Though O'Leary professed to have connections here at Boston College, Zafir was still somewhat on edge. He had given this pig one million dollars already –in cash. Once the crates of weaponry got loaded into the van, Zafir had promised to disclose the location of the other duffel bag of cash.

Once inside the main entrance, a guard booth did appear on the right. They made a left. O'Leary drove around a tree-lined street on campus and made another right into a half empty parking lot. He turned the van off and looked for his cell phone. During the last hard turn, the phone had slid across the dashboard to Zafir's side. Zafir leaned forward, collected the phone, and handed it over to O'Leary.

Jimmy Junior dialed a number from his directory. When his associate picked up, all Junior said was, "Make the call." Then he ended the call and stuffed the phone into his pocket. When he did, he felt the lump of his revolver. He looked over at Zafir.

"Listen, once we get this shit loaded up," he pulled out the gun, "I need to exchange this for a new one." He grabbed a napkin and wiped his prints off the old revolver. "This one has a body on it, now. I need to get rid of it, understand? Ballistics, know what I mean? I don't know what kind of pistols or whatever we got coming here, but I'll need at least one to keep me going, all right?"

Zafir nodded. Junior put the gun away and pulled his

phone out again. He stared at it, waiting.

His granduncle, Seamus –the first, would be sound asleep for the remainder of the day. Maybe more. Junior smiled. He had slipped the old man a couple of sleeping pills. The old man usually took half a pill to get to sleep at night, but Junior had dissolved two of them into his morning coffee. *If it kills him, too fucking bad, Junior thought. His time was about up, anyway.* The phone rang. Junior answered it, but only put it to his ear and said nothing.

Then the caller spoke: "Seamus?"

"Oh, hey, Uncle Mike. Yeah, this is Jimmy Junior; what's up?"

"Oh. Hello, Seamus. I need to speak with my brother, it's very important."

"Oh, yeah, you can't. He's out like a light, Uncle Mike. He took a couple of pills and laid down; you know how he gets. But yeah, he told me you'd probably be getting a call. Said you've always been a careful guy and all that, you know?" Junior shifted in the seat. "If this is about the guy visiting from Northern Ireland who needs to listen to some tapes or something, Uncle Seamus, before he checked out, he told me to tell you that the guy's legit; to give him the green light. That's all I know, Uncle Mike: the old man told me to tell you that the guy looking to listen to your tapes is legit; he's got a real dire need to know or something, and that you should go and get the tapes and lay them out for the guy. That's all I know. Uncle Seamus gave the guy your direct number and all that. That's all I know: guy's legit."

There was a long pause. Then Father O'Leary spoke. "When do you expect your granduncle to wake?"

"Oh, I don't know, Uncle Mike; probably not until tomorrow, you know? He was having a bad day and then this guy from Northern Ireland called and the old man got all stressed out. Said he was tired of dealing with all this life and death political stuff and all that. He took two pills, Uncle Mike; he usually only takes a half. Nah, he won't be up until tomorrow sometime, you know?"

"I see. Very well. Seamus, take care of yourself, and stay out of trouble young man."

"Oh, yes sir, Uncle Mike. I'll do that. You take care, too." Junior hung up the phone. He turned to Zafir and smiled.

"So, Zafir, if you were hiding something real, real important for a long, long time, you'd pick the best fucking hiding spot you had, right?" Zafir did not respond, but again only nodded. Junior continued. "So then you get something else real important, like some audio tapes that half the fucking world is looking for, where you gonna put those, huh?" Junior nodded and checked the doorway of the building across from them. "That's right: the same fucking place, right? I mean, you got a great hiding spot picked out already, why go look for another one? Just put them where the other thing is, right?"

Junior kept his eyes on a door under a stone trellis walkway and kept smiling. "Any minute now, Zafir baby; any minute now."

20

Early autumn hints of red and yellow dotted the green splendor of Commonwealth Avenue. Frank drove. Jimmy drew a long, deep breath and relaxed.

A procession of magnificent brownstones lined either side of the boulevard and rows of abounding trees harbored the wide-open center lawn. The tall elms, green ash and maples conspired at every crossroads with sculpted monuments in tidy esplanades to bestow the countenance of grandeur.

Driving with the flow of traffic along the majestic promenade, Jimmy noticed that every so often Frank would lean forward and glance up through the top of the windshield.

Finally, Frank turned to Jimmy:

"You're telling me we're going to see the Citgo sign from here?" He shook his head. "…can't picture it."

Jimmy shrugged. "That's what the guy said: bear left at the Citgo sign onto Beacon Street; it'll run us right into the place." Jimmy finished typing a text message and put the phone down on the center console.

After billing last night's hotel stay to the department's credit card, he had to check in with his Chief. Generally, Jimmy enjoyed autonomy in his investigations. He was trusted. His superiors knew that even if he wasn't always on the right track, he was always doing the right thing. No one was right every time, but Jimmy had a damn good track record.

Finally the tall trees gave way to an interstate overpass,

and Jimmy leaned up toward the windshield himself. He pointed outward and turned to Frank. "Oh, ye of little faith."

Frank nodded. "Okay, Citgo sign. So where's Fenway?"

"Should be over on the left somewhere."

They entered Kenmore Square, with its choice of ten lanes of traffic. Frank studied the signage and veered left onto Beacon Street, following the signs for Boston College.

"There it is, you can just see the lights." Jimmy pointed to the left. "See it?"

Frank hit the gas and just made it through the busy intersection before the light turned red. "Little busy at the moment, there, Yankee fan." Once it was safe, he glanced back over his shoulder, but it was too late to glimpse the Ballpark. "Fuck the Red Sox anyway."

Jimmy raised an eyebrow. "Don't say that too loud in this town. I think that might be a felony on the books, up here."

Less than three miles later, Beacon Street curved around a reservoir and brought them to the campus of Boston College. Jimmy left the phone on the console. Frank turned to him. "So, where do we begin?"

"I want to go in soft, at first. I told Jack to restrict his research to the internet, and not to make any calls yet. I don't want to raise anyone up. Let's just ride around campus a bit and get a feel for the place. After a while, maybe we stop and talk with their security people; we'll see. The less we say about secret IRA tapes, let alone the possibility of an old secret stash of guns, the better. Eventually we might have to sit down with the head of security and some people in administration, but let's take our time for now."

They turned into the campus through a service entrance

opposite the edge of the reservoir and rolled slowly along past rows of modern, semi-high-rise buildings. Frank commented, "I expected something, I don't know, older?"

"Yeah," Jimmy agreed. After a few minutes of driving on and off the campus and around the immediate vicinity, they turned onto a narrow lane and passed a stately old cathedral-like structure. Jimmy pointed up. "Here you go."

Frank looked up through the windshield. "I wonder what that Latin inscription says."

Jimmy concentrated on the lettering. "You know what, that might not even be Latin; it might be Gaelic."

"Gay-lick?" Frank smirked. "Is that what you just said? Gay-lick?"

Jimmy shook his head at Frank. "That is how you pronounce it, but Gaelic is the ancient language of Ireland."

"Oh, sorry." Frank tried not to smirk. "I didn't know the Irish had a language."

"Yeah, it was one of the last things to go after the British took over. You can take over a country using men with guns, but the British liked to conquer cultures, too, you know? They outlawed the use of the Gaelic language."

Frank just looked at him. "Whatever you say, man." Then he snapped his fingers. "That reminds me, what the fuck does 'om-ba-than' mean?"

Jimmy laughed. He turned sideways in the front seat and looked Frank up and down. "How fitting you should think of that now. It means 'big, sloppy idiot'."

Frank sigh-laughed, shook his head, and turned to look out his driver side window. "Big and sloppy, maybe…" he said under his breath.

They got to the end of the narrow lane and pulled up in front of a tall obelisk with a giant gold eagle on top. Beyond the monument, a spectacular Gothic Cathedral spread out almost to the campus fence on the right.

"Holy fuck." Jimmy stamped his foot down on the floor as if there was a brake pedal there. "Frank, stop." Jimmy bolted upright in the seat like an electric charge shot through him. Jimmy pointed to the back of the cathedral. "Is that who I think it is?"

"Jesus Christ." Frank stopped the car. "Are we that lucky, or are we just good?"

Jimmy couldn't believe his eyes as he watched Zafir and another man stroll onto campus from College Road, the other man pulling an empty hand truck behind him. "Ten to one says that's O'Leary with him."

"Yup, fits the description all right." Frank put the car in park. "Though he's not dressed like I imagined; not according to your little friend back at the restaurant."

Jimmy opened the door. "Alright, let's go." They moved quickly, but tried not to look hurried. Jimmy saw that O'Leary's gaze didn't waver as he walked, but Zafir turned his head every few steps. Jimmy and Frank split to opposite sides of the small plaza and closed the distance.

Zafir and O'Leary disappeared behind the cathedral. Jimmy and Frank ran to each other and met at the giant cornerstone. "We don't want to grab them yet," Jimmy whispered. "Let's follow them and see where they lead us." Frank nodded. They turned the corner.

Zafir's mind raced as they entered the building the second time. He had glimpsed two men, obviously policemen, getting out of a car easily characterized as an unmarked police vehicle. If it was him they came for, this could be the end.

On the way in the first time, as he and O'Leary had surreptitiously followed the priest, Zafir took note of a restroom in the hallway just before the stairwell door.

The policemen were too close now, but Zafir believed he could find success –somehow. The available seconds ticked away. His trainers had drilled into him the idea that when there is no time to plan, act. Take action and pray to Allah for guidance.

Zafir stopped and very calmly feigned exhaustion. After carrying such a heavy crate out to the van, he pleaded with O'Leary that he absolutely had to use the restroom. He pushed open the bathroom door and assured O'Leary that he knew the way now, and would meet him downstairs where the priest was tied up in the small anteroom just outside the secret crypt.

O'Leary protested, but Zafir grasped his crotch and insisted. The young criminal turned in disgust and went down the stairs. Zafir opened the door to the restroom, but didn't enter. He listened until he heard O'Leary's footfalls on the stairs. But footsteps came also from the start of the hallway directly behind him. No time.

Zafir ran to the stairway door. He shoved it hard and sprinted back to the bathroom. By the time the door slammed loudly into the wall of the stairwell, Zafir had stepped back into the restroom and gently closed the door behind him. Then he heard a voice right in front of him in the hallway: "The stairs."

It worked. Once the sound of footsteps hurried past him and descended the stairs, Zafir opened the restroom door and sprinted for the rear entrance of Gasson Hall.

The rented van was parked in the bus stop on College Road just beyond the campus gate, a mere two hundred feet from the building. The keys were in the ignition and the first crate of weaponry was in the back.

Zafir climbed behind the wheel. He didn't know who would die at the bottom of those stairs; nor did he care — but he knew someone would. He put the van in gear and smiled, knowing, at least, that the confrontation taking place down there right now would provide him with the valuable seconds he needed to slip into traffic and begin his journey back to New York City. With a crate of guns.

Halfway down the stairs, Jimmy stopped suddenly and turned back up into Frank. He put his hand on his partner's chest and stared wide-eyed at the top of the stairs, listening. Without a word, Frank picked up on the sound of feet sprinting away in the hallway behind them. Frank nodded and took off, back up the stairs.

Jimmy turned and ran down to the basement. The hallway at the bottom of the stairs made an immediate left. Jimmy stopped before he turned into it. He peeked around the corner first and, seeing no one, stepped out into the hall. After a twenty-foot run, the hall ended at an open door. Jimmy walked carefully toward the small room. As he proceeded down the hall, more and more of the room became visible. A few feet out, a lone desk appeared in the middle of the room.

He got closer, and the robes of a priest sitting on the ground came into view. Jimmy froze, but then crept up slowly. After another step he could see nearly all of the priest, an older man, sitting on the floor in front of the desk, his hands tied together in his lap.

Jimmy scanned the room and his eyes lit up when he noticed a handgun sitting on a napkin on top of the desk.

Jimmy didn't hesitate. He boldly stepped right into the room and went directly to the desk. Head on.

The rest of the room came into view and a gaping hole appeared in the back wall. Jimmy reached for the revolver and heard cracking sounds coming from inside the crypt.

He snatched the gun off the desk and the priest startled up at Jimmy. The old man's eyes lit up, but he didn't make a sound. The priest furiously tilted his head to the opening in the back wall. Jimmy nodded to him, held the gun out in front, and tiptoed to the opening.

The lone light in the anteroom lent nothing to the crypt, and Jimmy closed his eyes for a moment to try and adjust them before entering. A muffled shot spat out. Jimmy heard the slug slam into the stone wall behind him. He dove back for cover behind the desk. He got to his knees and laid his arms out across the desk, pointing the old revolver at the opening.

From out of the crypt, the gun appeared first, then the laughing man holding it. The gun wasn't pointed at Jimmy, though; it was pointed at the priest. Jimmy yelled, "Police – drop the gun."

The smiling man kept the shiny new semi-automatic pistol with the long, thin silencer trained on the priest and sneered at Jimmy, "New Yawk, huh? Pretty far from home there, cowboy." Then he lost the smile. "Drop the fucking gun before I blow the old man's head off." The man stepped directly up to the priest.

Jimmy stood up from behind the desk. "Easy, easy. No has to get shot, here."

The man jammed the tip of the silencer into the priest's temple. "What are you, fucking deaf? I said drop the gun, asshole."

The priest spoke. "Seamus, stop this madness." Without moving his gun hand, Jimmy Junior squatted and launched a left jab directly into his granduncle's nose. The priest's head snapped back against the desk and blood burst forth onto his robes. Junior never took his eyes off Jimmy. He smiled again and waved his left palm out. "Now, drop it."

Jimmy pulled the hammer back on the revolver with a loud 'clack.' "That ain't happening, tough guy."

Then Jimmy noticed the golden gloves pendant on the man's chest. "Tell me something." He pointed the cocked revolver at the man. "What kind of a pussy holds a gun on an old man when he's facing another man with a gun? Huh?" Jimmy took a step closer. "…pretty soft, you know?"

The priest raised his eyes to Jimmy. Jimmy noticed the old man purse his lips and nod, ever so slightly. Jimmy kept his eyes on the priest, but spoke to the gunman: "You ain't got the balls, pal."

Junior pointed at Jimmy with his left hand. "Back the fuck up. I'll kill him. I got no problem killing people, mister. Just ask Johnny Dineen." Junior puffed out his chest. "Most powerful gangster in Boston, and I killed one of his lieutenants —I'm movin' up in the world." Junior snarled at Jimmy. "You and this old fuck ain't nothin' after that. I'll kill yas both, no problem."

The priest continued the almost imperceptible nod. Jimmy continued, "So you're into killing old men, huh?" Jimmy slid another step closer. "Boy, that takes balls all right. You're one tough little punk, huh? Why don't you try that shit with me?"

Jimmy dared another step and kept a laser-like glare on the tip of the silenced pistol. If this guy was insecure enough to move the barrel away from the priest and toward Jimmy

—even just for a split second —that would be all the time he needed to take his shot.

Junior kept the gun poised on Father O'Leary but took a step back and emphasized his left arm outward. "You think I won't do it?" The priest suddenly ducked forward. Junior fired. The bullet hit the priest toward the back of the head and Jimmy Gallagher fired two shots from the old revolver, center mass, and killed Seamus O'Leary —The Third.

The acrid smell of gunfire filled Jimmy's senses. Again. Boston Detective Pete Wallace had to straddle the body to get his two feet into position. He looked up at Jimmy again and, without saying a word, asked if this is the exact spot where the man was standing when Jimmy shot him. Jimmy nodded. Wallace frowned.

The priest had long since been removed, still breathing but unconscious. The prognosis for the old Jesuit wasn't good, but the responding EMTs said they'd know more once they got him to the hospital.

Jimmy understood Wallace's frown. The shooting was obviously justified. It wasn't that, but Wallace apparently had a lot of other questions and, Jimmy could see, didn't know where to begin.

Jimmy had been supervising detectives for a number of years now, and had seen that look before. Wallace was one of those nine-to-fivers in a local district, who preferred to stick with the everyday assaults, domestic cases, and the like. Boston PD, like so many other big city police departments, had special units to handle the big cases, and Wallace kept looking at the door, waiting for someone from Homicide to come in and take this bag of shit off his parochial hands.

The detective held onto the .38 caliber revolver Jimmy used to shoot O'Leary. "So you're telling me this isn't your gun?"

"No. I found it right there on the desk."

Wallace just stared at him. Jimmy continued, "I have a Glock." Jimmy opened his jacket to show Wallace his service weapon.

Wallace frowned. "You don't carry a back up? Most guys I know carry a back up. Usually a .38, too."

"Yeah?" Jimmy said. "Where's yours?" He figured Wallace as a cop who's not running around out there looking for trouble. He figured right. Wallace just exhaled. Jimmy pulled his jacket closed and sat back on the desk.

Again, Wallace asked Jimmy why he didn't draw his .9mm Glock when he entered the room. Jimmy's answer was what had caused all the other questions to start pinging around inside Wallace's head: Not my jurisdiction; only had suspicion on the guy, no proof; came up here to do interviews, not to arrest anyone; didn't know what I had; and so on.

It was when Jimmy had told Wallace about the places he'd been and the people he'd been asking for the night before that Wallace had put a second call in to the Homicide Unit from the Bureau of Investigative Services. That, and the crate of guns and ammunition in the little fucking cave behind him.

Wallace stepped carefully away from the dead man's legs. "So you don't know who this guy is, but you think he works for Johnny Dineen, that right?"

"I don't know who he is," Jimmy agreed. "And I believe he was seen at the Saints and Scholars last night with Johnny Dineen and a few of his people. I believe." Jimmy sighed. "If you let me get a picture of him, I can verify that with the Maitre'd there."

Wallace walked over and peeked inside the crypt again, but didn't enter it. "Yeah, right, no problem, guy. Let's just wait for the Homicide Unit to get here before we go taking any pictures, all right?" He glanced at Jimmy, but quickly looked away. He checked his watch for the umpteenth time.

Campus security had already designated the entire basement and the stairs leading to them as a crime scene. Frank Ramirez stood in the far corner of the anteroom, again telling the security guys, mostly retired Boston PD, that the possible terrorist might have fled in a white van. Possibly. That's all he had, after he chased the footsteps he heard in the hall; he saw a white van pulling away from the curb —and no, he never actually saw anyone. But he was sure it was Zafir, the terrorist from Brooklyn. Then he'd heard the shots and came running back down here.

Security had politely written it all down, but didn't have much else to say. Jimmy could just feel the skepticism in the room.

Finally, two people entered. A man and a woman. The man was the very picture of quiet self-confidence. In his late forties, he wore a plain but crisp business suit and stood just under six foot. His partner, about ten years younger and a couple of inches shorter, was drop-dead gorgeous.

Her hair was tied back in a loose bun and her nails were plain and trimmed. She wore no makeup nor jewelry, but the moment she walked into the room —any room, Jimmy guessed —she snatched everyone's attention —immediately.

Her hair was jet black, her eyes bright green, and the wrinkles that barely showed around the edges of her soft, red lips did nothing but enhance the striking symmetry of her face. After taking stock of the room and the people in it, she walked up as far as the desk and extended her hand over it to Jimmy. "Detective O'Neill, Boston Homicide."

"Captain Gallagher, NYPD." They shook hands across the desk. She motioned to her partner. "Detective Ranaghan." Ranaghan stepped around the desk and shook

Jimmy's hand. "Brian," he said; and then went over and took possession of the revolver from Wallace.

Detective O'Neill took out a narrow notepad and wrote something down as she walked around the desk. She wrote hurriedly, sighed, and when she got about two feet away from Jimmy, looked up quickly.

The sudden brightness of her green eyes nearly knocked him over. Jimmy was sure he'd never seen eyes that green – they were nothing but green, not hazel, not any other shade –and so bright. He looked down into them for a moment.

He saw a woman like very few he'd seen before. She seemed completely aware of how attractive men found her, and completely unconcerned about it. "Uh," Jimmy tried not to stammer. He pointed across the room. "My partner, Detective Frank Ramirez." O'Neill looked over her shoulder and nodded at Frank.

Then she turned to Detective Wallace, who was still standing by the crypt, refusing to set foot inside it. "Wally, you got anything else other than what you told me on the phone?"

"Nothing." He threw up his hands. "Not a thing, Sheila."

O'Neill nodded. "We'll take it from here."

"Right." Wallace headed for the door. As an apparent afterthought he turned to Jimmy. "Good luck, man."

Jimmy nodded.

O'Neill watched Wallace leave and settled back onto the desk behind her. In her left hand she held the notebook, and in her right, a pen. She half sat on the desk and rested the heels of her hands onto the edges on either side. "So," she began, "who's your friend, Jimmy?" She tilted her head to the dead body on the floor to her left.

Jimmy raised an eyebrow. Before responding he smiled at O'Neill. "So you did some research on the way over here, eh, Sheila?"

She tilted her head, "Research?"

"My name. I didn't tell you my first name, but you just called me Jimmy."

O'Neill smiled and stood up from the desk. "Jimmy Gallagher." She flipped a page in her note pad, nodding. "Super hero. Terrorist hunter." She walked halfway around Jimmy so that she now stood squarely on his left side. "By all accounts, Jim, you're the man. No doubt." She crossed her arms, just under her breasts. "But you still didn't answer my question: who's your friend lying over there?"

Jimmy shrugged. "I was hoping you could tell me."

Detective Ranaghan already knelt over the body, inspecting it. "That's Jimmy Junior, Sheila, from Dineen's crew." Ranaghan said, without looking up.

"Dineen's crew?" Sheila turned to her partner without looking down at the body. "Really." They exchanged glances. O'Neill pointed with her chin. "What kind of gun is that?" Ranaghan nodded slowly as he looked down at the gun in his hand. "Yeah, thirty-eight caliber revolver."

O'Neill raised an eyebrow and, without turning her head back to Jimmy, looked sideways at him. "You know Johnny Dineen?"

"No. I mean, I know who he is, but I've never met the man."

"No?"

"No."

Then Sheila stepped back around to the desk. "What about Dermot Casey; you know him?"

Jimmy nodded. "Yeah. I mean, I don't know him, but I

understand he's one of Dineen's men. I was looking for him just last night."

"So you're the guy who was looking for Dermot Casey." It wasn't a question. She turned to her partner, who stood up and weighed the .38 in his open hand. She looked back at Jimmy, but pointed at the gun. "You have that .38 with you when you went looking for Dermot Casey?"

"What? No. I found that thing here. Right here on that desk.

"On this desk?" Ranaghan acted surprised; dumb almost. "What, like this?" The detective placed the revolver on the desk. Then he pointed at it. "That's where you got this gun? You didn't have it with you when you were hunting all around town last night, looking for Dermot Casey?"

Sheila stepped in closer to Jimmy. "Tell me again: when did you last see Dermot Casey?"

Jimmy dropped his head with just the first half of a nod and froze it there. "I already told you I never met the man."

O'Neill mimicked Jimmy's head movement and said, "I didn't ask if you ever met the man, Jim, I asked you when you last saw him."

Ranaghan stepped over from the desk. With an almost imperceptible touch of body language, he told Sheila that he'd take it from here. Jimmy sensed the relationship right away. Ranaghan was the old warhorse and O'Neill was the up-and-comer. Maybe Ranaghan was even training O'Neill.

Ranaghan stood squarely in front of Jimmy and put his hands in his pants pockets, crimping his suit jacket forward. "Let's start at the top. What brings you to Boston today, Jim?" Ranaghan gestured without taking his hands out of his pockets, friendly as could be. "May I call you Jim?"

Ranaghan was an old pro. Jimmy appreciated his style, but was uncomfortable being the subject of it. Jimmy just lowered his eyelids and nodded at the detective. "Sure, Brian, you can call me Jim."

Half way through his return smile, Ranaghan stopped and raised his eyebrows. He tilted his head forward in patient anticipation.

Jimmy sighed. "I'm following a terrorist target. We believe he came up to Boston yesterday."

Ranaghan nodded, but didn't move. After a moment of just staring at Jimmy, he finally asked, "So what was your first stop?" Ranaghan took his hands out of his pockets and clasped them together in front of himself, below his waist. "And how did you end up here?"

"Well," Jimmy shifted his feet a little. "My subject is in the market for handguns. He's looking for a large shipment. We think there might be a connection with the IRA; maybe from the old days, you know?"

"Okay." Ranaghan nodded again slowly. "I get all that." Ranaghan kept his hands clasped in front of him and leaned forward with just his head and shoulders. "But, Jim, my question was: what was your first stop? And how did you end up here?"

Jimmy sighed. "Well, we figured he's not going to a gun store, right?" He put his hands in his pockets and shrugged. "You gotta start somewhere."

Ranaghan took a long moment and studied Jimmy's face. Then he said, "You know, Jim, you could drop me just about anywhere in New York City and I wouldn't have the vaguest idea where to look for my friendly neighborhood gangster hangout. I'd have to ask someone. I'd have to have some kind of information on that, you know?" He tilted his head forward and to one side like a period at the end of a sentence and brought it right back.

Jimmy blinked slowly, growing impatient. "A friend told me —"

"A friend." Ranaghan cut him off. He raised his right hand and made a circle, index finger extended. "A friend of a friend told you to check the Mayo Inn. And you mentioned the name Dermot Casey while you were there. And you flashed your hardware," he widened his eyes and pointed at Jimmy's waist, "and then you ended up here somehow?" Ranaghan stopped speaking, but kept his hand in the air, mid-circle. He stared at Jimmy with the question frozen on his face.

"How is it that you know so much about my trip last night?"

Ranaghan smiled broadly. "I'll ask the questions for now, Jim-bo."

Jimmy shook his head. "All right, now it's Captain Gallagher from here on, Detective."

Ranaghan said nothing at first, but closed his eyes, pursed his lips, and nodded once in compliance. Again, he smiled broadly. "No problem, Captain. I'm just trying to understand. I need to understand how it is that you ended up here, killing this guy." He swept his left hand behind him towards the body of the deceased Jimmy Junior. "Hours after his partner, Dermot Casey —the same Dermot Casey you were looking for just hours ago —turns up dead nearby."

Now Jimmy raised an eyebrow. "Dermot Casey's dead?"

"Shot through the heart, Jimmy," he picked up the revolver from the table, "with a .38 caliber revolver." He held it out in his palm and stared hard at Jimmy. "Just like this one."

The room began to fill up with technicians from the Boston PD's Crime Scene Unit, followed immediately by a team from Ballistics.

Ranaghan handed the .38 to Sheila and put his hand on Jimmy's elbow, nudging him away from the crypt and the busy technicians.

"Listen, Captain," he spoke in a hushed tone, "we've all got friends in low places." Again, that broad smile. "Am I right?" He pulled his hand off Jimmy's elbow and held it open. He turned fully around and put his back to the wall. Then he looked down at Jimmy Junior, practically at his feet. He crossed his hands down low again, but seemed to drop all pretense. He frowned at Jimmy and nodded.

"Look, Jim, this is really what we call a public service homicide. This dirt bag," he waved down at the body, "is probably responsible for at least two, maybe three, homicides we could never prove." He stood up off the wall. "And Dermot Casey was no better; in fact, he was this clown's boss." He crossed his arms in front of his chest. "This is no one's loss," he leaned his shoulders forward again, "you know what I'm saying, Captain? Public service homicide? Justified? Just tell me how the Dermot Casey one went down. I'm sure we can justify that one, too. Understand?"

By now, Sheila O'Neill had made her way into the space. She was aghast at her partner's words. "Jesus, Brian, what are you trying to say?"

Ranaghan tried to hide his frustration.

Jimmy couldn't help but laugh out loud. Just once. Then he smiled at O'Neill. "It's called cajoling the witness, hon." Jimmy smiled at Ranaghan. "I did mention that I'm a Captain of detectives, right?" Then he turned back to Sheila.

"He was trying to get an admission the nice way." He smiled at Ranaghan again. "You're good. But I wonder how good."

Jimmy stepped out of their little circle. "Have you even considered what was in the crate that they apparently loaded into the van on their first trip up the stairs here? Have you broadcast a description of the van?" Jimmy looked back and forth between them both. "Anything?"

Ranaghan smiled and waved his hand across the entrance to the crypt, where at least six Crime Scene and Ballistics experts donned surgical gloves and masks. He smirked at Jimmy. "You know what the DMV told me on the way over here, via their database that I accessed through my radio car's terminal? Right after Wallace mentioned something about a white van? They told me that there are over three thousand such vans registered in the greater Boston area. Can you imagine that, Jim?"

Now he stood squarely in front of Jimmy again; hands in pockets, jacket crimped. "Just tell me one last time, Captain: where exactly did you get this .38; this gun that killed Dermot Casey, the guy you've been running all around town asking questions about?"

"Right there, on that desk," Jimmy pointed. "It was wrapped in a napkin."

Ranaghan said nothing, made no gesture. He just stared at Jimmy, and then repeated him. "Wrapped in a napkin."

22

Siban waited patiently for the three FBI agents to complete their interrogation. One sat across from him at the old, worn desk in the small, musty room and stared directly into his eyes. The other two huddled in the corner and whispered.

Though they had not yet threatened him with arrest, their tone was such that Siban knew he could not trust them with the truth. Their interrogation, thus far, had lasted only twenty minutes, and they appeared to be on the verge of bringing it to a close.

Though he did not trust these men, Siban did not view them as the enemy, either. Not anymore. The killing had to stop. And, contrary to what these men believed, they could have no hand in bringing that about. That was up to Siban and his fellow Imams and other leaders of the community.

Siban understood inherently that these agents did not care to work with him toward that goal; they desired only to accomplish a victory of their own accord. They wanted no input from those whose lives and futures were at stake; they wanted only to win. Siban had decided to remain silent.

He glanced down one last time at the picture of Zafir which the agents had put before him. Siban had learned over the years that though the FBI was meticulous in its efforts, it was also slow. He nodded to himself, realizing that the latter attribute was a function of the former.

The federal agents had obviously perused the surveillance footage from the UN demonstration and documented persons in attendance that did not appear on the witness list developed by the police that day. Siban surmised this from the nature of their questions over the last twenty minutes. He realized that he must be one of many. They could not possibly know that he could identify Zafir. They were fishing. And he knew it.

Siban sighed and pushed back from his desk. "I truly am sorry, gentlemen, but there were hundreds of people at the UN that day." He stood and pushed the picture back towards the far end of the desk. "I wish I could identify this man for you, but I do not recognize him." He glanced at his watch. "I really do have many tasks to perform today." He motioned toward the office door, raised his eyebrows, and smiled.

The agent at the table frowned and looked over his shoulder at his counterparts. The agents came together and prepared to leave. One gave Siban a business card. Then, with many instructions, veiled threats, and polite promises from all three agents, they turned to leave.

Siban walked them to the door and bid them a polite and professional farewell. Though a little nervous about it, he was comfortable with having lied to the FBI. He knew that if he were to identify Zafir to these agents, they would not use that information with Siban's safety or his mission in mind. No, he would leave his trust in Captain Gallagher and hoped that was not a mistake.

23

Jimmy pushed the 'up' button at the elevator bank in the lobby of One Police Plaza and stood back to wait. It usually took at least three or four minutes for an elevator to arrive. Members of the gathering crowd either stared at their shoes or affected a confident glare at anyone willing to make eye contact. Cell phones were the newest addition to these moments, Jimmy observed, giving people something to do with their attentions.

The elevator door nearest Jimmy finally opened and a small throng poured out. Jimmy crowded on the elevator and pressed thirteen, the next-to-highest floor. Fourteen, the top floor, housed The Office of The Police Commissioner, which had nothing above it but the long-abandoned helicopter pad. You only pressed fourteen if you were ordered to.

The 'Super Chiefs' –The Chiefs of the Patrol, Organized Crime, and the Detective Bureaus –were on the thirteenth floor. Jimmy had been summoned to The Office of The Chief of Detectives this morning. The Chief probably had a few questions about his trip to Boston and the progress of the investigation of the UN shooting. Jimmy had the investigators in his office open a folder to document the steps taken so far, and he had read it again just before coming across the street. Not quite routine, but not the fourteenth floor either.

Jimmy got off at thirteen and had to be buzzed in through the etched glass, floor to ceiling partition. He got as far as the receptionist outside the Chief of Detective's office when an Inspector from the Inter City Correspondence Unit came hurrying out from the depths of the office. He looked Jimmy in the eye as he approached, but didn't slow down.

"Venue change, Gallagher." He brushed past Jimmy. "Fourteen. Let's go." Jimmy quizzed at the receptionist who just shrugged. Jimmy turned and followed Inspector George Christakos to the stairs.

They jogged up the one flight, and no one had to buzz them through the glass partition on fourteen. Christakos' ID card was programmed for the swipe pad next to the buzzer. Down the hall, through the Roosevelt Room, with its nearly one-hundred-and-fifty-year-old commander's desk, and up to the door of the Police Commissioner's Conference Room. Christakos knocked and waited. Jimmy recognized the voice from within as that of Jim Shea, Chief of Detectives. "In."

Chief Jim Shea had, at one time, been in a similar position to Jimmy when he commanded the Joint Terrorist Task Force –JTTF, years ago. Chief Shea shot right up through the ranks over the years and now sat as the highest-ranking detective in the NYPD.

Shea sat at the far head of the table. Mike Gonzalez, a one-star chief who ran the Commissioner's office, sat on Shea's right. Christakos stepped around and took a seat opposite Gonzalez. Shea motioned for Jimmy to take the seat directly inside the door at the foot of the table. The hot seat.

They all exchanged greetings, and Shea began. "Jim, Inter-City Correspondence has raised some issues."

Christakos opened his folder and waited for Shea to give him the nod. Christakos couldn't wait to start, Jimmy noticed. Chief Shea nodded and Christakos turned to Jimmy, "Captain, you did fail and neglect to inform my office that you were leaving the jurisdiction to take enforcement action."

Christakos obviously wasn't done, but Jimmy chimed in anyway: "I didn't go up there looking to take enforcement action, Inspector, I was just investigating, following a lead. I didn't think —"

"Not taking enforcement action? Christakos cut him off. "You call shooting and killing someone not taking enforcement action?"

"All right, hold on," Chief Shea cut in. "There is a difference, Inspector, between the intention at the outset and the eventual outcome. I said you could address your issues with my Captain, but any disciplinary talk will —"

Jimmy interrupted, "Discipline?" Jimmy opened his hands on the table toward Shea. "Chief."

"Relax, Jimmy." Shea blinked slowly. "ICCU was brought in by the Police Commissioner initially, but he asked me to take care of it."

Chief Shea didn't appear to be finished speaking but, at the mention of the Commissioner, Chief Gonzalez put up a hand. "Uh, Chief, may I?" Although Chief Shea outranked Gonzalez by at least three steps, he knew, as did everyone in the room, that Chief Gonzalez carried with him the authority of the Police Commissioner. Shea sighed and nodded. "Go ahead, Mike."

"Captain," Gonzalez began. "The Police Commissioner has been requested to cooperate fully with the demands of the Boston Police Department in this matter. Their Mayor has been in touch with ours. This is why Inter City Correspondence is involved. Boston has questions, but they've agreed to let us ask them." Gonzalez then turned back to Shea.

"Alright, Jimmy." Chief Shea opened a folder on the table in front of him. "Tell me what brought you up to Boston in the first place."

Jimmy sat up. "Okay, well, from the surveillance tapes from the UN shooting our witness pointed out a radical who may have set up the shooting, compelled the actual shooter to act as, like, a suicide shooter –"

"Tell me about your witness, Jim. Where'd you get him?" Shea interrupted.

"He's known to me from past investigations, Chief. I caught up with him around the corner from the UN."

"Did IAB speak with him first?"

Jimmy just stared at Shea for a moment, then responded. "No. But –"

"No?" Chief Shea flipped through the sheets in his folder. "So he was at the scene of the shooting, but IAB didn't debrief him? And you did? And you didn't give him over to IAB?"

"Chief." Jimmy didn't stammer. "I asked him if he actually witnessed the shooting. He didn't. If he had anything to add to IAB's investigation, I would have marched him right over to them."

"That's outside the protocol, Jimmy; you're on thin ice already, here. But go on: tell me how this directs you to Boston."

"The witness identified the possible bad guy and, my investigators pulled a still photo out of the footage, and scanned surveillance resources from transportation hubs. We got him getting on a train to Boston the next day."

"Okay." Shea flipped back to the first page of the folder.

"Now, what about taking police action without notifying the locals?"

"I didn't really consider it 'taking police action,' boss. I didn't have anything solid yet. I just wanted to see if I could find the guy without raising anyone up." Jimmy shifted in his seat. When he got on the elevator this morning, he was not expecting a full-blown 'Q & A.'

"So why the Mayo Inn? What brought you to that place in particular?"

"I needed to tap into the underworld up there. My witness said the perp was on a mission to procure weapons."

Shea perused the top sheet in his folder. Jimmy assumed it contained a list of questions the Boston people wanted answered. Shea continued, "So how did you know which place to go to?"

"My Dad's people, Chief. You know he runs a PI firm that just branched out up there. He pointed me in the right direction, that's all. I got lucky, I guess: only had to go to two places 'till I got confirmation on my subject." Jimmy shrugged.

Shea sat up. "Okay. Now tell me specifically about the shooting."

"Alright. I followed my mark down into this basement and —he must have doubled out on me somehow, 'cause he wasn't down there. Anyway, I come upon this priest tied up on the floor and some psychopath takes a shot at me from inside this, like, cave or something.

"There was a revolver sitting right there on the desk in front of me, so I grabbed it and drew down on him. He emerges from this black hole and draws down on the priest. Words are exchanged and the guy lets one go, right into the priest's head. So I put two in his chest. End of story, Chief." Jimmy sat back. "Listen, I only wish I didn't wait for him to shoot first. I'm sorry the priest got hit."

"He's alive, you know." Chief Gonzalez said. "He's in a coma, but they say he's going to make it."

"Yeah, I'd heard that. Thanks." Jimmy nodded at Chief Gonzalez.

"Jimmy." Chief Shea closed his folder. "How do you know Dermot Casey?"

"Boss, I don't." Jimmy sat back up. "Let me say it this way: I never laid eyes on the man in my life. I asked for him at that bar because I got his name along with the name of the bar. That's all."

Shea sighed and tossed the folder out onto the desk. "Jimmy," he spoke softly, "there's no easy way to say this. The ballistics are a match between the gun that killed Dermot Casey and the one you used to kill the other guy. Boston likes you for the Casey homicide."

"What?" Jimmy put his hands flat on the table and started to stand.

"Remain seated, Captain." Chief Shea waited until he regained complete control of the room, then he continued. "It's ludicrous, Jimmy; I agree. Everyone in the department agrees. There's no doubt in anyone's mind that you picked that gun up off the table in that room and shot the perp with it. I personally have no doubt, let me assure you of that. But Jimmy, the ballistics are a match, and they don't know you up there like we do. Look." Shea drew the folder back in toward himself and opened it.

"Boston PD has O'Leary —" he looked up at Jimmy for a second, "—that's the guy you shot; right, O'Leary?" Jimmy nodded. Shea continued. "They have him listed as a possible perp in the Casey shooting." He flipped a page in the folder. "But they have no prints or other hard evidence to prove that beyond any doubt." He closed the folder. "I don't think they're going to push you on this, but you are listed as a possible shooter. All they've asked is that we do the 'Q and A' with you here and transmit the results.

"For now, anyway, they're going to leave it in our hands. But," Shea looked at Gonzalez, "there are other issues raised here now, Jimmy." Shea stood. "You're a good Captain, Jim; one of my best. But when you go trotting off like a lone wolf, it raises eyebrows." Shea looked like he wanted to say more. Instead, he pushed his chair in and signaled the end of the meeting.

"Jimmy, you work for me. I'm behind you. But you have to realize that we both work for the New York City Police Department. That's not *your* badge you have in your pocket, or *your* gun either, son: they were bestowed upon you –and they can be removed. Remember that."

They all filed out and Jimmy headed to the elevators, alone. He pushed the button and waited, thinking. Everyone has a hundred open cases in this world. All anyone cares about is closure. Close the case, that's it. Just like IAB could care less if the UN shooter was part of something bigger than just a random suicide job.

And Boston –hell, Jimmy wasn't even sure they believed him that a Middle-Eastern terrorist was in their jurisdiction at all; let alone procuring guns. Boston identified the shooter on the O'Leary shooting all right, and all they cared about was closing the Casey shooting. *Can't pin it on a dead man who left no prints; so follow the ballistics to me and make a case of it? For God's sake.* Jimmy hit the button again.

He knew he should head back to the office and check in

with Clark and Donohue; see what's going on with the case. He stared up at the elevator lights, waiting. *I'll stop in with the guys later,* he thought. *I need to do something else, right now. I need to go see Jessica. Life is too short.*

24

"You stu-pid bastards." Johnny Dineen walked around behind the two chairs. "A simple fucking task and you blew it." He stopped behind the chairs and looked at his guy with the knife. After a moment, he continued to circle. "A simple fucking task." He stood before Coghlan and Duffy and shook his head at them.

They were bound and gagged, and so couldn't say a word. "I left you two idiots to watch out for my fucking brother-in-law and now he's dead."

He turned to the guy with the knife, who was now behind him. "What should I do about that?" He turned back to his two goons. "Really, I should have him slit your fucking throats. But you know what? Normally, I'd have Junior do it for me. But you know what else?" Dineen bent over and put his hands on his knees and looked each of them in the eye. "He's fucking dead, too."

The two men tied to the chairs vehemently shook their heads. Their eyes were as wide as could be, and they nearly hopped the chairs in place. They adamantly tried to communicate, but Dineen turned away from them.

Johnny was in a tough spot. He knew that to maintain control over a bunch of savages, you had to be the biggest savage. But he didn't like killing people. It was the one part of being made boss that didn't sit well with him.

They were in the basement of the Mayo Inn. The walk-in freezer hummed away behind him. Cases of beer and liquor lined the far wall. He stepped back and turned sideways. With his hands on his hips, he surveyed his two idiot prisoners and their potential executioner. He thought it through. He knew that if he let these two come up out of the basement alive, he would possibly lose standing with the rest of them.

He had to take dramatic action, but didn't want to commit murder. He was strong and he was willing, but he wanted to be above that. He would let them live. But he would save face. He got an idea.

"Put that away," he told the man with the knife. Then he turned to Coghlan and Duffy. "These two jerks dropped the ball, but they didn't kill anyone. That Gallagher cop did." He looked past the man with the knife and over to his remaining Lieutenant, Peter Flynn, standing guard at the door to the upstairs. "Our connections in the BPD confirm that the ballistics are a match, right? The same gun that Gallagher used to kill Junior also killed Dermot?"

Flynn didn't say a word; just nodded.

Dineen sighed and dropped his hands off his hips. He turned to the man who had put away the knife. "Break their noses and cut them loose." He stepped toward the door.

He stopped next to Flynn. "Somebody killed two of our people." He said loud enough for all to hear. "I need to take care of that." He opened the door. "We'll need all hands on deck. I've got a plan."

25

Mike Kelly's office was actually over in Hoboken, New Jersey. Because much of what they suspected he controlled was based in Times Square, the Feds insisted he not set up shop anywhere on the West Side of Manhattan. No problem. Although the Feds had recently dismantled his Carpenters Union, he still had his hands full with the unions that ran Broadway. The Theatre District was still good to Mike, and, for public meetings like this one —meetings that had to look random or casual —Rosie's was the perfect spot.

Rosie O'Grady's Irish Saloon proudly occupied the corner of Seventh Avenue and Fifty-Second Street. It was within shouting distance to the bright lights of Broadway, but far enough up the street to allow plausible deniability. Besides, it was a tourist spot. No real inference could be made from any associations he made there; not even by a Grand Jury.

Mike decided to forgo the grand dining room for a bar top table in the back corner along the windows looking out on 52nd Street. From his vantage point, he watched his two guests cross the street and make their way through the crowded sidewalk and in the front door.

"Table for two?" The host approached Joseph Gallagher with two menus in his hand. Murray answered for them both. "No, we'll grab a table by the bar." Joseph and Murray turned left through the lobby, ignoring the dining room. They headed inside along the 52nd Street windows and found Mike waiting for them.

Kelly stood, but didn't smile. "Joseph? Fancy meeting you here, old friend." Joseph and Murray both smiled, pulled out stools, and joined Kelly at the back table. Greetings were exchanged, food orders placed, and the men settled in. Eventually Kelly leaned in close over the table. "Joseph, you know I trust you with my life, right?"

Joseph squinted and barely nodded. Murray pulled his stool in closer to the table. Kelly glanced around the bar and nearly whispered.

"Look, you know how my business works; a lot like yours in some ways, right? I mean, if I have business to tend to in someone else's jurisdiction, I have to check in with them before I do anything. Maybe even offer them a cut or, like, first shot at whatever it is, right?"

Again, Joseph barely nodded. Murray grabbed ahold of the table and pulled himself in even closer. Kelly looked down at the table for a moment. Then he looked back up and continued.

"Joe, this isn't easy for me, but it's going to be a hell of a lot harder for you. It's about your boy, Jimmy. I was approached this morning by my colleagues from Boston. They think he killed Dermot Casey. They know for sure he killed one of their top enforcers, a madman named O'Leary, and they're insisting that Jimmy capped Casey, as well."

Kelly glanced around the restaurant again. "And they're saying he shot the priest too. They put a hit out this morning, Joseph —not exactly on him, 'cause they won't hit a cop —for a variety of reasons —scrutiny, yeah, but… well, with a guy like your Jimmy, he's liable to hit back. I think they're afraid of him.

"Joe, I'm sorry to say but, there's a hit out on his girl, the doctor, Jessica. They came to me with a picture of her, thinking I didn't know who she was."

Kelly stopped talking suddenly when he noticed the table shaking. He shrank back a bit when he saw the whites of Murray's knuckles nearly ripping the edges off the wood. Kelly continued.

"Look, they're not onto us, you and me —they don't know that I know you. I politely turned them down and told them they'd have to take care of it themselves; that I wouldn't help them. But they're here. They sent a team of two down here this afternoon. I don't know what they're driving or where they're staying. I just know that they're here, and they're looking for her, right now."

Murray stood. Joseph spoke without taking his eyes off Kelly. "Go find them, Murray; both of them. And bring them in." He looked up at Murray. "The Department's Threat Assessment Unit won't take this; it started in another jurisdiction. It's not a threat against a member of the service, and –" he looked back at Kelly –"we don't have sufficient corroboration to lodge this as an official threat." He stood. "Find them, Murray. Now."

26

The tears rolled down Jessica's cheeks and onto Jimmy's chest. She cried like she'd never cried before in her life. Jimmy held her close and together they rocked softly.

"Where will we go?" she burbled through her sobs. "Where will we live? Should we move?" Jimmy squeezed her gently. "None of that matters right now, Sweetie; all that matters is that I love you. And I'm going to love you for the rest of my life." Jessica kept her body pressed against Jimmy's but pulled her face back slightly to peer into his eyes. "I love you, too." She worked a smile up through her tears. "This is the happiest day of my life." She held out her left hand and admired the engagement ring Jimmy had just slipped onto her finger.

Jimmy's cell phone rang again, for like the tenth freakin' time in the last two minutes. Jessica patted his arm. "You really should see who that is; they're being very persistent."

Jimmy sighed. "Yeah, you're right." Just as he reached for his phone on the nightstand, a loud thud came from the apartment door. Jimmy and Jessie quizzed at each other and Jimmy grabbed his clothes. They heard shouting from beyond the door, but couldn't make out the words. Jimmy got his pants on quickly and stepped out into the hall. He recognized the voice.

"Murray?" Jimmy called up the hall to the door. But apparently Murray didn't hear him. Jimmy got closer and then heard the words:

"Jessica, open this door now! God help me, child, I'm taking it down. If you can hear me, kiddo, back away from the door."

Jimmy ran up the hallway, shouting, "Murray. What the fuck. Hold on, I'm coming." Jimmy opened the door. It shocked him to find Murray with his gun out and two men over each of Murray's shoulders with their backs to him and their weapons drawn on the street behind them.

"Jesus, Murray, what the fuck is going on?" Murray didn't answer; he just bulled past him.

"Where's Jessica?"

"In the bedroom."

Murray signaled his men in and turned down the hall.

"She's not dressed, Murray. What the fuck are you doing?"

Again, Murray ignored him. He left one of his men on the front door and ordered the other down the hall to the back door. Then he turned to Jimmy.

"Get her dressed. We're leaving. Dineen's people put a hit out on her."

Murray looked Jimmy up and down. "And get yourself dressed too, Junior. We'll take care of the girl. And we'll deal with this fucking hit team and take them down, too." Then he stepped in close and put his hand on Jimmy's shoulder. "You go find your terrorist friend. I'll let you know when it's all clear."

Jimmy turned and ran for the bedroom but then stopped. "Where are you taking her?"

Murray frowned at him and shook his head. "You know how this works, kid. No more than three people on this fucking planet will ever know the answer to that. Now get your clothes on."

27

When Jimmy rushed into her bedroom and told her why she had to get dressed immediately and go with Murray, the tears had stopped. Jessica wouldn't cry for herself. She'd stay strong and show Jimmy she could handle it; that she'd be okay; that he didn't have to worry about her.

But now, after being in the back seat of Murray's SUV for the last twenty minutes with a stranger armed to the teeth wordlessly sitting next to her, she felt herself about to cry again. Just when life seemed to be coming together, suddenly she found herself in a whirlwind of uncertainty.

Murray had driven through the Holland Tunnel out of Manhattan and headed north about ten minutes ago, his eyes on the rear view mirror the entire time. Jessica realized that someone might already be following them. Murray had told her that he didn't know what the assassins would be driving; just that they knew where she lived and what she looked like.

But the way Murray drove, it didn't look to Jessie like he was trying to evade anyone.

It was too much for her to process without getting hysterical. She decided to leave her emotions out of it, for now. But when Murray turned east and headed for the George Washington Bridge back into Manhattan, Jessica began to worry again. "Murray, why are we going back into the city?"

Murray locked eyes with her through the rear-view mirror. "Don't worry about a thing, darling. You just be ready to get out when I tell you to." He looked out both side windows and then back up into the mirror. "Soon, Jess, very soon."

"Get out? What do you mean?" A cry creaked into her voice. "I thought you were taking me somewhere safe." She looked out the window. "We're on the George Washington Bridge, Murray. Why do I have to get out?" Murray looked up at her in the mirror again and spoke with as much confidence as she'd ever heard in a man's voice. "You just trust me, young lady. I'll take care of you."

Then Murray spoke curtly to the man in the front passenger's seat next to him. He pointed out the front passenger's side window;

"Now. Give them the signal." Murray guided the SUV out into the far left lane. At mid-span, he turned it sideways and stopped. Tires screeched all around them. Jessica hadn't noticed that another, identical SUV had been trailing along with them. The companion vehicle also turned sideways and blocked the remaining lanes of traffic.

It didn't take long for the inbound traffic on the George Washington Bridge to come to a complete, screaming halt.

"Go." Murray threw the car in Park. He turned fully around and leaned over his seat to her. "Sweetie, trust me, you have to get out of the car now." He turned back and jumped out of the driver's seat.

In a flash, the man sitting next to Jessica was out of the car and physically coaxing her to follow. Her head spun. She couldn't wrap her mind around what was happening.

"Murray? Why?" she cried. The tears came uncontrolled. Murray and the man from the back seat picked her up onto the three-foot high center median of one of the busiest interstate bridges in the world.

She could barely stand. Her legs wobbled with fear.

Murray held onto her and they stood up there, watching the traffic on the opposite roadway. She nearly collapsed when, right in front of her, two other SUVs, identical to Murray's, shrieked to a stop and blocked the four lanes of the outbound bridge.

Horns blared. People shouted. Distant sirens wailed. Murray and his partner gently brought Jessica down off the median and out in front of the newly created traffic jam.

The driver of the nearest SUV nodded to Murray. The driver then checked his mirror and, keeping his eyes on it, held up three fingers. They waited.

After a moment, the driver pulled down one finger. After another second, he pulled down another finger. Then he pointed his remaining finger out in front of his SUV, at the open roadway.

Murray escorted Jessica out to the center of the eerily empty span. She very nearly physically resisted. She was beyond scared; none of this made any sense. Her inner alarm screamed for her to break free and run.

A thunderous growl bellowed from the traffic jam and a huge old Harley Davidson motorcycle rolled out. A scraggly older man pulled the bike up a few feet past Jessica and put his two big boots flat down on the road.

The rider turned to look over his shoulder at Jessica and she read the colorful words painted across his back, 'Nam Knights.' The rider smiled back at her. "Hey, kiddo, tell Captain Kid we got you covered. Hop on."

Murray lifted Jessica up onto the back of the bike. It roared off onto an open road. And headed up to Rocket's place.

28

Zafir finished pulling on his gloves. Then he snatched the magazine from Mustaf's hand. He inspected it closely to ensure that it now contained the maximum number of bullets. It did. Mustaf remained seated at the small card table in the basement and looked up to Zafir, awaiting his approval. With a grunt, Zafir dropped the magazine on the table. "Now, load it into the gun." Mustaf snatched up the magazine and scrambled to do as he was told.

Still snarling, Zafir turned to the young man sitting directly across from Mustaf. Hamid held up his magazine, newly loaded –properly. Hamid attempted a smile as Zafir inspected the work. Zafir noticed this from the corner of his eye and nearly spat at the boy.

"Into the gun." He dropped the magazine on the table like it was garbage. He stood back and watched his two young soldiers slap their magazines up into the empty handles of their brand new Russian-made Makarov nine-millimeter pistols. New to them, anyway. Zafir figured the guns were about forty years old, but they had never been used. And no one in this country would even admit that they existed. Perfect.

Zafir left the two boy-soldiers waiting at the table and crossed the room. It was good to keep them waiting. And scared.

He went back to the crate and knelt down beside it. Again, he counted. After today's mission, there would be forty-eight of the Makarov semi-automatic pistols left and still close to ten thousand rounds of ammunition. But the gun and ammunition boxes took up only half the crate.

The suitcase occupying the other half remained a mystery. He had been able to open it earlier, when he was alone, but did not understand its function. He had placed a call to the homeland. Some of his father's cohorts would know exactly what it was. They were due to call back soon. But it annoyed him greatly that the key his father had given him all those years ago, the key he had left on that damned table up in Boston, apparently caused this device to function. He was disgusted with himself for not retaining it.

Over his shoulder, without turning toward them, he felt the intensity of his waiting soldiers. He would re-engage with the suitcase later, when he could be alone with it. He stood and turned to his fedayeen.

Mustaf and Hamid stood up from the table and tensed for their next command. Zafir looked them up and down, shaking his head in disgust. Then he threw his hands up at them. "Rack them."

The two boys looked at each other and then each took a step back. They pointed the guns at the ground, grabbed the rear of the long rectangular bar that formed the top of the weapon, and pulled it back. They released it quickly and the bar slapped forward, grabbing as it went and setting in place, the first bullet out of the magazine from inside the handle.

They looked at Zafir with wide eyes. The guns were now fully loaded and ready to fire. Smiles crept across their faces; evil smiles. Zafir stared hard at them and lowered his eyelids. He did not smile. Fear replaced the smiles of Mustaf and Hamid and they stood ramrod straight.

"Secret them," Zafir said, and turned his back to them. He walked to the front wall of the basement and began to climb the half staircase there. About three steps up, Zafir crouched under the outside cellar door and looked back at his young soldiers. They showed him their empty hands and nodded, ready. Zafir pushed open the cellar door above him and climbed out into the Brooklyn evening, heading for the Abra Zam Café.

29

"The Abra Zam Café," Jimmy repeated. He looked over at Frank, making sure he wrote that down in his notebook.

"Yes," Siban said. "This is where you may find him publicly, at the places our youth socialize —where he goes to impress and recruit them. His appearances are irregular at such places, but you should start at the Abra Zam. You will recognize him, yes?"

Jimmy sat back. The chair in the conference room of Siban's Coney Island Avenue office was padded but flattened. "Oh, I'll recognize him, alright. Just like in Boston. I knew it was him the moment I set eyes on him." Jimmy scrunched forward in the chair and leaned his elbows on the old, worn table. "I'm just finding it hard to believe that you don't know where he lives."

"Captain," Siban sat back. "Obviously I have made my decision to help you. I even lied to the FBI for your sake. Why would I withhold the location of Zafir's residence at this point, if I knew it?"

Before Jimmy could respond, there was a knock at the door. Siban's secretary poked her head in, reminding him of his next appointment. He engaged her in their native tongue and she entered the room with a sheaf of papers that she placed on the table in front of him. Siban held his hand up to Jimmy and motioned that he would only be a moment, but needed to look at these. Jimmy nodded and sat back.

He thought about Jessie. He took a deep breath and mentally reiterated his trust in Murray. Not even Jimmy knew exactly where Jessie was, but he had an idea. Either way, he knew she was safe.

As for the hit team from Boston, Jimmy agreed with his father to let Murray handle it. Jimmy was too close to it. They knew he would never lose his cool, but still, they'd rather take their platoon of retired Anti-Crime cops and Intelligence Division Detectives and track them down themselves. Jimmy had conceded. He knew that part of the case was in good hands.

The secretary left with the papers and Siban stood up from behind the table. "I must continue with my day's work, Captain."

Jimmy stood. "Got that." He stood up from the table and pushed the bent, stained chair in underneath. "I appreciate your help." He reached across the desk to shake Siban's hand. "I'd like to stay in touch, in case there's anything more we can do for each other." Jimmy held Siban's hand for an extra count. "I might need more help with this case." Siban released Jimmy's hand. Jimmy waited as Siban drew a deep breath and exhaled it slowly. Then he nodded. Jimmy smiled. "I'll be in touch."

30

Zafir strolled along Jefferson Avenue all by himself. He made his way to the corner of Bedford Avenue in the part of Brooklyn know as Bedford-Stuyvesant or 'Bed-Stuy,' for short. It was early evening and he knew that many of his potential young followers would be lounging at the outdoor tables of the Abra Zam Café across the street.

He got to the end of the block and stood directly across from the cadre of Middle Eastern teenagers gathered around the café. He stood with his hands in his pants pockets and his back to the corner he stood on. He stared across the street until his minions noticed him. They all stopped what they were doing and stared at Zafir as if he were in enemy territory.

For years, Zafir watched the strong young men of his community skulk about this neighborhood, cowed by the depraved language, violence, and demeanor of the local American drug dealers. His people feared these criminals. And that sickened him. Today he would show them what courage looked like. And then they would follow him – anywhere.

As expected, one of the American drug-dealing criminals approached from over Zafir's left shoulder.

"Yo, you coppin'?"

Zafir had observed enough of these drug deals to know exactly how this worked. The man addressing him, as yet unseen by Zafir, was known as a 'steerer.' This man, typically, would be unarmed. A potential drug purchaser would interact with this steerer and state the amount of drugs he desired. The steerer would then state the amount of money required for such a purchase, observe as the buyer counted out the correct amount, and then direct the buyer to put the money through a hole in the 'money door.'

The money door, Zafir knew, was directly behind him on Jefferson Avenue, just ten feet in from the corner.

The steerer would then direct the buyer around the corner to the 'enforcer.' That man, typically, would be armed. The enforcer would put his hands on the buyer, ensuring that he was not equipped with the communication gear or firearms with which the police normally outfitted their undercover officers.

Once cleared, the buyer would be directed to approach another door on Bedford Avenue, again ten feet down from the corner, where they would receive their drugs through a hole in that door.

The entire elaborate scheme, Zafir knew, was devised, in part, by the lawyers who regularly defended the drug dealers. The lawyers would inform their clients as to which actions would work against them in an American criminal court and which would not.

The steerer stepped up and stood directly next to Zafir. He repeated his pitch: "Yo. What's up? You coppin'?"

Zafir turned only his head and stared into the eyes of the young American. He said nothing for a moment. Then he turned fully toward the man and leaned his face in close. "If you value your life, never again address me as 'Yo.'"

From the corner of his eye, Zafir saw Mustaf and Hamid approach along Jefferson Avenue, on cue. They were still about fifty feet away and moving slowly amidst the other pedestrians. Zafir turned away from the steerer and crossed the street without uttering another word. He could hear the steerer calling out behind him.

"Yo. What the fuck?" By the sound of the criminal's voice, he knew the steerer stayed on his side of the street. "Yo! Motherfucker! I got your shit right here, YO!" Zafir finished crossing the street and arrived at the café.

By now, the group of his fellows had gathered outside the rails of the café, on the sidewalk. This would be a minor step in the coming war, but a necessary one. Yes, he had procured the weapons; they were all aware of that. He had actually allowed a few of the more popular youths, along with Hamid and Mustaf, to come to the basement and observe the crate and its contents. They were rightly impressed. But now Zafir would bring the whole community fully into the fold of Fateh. Now they will worship him.

Zafir stood before them and stretched out his arms. "Masaa el kheer." The young men just stared, wide-eyed, at Zafir as the drug dealer across the street continued to taunt. Some nodded; some returned the greeting. Zafir continued in English for the benefit of those American-born and not proficient in Arabic.

"I know you are not cowards. I know how brave you can be." He paused and looked each of the dozen or so young men in the eye. "Yet you have not shown courage in the face of these animals." Again he took a moment to look each man in the eye. Then he changed his demeanor and spoke with a stern authority,

"You disgrace Islam with your cowardice." He paused. "These savages," he waved across the street without turning, "are animals. They are animals and must be dealt with as such. I have had enough. Watch, and you shall see." Zafir turned from them and walked back across the street.

By now, as expected, a number of criminal aspirants stood around, laughing with the steerer and the enforcer. But they all fell silent as Zafir crossed back toward them.

Mustaf and Hamid had stopped just short of the money door, as instructed, and waited.

Zafir stepped up onto the far sidewalk and the steerer immediately approached.

"Yo." The steerer smirked at Zafir, his face just inches away. "Now what, Motherfucker?"

"I gave you fair warning never to address me as such, did I not?" Zafir stared.

The steerer sucked his teeth and backed up a step. Then, as quick as a man could possibly move, the steerer snapped a left jab directly into the center of Zafir's face. Zafir barely flinched. Blood immediately began flowing from his nostrils. He smiled and said, "You are– what is the word? A lightweight, yes?"

The enforcer and others in the small crowd laughed. The enforcer put his hand over his mouth and crouched in laughter. "Ho, ho shit, yo, that A-Rab dissed yo ass, boy."

The steerer took another step back and turned to his cohorts. "Man, that's just openers, yo. Givin' the boy a chance to run off." He turned back to Zafir. "But he too stupid."

Zafir hadn't moved and hadn't stopped smiling. Hamid and Mustaf were in position. "Mustaf," Zafir pointed first at the enforcer, "kill that man." Then he turned and pointed at the steerer. "Hamid, kill him."

Jimmy and Frank had just entered the intersection when they heard the shots. Frank spun the wheel and hit the gas. Jimmy pulled out his radio. "Shots fired. Bedford and Jefferson. Need back up, forthwith."

Frank jumped the curb onto the corner with a loud bang. He threw it in Park. The shooters were immediately to their right and their two victims were still just on their way to the ground.

Jimmy and Frank both jumped out, but didn't leave the cover of their open car doors. Jimmy's Glock came up to eye level over the top of the door frame. He pointed and shouted at the same time, "Police. Drop the gun."

Jimmy pointed at the shooter on the right, Frank at the one on the left. Both shooters turned to the radio car and raised their pistols. Jimmy wanted to shout another warning, but realized it would do no good. And it was too late. Jimmy could see the very pupils of the gunman's eyes. And nothing else. Tunnel vision. Jimmy fired two rounds. So did Frank. Both gunmen immediately collapsed with bullets in their chests.

Jimmy and Frank stepped out from behind their car doors. Cautiously. They kept their guns out in front and turned like tank turrets, covering the immediate vicinity. They blinked as they stepped forward, and the tunnel vision faded.

Jimmy noticed a man stepping lively away from the scene, crossing the street. Jimmy shouted, as much to himself as to his partner, "Zafir."

Frank and Jimmy both turned to pursue when the money door opened. A man wearing a ski mask stepped out, –firing a Mac 11 sub-machine gun. Indiscriminate firing. No training, no thoughts. The wild-eyed machine gunner just let loose at whatever was out in front of him.

From the first discharge onward, the barrel jumped up from the recoil and the shots immediately went over everyone's heads. Time to aim. Jimmy dropped low into the combat stance –like a basketball player defending a fast dribbler. Again, time stood still. Jimmy lined up his sights and exhaled. Two shots, center mass, and the Mac 11 flew up out of the man's hands as he dropped to the sidewalk.

Frank had also let a few rounds go. Jimmy stepped toward his partner. "You okay?" Frank kept his eyes on the machine gunner and the money door. "So far. I think. I'll let you know."

"Yeah, right." Jimmy said. Then he spun around toward the street, remembering Zafir. No sign of him. Jimmy was about to run across the street to try and see which way Zafir had gone when another door opened just ten feet off the corner.

A shotgun barrel came out first, wielded by a large, older man. The gunman stepped out onto the sidewalk and searched for a target. He found the enforcer laying dead and shouted.

By the time the gunman noticed him, Jimmy was squarely in his combat stance, his Glock pointed directly at the man's chest. In a normal voice, Jimmy just said, "Don't do it." The man froze and stared at Jimmy. He moved his eyes to the unmarked car half mounted on the sidewalk. He looked at Frank, then back at Jimmy. He didn't raise the shotgun; nor did he lower it. Jimmy just calmly told the man to lay it on the ground. The man clenched his jaw but still didn't move. Jimmy drew a deep breath and exhaled. He squinted his left eye closed and lined up his gunsights on the man's chest.

"Okay." The man lowered the shotgun. "Okay," he said again, and took one hand off the shotgun. Without taking his eyes off Jimmy, he crouched down and laid the shotgun on the sidewalk. Then he stood up and put his two hands out and said, "I ain't with these guys. I don't know shit about nothin."

"That's fine." Jimmy kept his sights on the man and stepped in closer. "Just turn around and get on the wall."

The man complied.

"Look at these stupid fucks," Dan Hearn, Murray's driver, said; and turned the corner off Hudson Street onto Duane. "Did they really think we wouldn't notice them?" Hearn drove past the windowless van with the antenna on the roof, three spots down from Jessica's place.

Murray grunted at Hearn, "They don't know we know, remember? They think they're taking out some defenseless woman and nobody knows they're here."

"Oh yeah, right."

"Go around the corner and pull over."

Murray had two more men in the back seat for a total of four. Armed and ready.

"How do you want to play it, Murray?" retired Anti-Crime Sergeant Joe Cain said from the back seat. "Do we just roll right up and jump them —old-school-like?"

"Gimme a minute." Murray stared out the windshield as they pulled to the curb on Greenwich Street.

"Yeah, then what." Hearn turned back to answer Cain's idea. "What do we do, call 911 and hand them over to a local sector team and have them arrested for gun possession? 'Cause that's all we'd have right now." He turned back and looked at Murray. "Gun possession, no way to prove their intentions —they'd get off with a fuckin' slap."

"Let me think." Murray smoothed his hands across the dashboard as if there were a map there. "Where are they, where are we, where is she —and why? What is each one of us trying to accomplish?" He gripped the dashboard and stared out the windshield.

Then he smiled. He leaned back and laughed out loud. "Okay, I got it. Go back around the corner."

Cain leaned forward. Hearn didn't move. "What –"

Murray barked, "Drive." Then he smiled again. "Have no fear, gentlemen, we got this." He pulled his cell phone off his belt. "Your job right now is to drive back around the corner and pull up in front of Jessica's place –directly in front." He dialed the phone. "And stay in the car 'till I tell you otherwise."

Hearn put the SUV in gear and rolled out. Murray's call was answered. "Rocket, how you doin my man?"

"Bored."

"Yeah? I'm sorry to hear that. How's the girl?"

"She's fine. But you got my guys all riled up, here. They're runnin around out here armed to the fuckin' teeth, Murray. Some of 'em even got camouflage paint on their faces, for chrissake."

Murray laughed out loud again. "Yeah, I figured that. Listen, Rocket, tell me again just exactly how safe she is if the shit hits the fan up there."

"You're kidding, right? They could drop a fucking nuke on us and she'd be the lone survivor."

"Right, okay. Yeah, I've seen that basement up at your place."

"Right now she's out there grazing in the fields like a lamb. It's all clear, we got our perimeter sensors and cameras rollin', nothing movin' but the occasional deer."

"So you're all bored, huh?"

"Yeah."

"All right, standby for a callback. Give me three minutes."

The SUV turned the corner onto Duane Street and

rolled right by the van. "Pull over." Murray pointed to the front door of Jessica's place. "Right here."

Hearn stopped the car and shook his head. He could see the hit team's van in his rear-view mirror, parked directly behind him. "Murray, what the fuck."

"Watch and learn." Murray pushed open the door. He got out and put his cell phone up to his ear. He walked casually up to the door of Jessica's place and tried the handle. Finding it locked, he turned and surveyed the street, ignoring the van.

With the phone up to his ear, he spoke loudly. Loud enough for the antennae on the van to pick it up.

"Hey, boss, it's Murray. Yeah, it's all clear here. She's gone, she's safe." He paused. "Yes, sir. Yes, that's right, they got her up at John Fahey's place. Right, right, the place behind the Pearl River Little League fields up in Orangeburg. What? Oh, yeah, Hunt Road; there's no number, it's the only house at the end of the dirt road. About a twenty-five minute ride up the Palisades Parkway."

Murray stepped away from the door and walked slowly back to his SUV. "Yeah, he's just an old man, but she'll be safe up there; that place is so tucked away, no one could ever find it. He's alone, but I really think she's safe. Okay. Okay, good enough then. All right." He hung up and got back in the car. "Drive."

Hearn did his best to suppress his laughter. Cain stretched out in the back seat. "Murray, you're a pisser." They turned the corner onto Greenwich Street. Murray turned back to Cain. "Call Rocket; give him a description of the van and an ETA for its arrival."

He looked back out the windshield and laughed. "Those poor fucks have no idea what's waiting for them up there."

33

Siban struggled through the crowd of onlookers and up to the yellow tape. The crime scene encompassed the entire intersection of Jefferson and Bedford Avenues.

Between the small talk in the crowd and the scene before him, Siban was able to surmise exactly what had occurred. He surveyed the crowd. Hundreds of people lined the tape, gawking at the five dead bodies strewn across the sidewalk. He found most of his neighborhood Muslims along the northern side of the tape. Segregation was a natural phenomenon. He sidled through to the north.

He settled in along the tape and made his presence known amongst his followers. Then he turned and scanned the police personnel within the tape. After a moment, he found what he needed.

He pushed forward until he nearly burst the tape. That got the attention of a young uniformed policeman. Once addressed, Siban requested the young officer to have the detective in the light blue windbreaker come to him.

Siban had been to the scene of police shootings before. In Brooklyn, almost everyone had. He knew there would be a detective from the Community Affairs unit present to stem the tide of whatever community unrest may have been stirred by such dramatic action taken by the state.

A middle-aged black woman approached from within the crime scene, her detective's shield pinned on her light blue Community Affairs windbreaker. Siban explained to her that he was the religious leader of the local Muslim community and that it was vital for him to enter within the police lines. She objected, of course. But when Siban explained what he needed to do and agreed to wait until the Crime Scene Detectives finished their explicit tasks, she acquiesced.

While he waited, Siban worked the crowd again. He let it be known to all that he insisted the state allow him to perform the basic Muslim rites of death before their brethren were removed to the city morgue.

Siban kept an eye on the proceedings, and after some time, the Crime Scene techs finished taking photographs and fingerprints from the two dead young Muslims. Siban again pushed up into the tape.

Community Affairs Detective Debra Wilson noticed him and nodded. She motioned for him to wait just another minute. Siban watched as Wilson spoke to what appeared to be a high-ranking police official within the crime scene. She then walked back over to him, lifted the tape, and Siban ducked under.

First, he approached Mustaf. The youngster had died with a look of surprise on his face. Siban knelt down next to him. With his right index finger, he gently closed each of Mustaf's eyes.

Then, with the palm of his hand shielding the young man's eyes, he called out for all to hear: "Laa ilaaha illa-Allah." A murmur of grief laced with satisfaction whispered up from the crowd. Siban stood. He stepped lightly around the crime scene and approached the body of Hamid. Hamid's eyes were already closed. He looked almost peaceful, but still, Siban knelt down and put his hands over the youngster's eyes. Again he professed the blessing for the dead. He stood, and the crowd of Muslims lining the yellow tape murmured loudly and applauded lightly.

Siban sauntered back across the sidewalk. People in the crowd scrambled to hold up the tape for him to pass under. He received many greetings and whispered a message in response to each one: "I must speak with Zafir, we have work to do in response to this." He repeated it many times as he made his way through the crowd.

He arrived across the street at the tables of the Abra Zam and took up position on the sidewalk. A small cadre casually surrounded him. Aahil Halim, a nineteen-year-old whom Siban knew to be one of Zafir's more trusted associates, stepped in close.

"He is gone, Sahid. He has left for the city of Boston. He is in search of a key that is of great importance." Aahil stepped back. "Come, I will show you."

Siban followed Aahil down Jefferson Avenue. Along the short walk, Siban told himself he would just observe. Whether he would report his findings to Captain Gallagher or not, he could not decide at this moment —he could not harbor the thought of deception while engaged with these young men. Certainly, they would sense it. He put any such thoughts out of his mind.

They arrived at a non-descript, three-story Brooklyn Brownstone. They turned down the driveway and Aahil led him around the back of the house to a cellar door. They descended into the basement together and Aahil greeted the small group of young men laboring therein.

A large crate sat half empty in the middle of the small, dusty room. Siban marveled and appeared to be impressed by the sight of almost fifty brand new handguns with boxes of ammunition occupying half the crate. He looked up at Aahil and gestured toward the empty half of the crate.

Aahil shrugged. "A large suitcase." Again he stepped in

close to Siban. "It is this item for which Zafir needs a key." He looked over his shoulder at the other men in the basement and then whispered to Siban,

"He received a call from the homeland just this past hour. He became delighted upon learning of the nature of the suitcase; but also frustrated. The key, apparently, is with someone in Boston and is necessary for the proper operation of the weapon. He left here," Aahil turned and motioned up the steps, "not long ago, headed for Boston."

34

Jimmy and Frank arrived back at 51 Chambers Street exhausted. The shooting investigation took nearly an entire workday. Then they had to gain medical clearance.

They pulled up right out front and left the car in the No Standing Zone. They got out and stopped to stretch at the curb. A long line of school children, all holding hands and led by an adult, crossed between them and the grand old Emigrant Savings Bank building.

Jimmy shuddered through a yawn and smiled down at the young children passing in front of him. From behind him on Chambers street, the sudden blare of a fire engine nearly lifted him off his feet. He cringed and looked at the passing FDNY truck. John Wilson hung out from the passenger's window. "There you go again, Gallagher; just hangin' around, huh?"

The rig got stuck in traffic. "Hey." Jimmy raised his arms. "New York's Noisiest, go back to bed, nothing's burning out here." Then Jimmy got an idea. He turned back to the sidewalk and bent down to the line of school-children. He got their attention in a hurry. "Hey kids, look at the big fire truck." The children all stopped and looked up at John Wilson in the truck window. "Yeah." Jimmy stepped around and crouched behind the line of children. "Now let's all wave at the nice fireman."

Jimmy stood up tall. The children cheered and raised their hands and waved. Behind the kids, Jimmy reached up and flipped Wilson the bird —with both hands. Wilson shook his head and sighed in defeat. Then he gave an overly demonstrative wave to the school-children. "Hi, kids." Traffic cleared and the truck moved on. Wilson waved goodbye to the kids. "We're just hangin' around out here."

Jimmy brought his arms down and waved at John. Wilson smiled and nodded in return. Jimmy and Frank turned and headed in.

When they arrived at the eleventh floor office, they found Lieutenant Clark and Sergeant Donohue in the bullpen.

Jack jumped up and approached Jimmy, wide-eyed. Clark smiled and stood. He looked down one side of Jimmy and Frank and up the other. "No holes in either of you?"

Frank patted his torso a few times and smiled. "Nope. Doc says we're okay."

Jimmy snatched a chair from along the near wall and spun it backwards between his legs and sat. "Where are we with ballistics?"

Clark shook his head and sat back down. "Don't you think you should take a break? At least a day?"

Jimmy snorted a half-smile. "C'mon, Kevin, where are we?"

"Okay, you're the boss." Clark turned back to his workstation and slapped the keyboard to wake it up. "We don't have much. The techs in the lab ran the ballistics every which way and came up with exactly nothing." He turned back to Jimmy. "I mean, on the Arab's guns. The drug dealers' Mac 11 and shotgun are well documented. In fact, the Mac 11 has a body on it from a homicide in The Bronx two years ago. The Gang Unit begged to run with those leads and we didn't argue. I told them they could take that part of it as long as they kept us in the loop." Clark made the statement sound like a question.

Jimmy nodded. "Agreed."

Clark continued, "Our ballistics people could only definitively say that the two pistols are not American made and they're old —not used, just old. They're checking with ATF and other places to try and get a better lead on them, but right now, nothing's coming back.

"I asked the detective out there in Ballistics for his best guess and he said they're probably cold war relics from the other side; Eastern European or Chinese, maybe, from the look of them, and were made around that time: anywhere from the 1950s to the 70s."

Jimmy frowned and nodded. Then he turned to Jack who, like always, was on edge, bursting to give a report. Jimmy smiled.

"Whaddaya got, kid?" he said, mimicking the street detectives of yore. Jack let loose. He had lists of details about the two dead gunmen: where in the Middle-East they were born, when they came to this country, where they lived, worked and went to school and their entire pedigree —height, weight, no criminal record —in this country, anyway.

"As always, Jack, good work. Nice and thorough." Jimmy leaned back and stretched. He finished his yawn with his fists on his thighs. "Okay, now do this." He glanced back and forth between Clark and Jack and said,

"Kevin, review everything Jack dug up; and Jack, take a look at the lab reports from ballistics." Jimmy stood and headed across the bullpen to his office. "I promised the Chief I'd check in once we got cleared by the Medical Division."

He went in his office and closed the door. He could use a minute alone. He walked around behind the desk and stood at the window. He was tired. He swiveled his executive chair around and took a seat, still facing the window. He'd forgotten how comfortable this chair was. He rubbed the armrests of the luxurious piece of furniture. He looked down at the chair and thought about the strict hierarchy of the police department. He thought it archaic that a Captain got better furniture than his subordinates, and that a Chief's office set was better still.

He stood up out of the chair and leaned on the window, resting his forehead on the glass. The view was the entirety of the Boss Tweed Courthouse. Jimmy sighed and stood up straight from the window. "I guess not much has changed around here, eh, Boss." He laughed out at the landmark and went back to his chair. He swiveled in and picked up the phone.

After a few minutes of updating the hierarchy down the block at the Puzzle Palace, Jimmy re-emerged into the bullpen.

Jack jumped up. He waved a ballistics report with a crime scene photo of one of the pistols attached. "No serial numbers."

"Okay." Jimmy stopped and listened.

"No, I mean there are none. It's not the usual, where they'd been scratched off. These guns were manufactured without serial numbers on them."

"Okay, that is unique. What did ballistics say about that?"

"Nothing. Nothing beyond the fact that they've never come across that before. Plus the fact that it makes it virtually impossible to trace them. These data-bases run on numbers, not descriptions."

Jimmy sat back on the edge of the desk next to Jack's

workstation. "So we need corporate memory, here. We need to find someone that can trace the gun based on personal knowledge."

Jack looked to Clark, who frowned at Jimmy. They all stared at the floor for a moment when Frank piped up from across the bullpen, "What about your old friend out in Brighton Beach, the Russian."

Jimmy's eyebrows went up. Clark pursed his lips outward like he'd just bit into something sour. Jack didn't say a word. Jimmy stood up. "Shorotov."

Frank shrugged. "Why not?"

"Because One P-P and the FBI told us to stay the hell away from that guy, that's why not." Clark spun his chair back around to the table behind him.

A few years back, during the Queen Mary case, they did more than just talk to Shorotov, the Russian crime lord in Brighton Beach —they'd kicked in his door and got their asses handed to them by the Mayor for it.

Shorotov was ex-KGB and had been feeding steady information to the FBI for years. They never did prove a direct connection between the Russian and the Queen Mary attack, so Shorotov had continued on with his ways out in Brooklyn.

Frank shrugged again and pointed at the picture of the pistol still in Jack's hand. "He'll know. Probably won't take him a second. Either him or his guys will know all about that thing."

Jimmy smiled at Frank for a second before responding. "You're such a street cop, Frank, you know that?"

Frank put his hands out at his sides. "Just saying."

Jimmy kept smiling at him and nodded. "From the ground up, Frankie; that's how you work it: from the ground up. I love it." He turned back to Clark and Jack.

"Get someone on the horn out there and let them know we're coming. I don't want to surprise him this time; don't want him thinking I'm out there to mess with him." He headed for the door.

"And don't tell him what we want, either: just tell him I need a favor." Frank pulled opened the door and Jimmy turned back to his lieutenant. "And give me a heads up; let me know that you got through." They left.

35

It had been a few years since Jimmy walked through the doors of The Bear's Den. The front of the two-story reception hall took up half of Brightwater Court just in from Coney Island Avenue. The back looked out over the Atlantic Ocean.

As he pulled open the front door, Jimmy noticed the daily 'number' was still being posted in the front window. Each morning in 'numbers joints' around the city, an index card was taped in the window showing a three-digit number; the last three digits of the number of shares traded on Wall Street the previous day. That's how the underground lottery or, as law enforcement called it, the 'numbers game' picked its winner. Honest enough pick, Jimmy thought as he stepped in and held the door open behind him for Frank.

The first thing Jimmy noticed was not something immediately present, but rather the absence of Shorotov's main muscle, a guy named Grigori. Jimmy fully expected the giant to meet them at the door as he usually had in the past.

But the place was completely empty; not even a bartender. The layout inside hadn't changed one bit. The red flag of the defunct Soviet Union anchored the wall behind the bar running along the left. The opposite wall on the right hosted a series of wooden plaques, each displaying the seal of every new republic formed with the dissolution of the Soviet Union. A number of the seals had at their center the familiar Islamic Crescent Star. In the center of the entire collection, of course, sat the seal of the Russian Federation.

Jimmy and Frank made their way past the bar stools on

their left and a line of small tables and chairs on the right. The entire barroom ran more than fifty feet deep and maybe thirty feet across. Behind the left wall, Jimmy remembered, was the huge catering hall.

Jimmy had seen that room filled with a thousand people the last time he was out here. When they got about halfway down the bar, a door on the back wall opened and a disheveled-looking older man wearing an apron ambled through it. He mumbled something to them and walked past the double set of glass doors leading to the reception room. He stepped in behind the bar and looked up at Jimmy with expectant eyes. Jimmy had put his hand up to motion that they wouldn't be ordering a drink when the back door opened again. Grigori stepped in the room.

"There you are." Jimmy smiled. "How've you been, old friend?"

Grigori did not smile. He stood by the open door and motioned them up the stairs. "Mister Shorotov awaits."

Jimmy nodded and walked past Grigori. "That's a fine 'how-do-you-do' there, big fella." Frank walked past Grigori without looking at him and the three men headed up the stairs.

Jimmy stopped at the second floor landing and let Grigori get past him. Jimmy and Frank then followed the large Russian down the hall, past a series of motel room-like doors used, Jimmy knew, for the purposes of prostitution – another of Shorotov's mainstays along with running numbers.

The upstairs hallway ran straight back above the bar below, so the window at the end looked out over the street. They went through the last door on the right and walked into Shorotov's office.

The giant space covered almost the entire ballroom below. The long row of windows on the left, the side facing the street, was heavily draped. The wall on the right, opposite the street side was occupied almost entirely with a movie screen, and rows of velvet seats backed right up toward them.

Shortov's desk faced them from the center of the far wall. Off to each side of the main desk sat two smaller but very professionally laid out desks. Behind each of those desks, in each far corner of the room, a door opened onto the back wall.

Vladimir Shorotov stood up behind his desk and Grigori escorted Jimmy and Frank across the room. He led them around in front of a curved row of six plush leather chairs facing the desk.

The bare brick of the wall behind Shorotov sported the occasional stained wood beam, which gave the room a grand, rustic look. The center of the wall was sheet rocked and painted a deep green. Tall flagpoles stood on either side of the sheetrock.

The one on the left presented a flag exactly like the Soviet flag downstairs behind the bar, except that it had a light blue stripe occupying the first one-eighth of its width. The flag on the right was something colorful that Jimmy couldn't quite make out.

In the center of the sheetrock, between the flagpoles, hung a large wooden plaque. On the plaque hung an official-looking symbol. Its main ingredient was a long, silver shield like a warrior would carry. From top to bottom, a brass-handled sword traversed the shield. In the very center of the symbol, covering the middle portion of the sword, shone a gold five-point star with the hammer and sickle imposed in its center. KGB.

"Captain." Shorotov extended his hand to Jimmy across the desk. Vladimir Shorotov was a short, thin, balding man in a tailor-made suit. Jimmy remembered the first description he ever got of the ex-KGB leader. He heard it from a vice detective some years ago: "A little old man with missiles in his eyes. Five-seven, maybe a hundred fifty, balding. Like a C-E-O except he's got, you know, the look. Like you'd know he's a killer." Jimmy smiled and shook hands across the desk with the Russian crime lord.

"Please." Shorotov motioned to the visitors' chairs opposite the desk.

Jimmy glanced at Frank, unbuttoned his suit jacket, and backed down into a seat. Frank followed suit.

"You have been taking care of yourself," Shorotov smiled. "You have not aged." He turned to Frank. "Either of you."

"Yes, yes," Jimmy nodded. "You, too."

"Thank you." Shorotov folded his hands across his midsection. "The years have been kind."

"So." Jimmy pulled a folded piece of paper from inside his suit jacket. "I need your help with something."

Shorotov didn't move; nor did he say a word. He just pursed his lips and waited.

Jimmy stood up and walked the two steps to the front edge of the desk. He extended the paper across. Shorotov unclasped his hands and reached out to receive it. Jimmy pulled it back and left Shorotov with his right hand outstretched across the desk. "I'm going to trust you, here. Tell me I'm not making a mistake."

Shorotov laid both his hands flat on his desk. He took a moment and stared at Jimmy. "You have made this decision already." He lifted his hands momentarily off the desk, turned them palms upward, and then returned them to his desktop. "You are here."

Jimmy leaned in and put both his hands, knuckles down, on the front of the desk. "Ya know, Mister Shorotov, there's something I've always admired about you." He paused and stared hard into Shorotov's eyes.

He sensed a movement behind him and knew that Grigori was never far off. Then he felt and heard Frank standing up behind him. Jimmy didn't move. He just stared at Shorotov.

"What's that, Captain?" Shorotov nearly smirked.

Jimmy stood back. "You don't deal drugs."

Shorotov raised an eyebrow at Jimmy. Then he glanced over to where Grigori obviously stood and blinked very slowly, leaving his eyes closed for just a moment. Then he sat back. "No, I do not."

Jimmy stepped closer so that his thighs rubbed against the front of the desk. "What about guns?"

Shorotov frowned and tilted his head. "Professionally, Captain, as an experienced Russian leader, I find private gun ownership to be an appalling idea. In Russia, we do not allow citizens to arm themselves."

He kept his elbows inside the armrests of his chair and spread his hands out to either side from the forearms up. "I am an American businessman. But some things are far outside my range of vision."

Jimmy stared at him for a moment before continuing. He knew the Feds allowed Shorotov some leeway with his lucrative vice operations as long as he kept them in the loop with vital information from overseas. But they'd never let him deal in guns. Besides, Jimmy did know, it was something the Russians didn't have a history of being involved in. He decided to trust him.

Shorotov nodded thoughtfully and stood. "So." He slipped his suit jacket panels aside and slid his hands into his front pants pockets. "What can I do for you today, Captain?"

Jimmy flapped open the now-crumpled sheet of paper. It was a crime scene photograph showing of one of the pistols used by Zafir's men at the Bedford Avenue shootout.

"No serial numbers. Not American. Hard to trace. My ballistics people tell me it might be Russian-made, cold war era, post-world war two; around there."

Shorotov took the sheet. Jimmy now pulled his jacket open and put his hands on his hips. "I need to know all about it and how a kid on the streets of Brooklyn came to have it in his hands."

Shorotov responded without hesitation. "It is a TT-33. A Makarov. You are right, it was made in Russia; but we stopped making them in 1954." He looked closer at the photo. "Though this weapon appears to be new." He looked up at Jimmy.

"Right, ballistics says it may never have been fired before until now."

Shorotov dropped the sheet to the desk, but still held it. "And how did you come to possess this?"

Jimmy shook his head. "If you don't mind, I'll ask the questions for now."

Shorotov left the sheet on the desk and put his hands up. "Yes, yes, this I do not need to know." He looked down again at the photo. He began nodding. "No serial number, you say?"

"Right, why?"

"That means it was an officer's gun. It must be even older than the 1950s." He picked up the picture again. "Whenever we introduced new models of side arms, we first issued them to officers. Depending on the manufacturer and his history, there were times when we issued them only to members of the high command. Those first high-level test-pistols were without identifying marks. There couldn't have been more than a hundred of them made."

"A hundred is a lot."

Shorotov looked up. "In New York City, maybe, Captain, but not when you are contemplating outfitting an army."

"Right," Jimmy nodded. "But I need to know how they got here. How some kids up in Bed-Stuy got their hands on them."

Shorotov raised his eyebrows and asked, "Them? You have more than one?"

"Right now, I have two. But I have a feeling there are more out there."

Shorotov motioned with the paper, silently asking if he could keep it. Jimmy nodded. "So, can you help me?"

Shorotov folded the photo and slipped it in his inside jacket. "I can try, yes. I can certainly expand on the history of the TT-33 and then explore how it may have arrived here at this time and place."

36

Frank had one hand on the gear shifter and one hand on the door handle, –ready to go either way. Jimmy folded the warrant, leaned forward to the dashboard, and stuffed it in his back pocket. Then he sat back and watched the scene unfold before them.

They had three warrants for today and the first two were being executed in the normal fashion –overtly. The last one, the one Jimmy had in his pocket, would be done covertly. Soon.

In the aftermath of a police-involved shooting, let alone a quintuple homicide, the Department turned the neighborhood upside down –as a matter of course. Every resource imaginable was deployed to the immediate vicinity.

The more arrests you made, the more debriefings you conducted. The more debriefings you conducted, the more confidential information you got, which, ultimately, led to at a least a few search warrants.

The Gang Unit had come up with one for human trafficking: there was an illicit massage parlor on Jefferson Avenue in the basement of a building a half block down from the Abra Zam Café. After the Gang detectives debriefed the girls, they arrested the Madam. And she was a font of information.

Subsequently, the Narcotics guys came up with a warrant for a stash house around the corner on Bedford. The Narcotics detectives weren't sure if it was the supply house for the money door where the shooting took place, but the judge agreed that it didn't matter: their informant gave enough details on the location to give them probable cause that there was a significant amount of drugs in the apartment.

So, they had two warrants —all they needed to get started. Then Jimmy went before the judge himself for the third. He was disappointed that he couldn't convince Siban to appear before the judge with him. So was the judge. Jimmy ended up having to present the evidence as being from a 'reliable confidential informant.' The judge didn't like that but since the information was so complete, she signed the warrant anyway.

Jimmy watched while the operation unfolded half a block away on the other side of Bedford. He had specifically ordered two separate Entry Teams from the Emergency Service Unit. Purportedly so that both warrants could be executed simultaneously; but really, he wanted twice as many cops in helmets, ceramic vests and machine guns roaming the area to set the stage properly. Now the overt warrant operations began wrapping up.

The Narcotics guys already started carrying out boxes of evidence and the Gang Unit had previously removed their prisoners.

And even though the ESU Entry Teams were finished, as ordered, they remained locked and loaded. The 79th Precinct Special Operations Lieutenant and his Anti-Crime Sergeant led each ESU team up and down the block, stopping occasionally and directing them to check on random stores and buildings.

They didn't actually make any entries. They understood the orders Jimmy had given them: it was a show. And it was working. The intensity on the street was palpable.

Teenagers hopped from foot to foot on the corners,

older heads swung like pendulums out the windows up and down the block. The street was closed to vehicular traffic. Pedestrians scurried along, craning their necks every so often at so much police activity.

It was time. Jimmy picked up his radio and called out his two 'uncles'.

"OCTU 1 to OCTU 2, come in?"

"OCTU 2 on the air."

"Move in."

"Ten-four."

Jimmy watched as his two undercover officers emerged from a laundromat a block to his left, on Putnam Avenue. Their purposefully nonchalant pace would get them in position in another minute and a half. Jimmy pulled out his warrant and took one more look.

He looked at the judge's signature and sighed. Then he folded it and stuck it in the glove box. He was surprised at Siban; he didn't expect him to be so nervous. It was out of character for him. Jimmy thought maybe it was the sight of so many guns in the hands of his young followers, but then, when Siban nearly had a nervous breakdown when Jimmy asked him where Zafir had gone, he realized it was because Siban felt like a traitor.

All the holy man could get out was the location and description of the guns in the basement. After that, he fell apart. Very unlike him. But Jimmy didn't have time to waste. He took the info on the guns and ran off to get the warrant and make the necessary arrangements. He would debrief Siban later. The undercovers turned the corner.

"OCTU 1 to 7-9 Special Ops. You on the air, Lieutenant?"

Jimmy could actually see the Precinct Special Operations

Lieutenant down the block reach for his radio in response. "7-9 Special Ops on the air, Captain."

"Uncles are approaching. Enact the final diversion."

"Ten-Four."

Nearly a block away, the uniformed lieutenant turned in Jimmy's direction and walked toward him down the middle of the street. The lieutenant could obviously see the team of undercovers approaching —and ignored them. When the target brownstone was just about directly on his right, the lieutenant turned left.

He bent down and looked under a parked car. Then he got down on all fours and looked closely under the car. Then he stood up and funneled his hands on the car window to look inside. Then he stepped back.

He stuck his right arm straight up in the air, circled his hand, and whistled. The nearest ESU team turned and trotted over in response. The lieutenant stepped back and pointed his right hand down, directly at the car.

ESU moved in tactically and launched a full search of the car. The attention of the entire block focused on it. The undercovers walked by the target brownstone on the other side of the street. No one bothered to look their way.

One of the 'uncles' dropped a small metallic object on the sidewalk at the top of the driveway and the other tossed an identical item a few feet down the driveway. They kept walking. No one noticed.

ESU finished searching the car and gave the lieutenant the all-clear. The crowd loosened their attention and the block came back to life.

The Anti-Crime sergeant sidled away from his lieutenant and over toward the target brownstone. Then he just hung around, waiting for the right opportunity. He waited until a random pair of pedestrians, a middle-aged couple, was just about to walk past the driveway.

He jumped in front of them and held up his hand. He yelled at them to stop as he stared hard at the sidewalk directly in front of them. His actions garnered the attentions of the street. He squatted low and stared at the 9mm cartridge dropped there by the undercover. He stepped back and began scanning the immediate vicinity of the sidewalk. He kept it up until a small crowd formed –all eyes focused on the 9mm cartridge.

The sergeant purposely kept his eyes on the sidewalk and away from the driveway, but kept searching until someone in the crowd spoke up and pointed down the driveway at the other bullet dropped there.

The sergeant looked up at the passer-by and thanked him. Then he mimicked the lieutenant's earlier hand signal to mobilize the ESU entry team. After circling his right arm high, he pointed down the driveway and to the basement entrance.

"Show time," Jimmy said. Frank pulled the gear shifter into Drive.

With two entry teams on site, the execution took only a few seconds. One team went in the front and the other through the back and down the basement stairs. They went in hard, lasers flashing, machine guns leveled.

Once they declared the basement 'clear', Jimmy entered with his investigators. There were only two young, now thoroughly frightened, Arab men present. And the entire crate of guns and ammunition was still exactly where Siban had said it would be. Jimmy had his first team handcuff the youngsters and lead them out of the basement.

A moment later, Sergeant Donohue came down the

stairs with the evidence collection people. Jack looked over his shoulder at the two prisoners being escorted up the basement stairs and then turned and whispered to Jimmy, "That was some show out there."

Jimmy smirked. He watched until the prisoners were completely out of the basement and said, "Yeah, you gotta protect your source. These guys can't know that Siban gave us this information. Otherwise, he's a dead man. Had to make it look like a random find."

"Nice job." Jack joined Jimmy next to the crate and observed the start of the inventory. Jimmy picked up one of the guns and examined it himself. He weighed it in his hands and turned to Jack. "Makarov."

"No shit." Jack nodded at the crate of almost fifty handguns. "Jackpot."

Frank walked over and joined them at the crate. He stared down at the guns and nodded slowly. "Russian?" He looked up at Jimmy.

"Yeah."

"Nice."

"Yeah."

Then Donohue looked closely at the evidence. "Yeah, those are Makarov TT-33s, all right." Then he pointed to the other side of the crate. "Any ideas on the empty half?"

"Not yet. Once we find this prick Zafir, hopefully we can get it out of him. But the pressure's off now; we got his guns," Jimmy smiled. "We'll have to talk to Siban more when he calms down."

"Oh yeah, that reminds me: apparently he's doing much better," Jack said. "I just got off the phone with Clark a few minutes ago. You launched the raid just as we were talking, but he said Siban now remembers where Zafir was going.

Something about a key? I'm not sure. Also —"

"Where did he say Zafir was going?" Jimmy cut him off.

"Back to Boston."

Jimmy headed for the stairs. Jack called to him, "But also, Captain, Clark said that Shorotov called. Said it's important. Said you should call him as soon as possible."

37

Zafir ignored the speed limit. Go with the flow, he was told. Your speed should be commensurate with the speed of the cars behind you and before you. Don't be nervous; going too slow would also attract the attention of law enforcement. And choose interstates over parkways. And stay out of the left lane.

Zafir tried not to get caught up in too many details. He had to appear calm, like a typical American on a holiday drive. But he was not calm. He was exhilarated at his prospects. He had lost his guns –all of them –but his handlers in the homeland were surprisingly at peace with that. And then they informed him why.

Then the conversation at once became joyous and desperate. He needed that key. He was chided severely for leaving it behind in Boston. Yes, he would retrieve it. No, he didn't know precisely where it was, but would they support him? Thank you, thank you.

That pledge of all the support and resources he would need in Boston put him on the proper footing to then divulge to them the greatest example yet of his brilliance.

Finding employment for Nagreb near that building in lower Manhattan was entirely his idea. The leaders at home did not know of it. And then he revealed it to them.

He'd had Nagreb lay in wait these two years on the remote possibility that they would be so fortunate to find a nuclear device. And now they had.

And now, because of his patience and foresight regarding Nagreb, he had access to what his fellow jihadists around the world believed was the greatest American target for such a device.

His handlers were astonished at his cleverness. Now it was just a matter of getting the eyes of the world onto that building and setting the device off in such a manner as to bring attention to its significance and, at the same time, do the most damage.

The rudiments of a plan were already in his head. But he did not divulge all to them. Not yet. Let them remain impressed. Now he demanded unadulterated trust and respect. It worked. The plan was his to devise, and they would supply him with whatever he requested.

He gripped the wheel harder at the thought of his new potential. The speedometer slid past seventy. He caught himself and fell back in with the flow of traffic.

38

This time Grigori paced the sidewalk, waiting for them. Jimmy had detected anxiety from Shorotov on the phone. Another guy out of character. Jimmy watched Grigori whip open the door to the Bear's Den at his approach. "What's up big fella; why the long face?"

Grigori held open the door and motioned Jimmy and Frank inside. "Please."

They found Shorotov sitting alone at the first table, just inside the door. Shorotov stood. "Captain," he motioned to the opposite chair, "please."

Jimmy pulled out the chair and sat. Grigori locked the door behind him. Frank stood over Jimmy's shoulder and Grigori watched out the front window. Shorotov picked up a short stack of papers from the table in front of him.

"Captain, I may have devastating news for you. It depends on what you can tell me about where and how you came to possess these two Makarov pistols."

"It's not just two anymore, Mister Shorotov; I got the whole crate just this morning. We recovered a total of fifty pistols and ten thousand rounds of ammunition."

Shorotov leaned back in his chair. "When you say the 'whole crate,' tell me exactly what you have recovered."

Jimmy tilted his head and pursed his lips.

Then he shook his head. "We're talking evidence here, proceeds of a 'no-knock' warrant we –"

"Captain," Shorotov interrupted him, "it is vital that you tell me what you have found so that I can tell you what you have not found. There is much more to this particular shipment of Makarov pistols than you may realize." He shook the sheaf of papers in his hand.

Jimmy exhaled. He had trusted Shorotov to this point. Now he was being asked to go a step further. He looked into the eyes of the man who had once been the head of the KGB. He hesitated. But only for a moment. Shorotov was a shrewd, double-dealing criminal; Jimmy knew that. But his instincts told him he could trust the old Russian further.

"Okay, we recovered an old wooden crate; half of which was filled with boxes of ammunition totaling about ten thousand rounds; and boxes of these Makarov handguns, totaling almost fifty."

"And the other half of the crate? What did it contain?"

"It was empty."

Shorotov's shoulders dropped. His hands slid off the table, the papers crumpling as they disappeared beneath. "We have a problem," he remained slumped, but looked directly in Jimmy's eyes, "of global proportions."

"Okay, you need to be very specific with me right now, Mister Shorotov."

"As do you, Captain. What ever more information you may have about the origins of this half-full crate —where it came from, how it came to be in America, in New York — you need to inform me of those facts right now if I am to be of any further assistance to you."

Jimmy looked over his shoulder at Frank. Frank just stared back. Jimmy frowned and turned back to Shorotov. He leaned in. "All right." He spread his hands flat on the table. "Middle Eastern terrorists. A guy named Zafir, young guy, went up to Boston to make contact with some old IRA contacts up there. He went looking for this crate of guns and we, well…" he glanced up at Frank again, "we got lucky.

We walked in on them, pretty much during the exchange."

"The IRA granted this Zafir person access to these crates of weapons?"

Jimmy sat back. He stared off in the distance for a second. "You know what, I'm not sure. It looked that way to me. But now that you ask it that way, I'm not actually sure. There definitely is more going on up in Boston than meets my eye, anyway."

Shorotov drew a deep breath. He laid the papers on the table. "Okay, Captain; cards on the table, literally." He put his hands over the sheets. "Tell me exactly every detail and I shall then respond in kind."

Jimmy looked at the papers and noticed they were in the Russian language. There was not a chance at glimpsing their content. He decided to go with it.

"Okay. I found my terrorist talking with the IRA in Boston. I followed some leads and found him on the campus of Boston College with one of the Irish contacts. I'm pretty sure they had loaded up one crate already and were headed back in to this, like, secret hiding spot, with a hand truck. We followed and found the other crate. I shot it out with Irish guy, but the Middle-Easterner got away."

"With one crate."

"Yes. The crate I recovered this morning, I believe."

"And this crate of this morning: it was half empty but for Makarov pistols and their attendant ammunition?"

"That's right."

"Captain." Shorotov took his hands off the papers and pushed them toward Jimmy. "You have a nuclear weapon in the hands of your Zafir person. You need to make haste and find him."

"Nuclear?" Jimmy looked down at the papers. There

were three sheets; two of text and one with four photos. He couldn't make heads or tails of the text. Three of the photos showed different views of the same box. A box with a large handle, almost like a suitcase. One photo showed an odd-shaped key. Jimmy pointed at the key. "What's that?"

"It is the trigger. Consider it a detonator. Before the explosives necessary to ignite the nuclear device can be triggered, that key must first be inserted."

"Nuclear? Device?" Jimmy stared at the photos. "This can't be what I think it is." He looked up at Shorotov. "I was at a training session a few years back. We were told suitcase nukes didn't exist; that they were a complete fabrication. No facts: just fairy tales meant to scare Americans."

The look on Shorotov's face was more serious than Jimmy had seen before, if that was even possible. The old Russian leaned in on the table with his forearms.

"Politics aside, Captain, there is no time to explain or debate that point." He pulled up the two sheets of text. "This is a bill of lading. It details the contents of a shipment of weapons we sold to Libya in 1977." He pushed them at Jimmy.

"Take them; have whatever experts you employ study them. They are genuine. The Libyans sold the shipment to the Irish Republicans. There were three crates. Two contained one hundred Makarovs with ammunition. The third crate contained only fifty.

"That is because that third crate also contained what your people now refer to as a 'suitcase nuke.' It is a uranium device. Uranium does not deteriorate over time; it would remain functional for decades." He leaned back and sat up straight. "This is no fairy tale, Captain. I am greatly concerned. We are all Americans now. An attack of this magnitude would devastate many aspects of my business relations and also impact international relations with Russia, a condition with which I am partly charged. This cannot happen. You must stop it."

Jimmy nodded and looked up at Frank. "The Guns of Antwerp."

"… went back to Boston to get a key." Frank pointed at the photo. "Isn't that what Jack said?"

39

Jimmy tried to appear calm, but found it difficult. He glanced up again at the indicator on the elevator wall. Eight and counting. A crowd of middle and upper managers surrounded him; all of whom recognized him. A few even said hello.

Being in 1PP was disturbing enough and, heading up to unlucky 13 again made it even worse, but his impatience at not being on the road to Boston yet was really killing him. He refrained from tapping his foot. Eleven and counting.

When Jimmy called Chief Shea to let him know there was a suitcase nuke hidden somewhere in the city, Shea called a meeting. Jimmy protested, but the Chief demanded he attend and personally conduct a briefing.

The real disagreement came when the Chief told Jimmy the FBI would be in attendance. Jimmy practically begged him to keep it in-house for the time being. Jimmy even played off the Chief's skepticism of a suitcase nuke being a viable threat and reasoned that, without further investigation, the FBI wouldn't care to get involved anyway. But Shea insisted they get input from the feds.

Jimmy wasn't used to that. His unit was unique in the world of counter terrorism in that it was not a joint unit. Unlike the Joint Terrorist Task Force that was half populated with NYPD Detectives and half with FBI agents, Jimmy's Organized Crime Terrorist Unit was a stand-alone operation tailor made for Jimmy Gallagher. Not that he couldn't play nice in the sand box. But he was at his best when unencumbered by the mores of other agencies. And the Chiefs knew it. And they gave him a long leash. Usually. But every time the shit was about to hit the fan, the bigwigs panicked and called in outside agencies. Which was entirely contrary to OCTU's mission.

Thirteen, finally.

Jimmy made his way through the glass partitions and down the hall to the conference room of the Chief of Detectives. A secretary at the top of the hall told him to go right in, they were expecting him. No-knock, eh, Jimmy laughed to himself.

He opened the door and stepped in. As expected, Chief Shea sat at the far head of the table and directed Jimmy into the opposite seat, directly inside the door.

Mike Gonzalez, the one-star from the Commissioner's office, was again on Shea's right. Next to Gonzalez, leading down toward Jimmy, were two men in suits from the FBI. Jimmy recognized the older one, Mark Neustein. Jimmy didn't like him.

The man considered himself an expert on all things related to domestic terrorism: the history, the players, the equipment. He may be knowledgeable, Jimmy could admit, but the man had showed himself to be a consummate bureaucrat as opposed to being a cop of any sort. Neustein would rather be right than find the truth. Image and reputation were everything to the man. A hallmark of the feds.

Opposite the feds, running along Jimmy's right, sat two uniform members of the NYPD. One was a Captain from the Motor Carrier Safety Unit; the other a Sergeant from the Emergency Service Unit – a HazMat specialist. Jimmy sat.

"All right, Jimmy," Shea began, "first tell me about your source."

"Shorotov, the Russian."

Both feds smirked and shook their heads. Shea turned to them. "Comments? Gentlemen?"

Neustein turned away from Jimmy and spoke to the head of the table. "Chief, the federal government has dealt closely with Mister Shorotov on a variety of issues over the years. He is known to be somewhat useful, but entirely self-serving. He has a history of being duplicitous if it serves him." He turned to Jimmy. "Therefore, he is considered to be unreliable."

"Why would he lie." It wasn't a question, the way Jimmy said it.

Shea put up his hand. "Okay, for now let's consider the witness' reliability to be debatable. Let's leave that right there." He pointed down to the table. Then he turned to the two uniforms on his left. "Tell us about the science."

The Captain spoke first. "It's a possibility, Chief. Notwithstanding the political skepticism surrounding the existence of suitcase nukes, I can tell you that plutonium and uranium do not degrade over decades."

"It's uranium." Jimmy said

Shea didn't verbalize a question; he just raised an eyebrow at Jimmy with an inquisitive gesture. Jimmy responded, "Shorotov told me." The two feds tried to remain professional, but Neustein let out a sigh. Jimmy turned to him. He pulled a slim sheaf of folded papers from his jacket and slid them across the table to the younger FBI man nearest him.

"Those are your copies; keep 'em. My people have been studying them for the past hour. So far, they appear to be credible." Jimmy turned to Chief Shea and opened his mouth to say something, but stopped. He turned back to the fed who was now scanning the sheets. "Get yourself up to speed and get back to me."

"That's enough, Jimmy." Shea then turned back to the MCSU Captain. "Continue."

The Captain sighed. "There isn't much more to say than 'anything is possible,' especially if you tell me it's uranium – that makes it more believable."

"Why is that?" Shea asked.

The Captain opened a folder in front of him. "Uranium is simpler. Let me give you the example. I say *the* example: Fat Man and Little Boy, the two bombs the U.S. dropped on Japan in World War Two.

"Fat Man, the one we dropped on Nagasaki, used plutonium; Little Boy, the one we dropped on Hiroshima, used uranium." He turned over a page in his folder. "Like I said, uranium is simpler. Little Boy, in contrast to the plutonium-based Fat Man, was a gun-type weapon, which is straightforward, if not trivial, to design and operate. I mean, really, once the uranium is put in place, all you have to do is flip the switch. They call it 'gun-type' because you need to have a relatively minor explosion to send two hunks of uranium at each other, through a cylinder –like a two-foot-long gun barrel at high speed. That's it. Boom."

"They don't exist," Neustein smirked, and pulled at his shirt cuff.

Shea ignored Neustein and turned to Chief Gonzalez. "Mike, anything?"

Gonzalez cleared his throat. "Yes, Chief. I spoke with the leaders of our Counterterrorism Bureau as well as the Intelligence Division. The Police Commissioner himself even went outside the agency to make conferrals on the matter." Gonzalez opened his hands to the table and shrugged. "No one claims to have the authority to state definitively that suitcase nukes don't exist. No one believes they actually do; but neither can anyone claim knowledge of their non-existence. It's a toss-up."

Shea turned back to Jimmy. "Captain, what was it you called the shipment this thing was supposedly in? The Guns of something? What was that?"

"Antwerp. The Guns of Antwerp. My information is —"

Neustein laughed out loud. "That old Irish fable?" He turned to Chief Shea and then back to Jimmy. "Are you kidding me? We put that folk story to bed years ago. It never happened."

Jimmy watched the younger FBI agent still perusing the sheets Jimmy had slid over to him. "You know what, Neustein, why don't you take a look at that." He pointed at the sheets. Neustein smirked. Jimmy continued. "That's the original Bill of Lading from when the Russians sold the shipment to the Libyans."

The younger agent looked up at Neustein, but shook his head. "It's in Russian. I'm a little rusty, but it does appear to list a shipment of weapons from 1977."

"I'm sure it does. But that makes no difference," Neustein said. "We know what happened in Antwerp. The Belgians got sticky fingers. End of story."

Now Jimmy sighed. He looked at Chief Shea. "Boss, this is all nonsense. No body knows if any of this is true or not."

"Finally we agree on something, Gallagher," Neustein said.

"You need to open your mind once in a while, there, fella."

"All right, that's enough." Shea again took command of the meeting. He stood. "Jimmy, go ahead on up to Boston and see if you can find your suspect. Bomb or no bomb, you like him for a couple of shootings, anyway. We'll keep our eyes open down here." Shea glanced over at the MCSU and ESU managers. "You guys have Radiation Detection Pagers deployed in and around the UN this week, am I correct?"

"Yes, sir," the Captain answered. "As a matter of course, the pagers are part of the UN deployment."

"Okay. Well, do pass along what you've heard here this afternoon to your Planning Officer. Make sure the people running that detail are apprised of any possibility."

The Captain nodded and stood. "Yes, sir."

40

Johnny Dineen strolled off Cambridge Street and onto North Grove. A hot dog vendor noticed him and nodded. The cart stood directly in front of a landscaped wrought iron fence hosting large brass letters announcing Massachusetts General Hospital. Johnny waved.

"Hey, how you doin, pal." Johnny stepped over to the cart. "Listen." He pulled out a twenty-dollar bill. "Can you tell me where's Massachusetts General Hospital?" He slapped the bill on the man's cart and walked away. The vendor laughed. "Thank you, Mister Dineen."

Johnny loved his notoriety. His many press appearances in the Boston media cast him as a criminal who couldn't be caught. But he worked toward changing that. A man had to make a living, that's for sure; but he saw himself as more of a 'man of the people' than a criminal. Corruption was a part of life. So was vice. People needed to wake up and admit that. He was just playing his part.

He continued his stride up North Grove Street. You could throw a stone in Boston and hit a hospital, but nothing like Mass General. The place took up a square mile; and in the middle of a crowded downtown, that was a lot.

He was proud of his involvement with the construction of some of the newer buildings and walkways. As were a lot of people.

But a place this big —the other unions, the service worker's locals, had a hard time getting in. Johnny's people weren't directly involved with those locals, but any time any union had specific problems, his people could always be counted on to lend a few hands.

Just ahead, on the right, a klatch of hospital workers sat on a low concrete wall. Lunchtime. Johnny watched as his presence became known. The gal closest to him made eye contact, said something to the group, and turned away. One by one, they looked over as he approached. One guy stood. A tall black guy in scrubs. Rough-looking guy without even the hint of a smile. Johnny noticed his ID tag —Maintenance. Good.

"Hey." Johnny stopped dead even with the man. He pointed up at him; the guy had at least four inches on him. "You're with Local Eleven-Ninety-Nine, right?" Johnny nodded in approval and stepped in closer. He put his hand out to the man.

"I'm right, ain't I? Didn't I see you at a business meeting once, maybe a few years ago?" Johnny brought out his subtle, sly smile; never having set eyes on the man in his life.

The man smiled and nodded. "Yeah, man, Eleven-Ninety-Nine all the way, bro."

"There it is." Johnny smiled broadly and shook the man's hand. Then he turned and surveyed the other hospital workers on their lunch break. He nodded to all of them and began to step away. He pointed at the tall guy. "You get any scabs coming around here, you let me know." He pulled on his shirt cuffs and shrugged his suit jacket snug. "I'll take care of everything, you got that?" Johnny didn't smile.

"Yes sir, Mister Dineen, we got you." The man smiled.

Johnny continued his saunter up North Grove, past Fruit Street. The main entrance of Mass General welcomed him like a giant U at the end of the dead-end street.

He smiled at how much concrete he had poured into the massive Lunder Building rising up on his left. Concrete had always been his thing. Construction, union no-shows; all big money. Then he was nominated to take over the real business when the last guy disappeared. Wasn't his idea. Johnny didn't like the idea of strong-arming people to gain their compliance. He'd rather do good things for the majority and gain their loyalty. But not everyone responded to kindness. Murder turned his stomach.

He glanced up at the Lunder Building again and thought of those few bodies mixed into the foundation. Concrete had always been his thing. No better way to dispose of the human wreckage left in the wake of success.

He approached the revolving door at the main entrance and made eye contact with a pair of hospital cops out front. Not real cops –kinda wanna be's; but law enforcement just the same. He stopped in front of them. He looked each one in the eye for a second and then clasped his hands together in front of his waist. "Everything as it should be today, gentlemen?" One uniform, a younger one, didn't smile, and turned away. The older one lowered his eyelids and nodded at Johnny. "No worries, Mister Dineen." He motioned to the doors. "All is well."

The doors came around and Johnny Dineen waltzed through them like he owned the place. He strode through the lobby and headed straight for the elevators. He knew what floor he was going to.

He passed the visitor's desk with a gallant wave to the young receptionist with the purple hair. The girl stood up and looked expectant of more –a hug, even. Johnny just strolled on by. Jeannie McCarthy, cousin to an in-law, poor kid. Johnny pushed for the elevator and looked back at her.

The kid was still looking at him and turned on the big smile again. Johnny smiled back. She had a set of parents that thought they did it right. Stayed together, worked hard, went to Mass every Sunday even. But, and Johnny knew 'cause he'd been over the house enough times, the kid was left to her room with headphones and such, hour after hour after hour. They did the right thing outwardly, her parents; but couldn't muster the patience to actually pay attention. Three rehabs later and the kid still couldn't stop trying to please the world.

Johnny looked away and pushed the 'up' button again. No, him and Margie decided early on they wouldn't try and raise kids. You can keep that purple hair shit. Ain't got the patience for it. And what's the use in pretending.

Off the elevators, down the hall, and after a few flirtatious comments at the nurse's station, he found what he was looking for: a couple of old Knights of Columbus sitting guard duty in the hall.

"Gentlemen." He pulled up just short of their chairs, one on either side of the private room. Though he wasn't a Knight himself, Johnny was well aware of the thousand-year-old secret 'handshake' which wasn't a handshake at all; but, rather, a wave of sorts. Johnny initiated the clandestine communication with his right hand and the man closest to him completed it with his right.

Johnny stared down hard at the man. He'd never seen him before, but knew a retired cop when he saw one – always. He pointed at him. "You used to be on the job up here, didn't you?" Johnny pulled out the old conspiratorial grin and shook his finger at the man. "Sure, I remember you." He gazed off to the distance for a moment, but came right back. "You were good, if I remember."

The man smiled and stood. "How you doin', Mister Dineen." He put his hand out to shake.

But Johnny stepped back and unbuttoned his suit jacket. He slipped his hands in his front pants pocket. "Why don't we do this. Since I don't like surprising people, you go ahead in there and announce my presence. Can you do that?" Johnny said without smiling.

The man just stared at him for a moment but then dropped his gaze and nodded. "Sure thing, Mister Dineen." He turned for the door.

The Knight went inside, and after a moment, the hospital room door opened and the Archbishop of Boston, Cardinal Seán Patrick O'Malley, stepped out into the hall, followed by two younger priests.

Johnny bowed at the waist. "Your Eminence."

The Cardinal stood straight and responded, "John."

Johnny motioned to the room. "I hope you're not leaving on my account."

"My visit has concluded John."

"Sure." Johnny looked up and down the hallway, then took a step back. "Just be sure you're not seen consorting with likes of me, though, right?"

The Cardinal sighed. "John, you're a decent man. I know you. But I will not give the impression that I condone the bad acts connected to you."

Johnny frowned. He had respect for the clergy. It was part of the reason he'd put the hit out on Gallagher's betrothed —aside from the fact that Gallagher had killed two of Johnny's men —no one should ever shoot a priest, for God's sake.

A number of retorts for the Cardinal came to mind, but Johnny bit his tongue. "No, I get that." He looked past the Cardinal and into the room. "How's he doing?"

"He just came out of the coma an hour ago." The

Cardinal also glanced back into the room. "I came as soon as I heard."

"Yeah, me too."

The Cardinal turned back to Johnny. "Amazing: after two days in a coma, he remembers everything."

The two men looked at each other for one awkward moment. Then the Cardinal put his hand on Johnny's shoulder. "Consider allowing your Savior into your thoughts on occasion, John." He patted his shoulder. "God bless." The Cardinal removed his hand and walked away.

Johnny watched him walk down the hall, past the nurse's station. "Yeah," he murmured to himself, "good idea." He turned and entered the private room.

A small bathroom crowded in from his left. On the right side wall, a couple of whiteboards offered up the names of the people assigned to the floor. Nurse Maura even threw in a nice little smiley face next to hers.

The curtains were all drawn back in the room. The empty space where a second bed would have been had a few low-slung chairs facing the occupied bed by the window.

Old Seamus looked up from the chair closest to Johnny. The old man looked at Johnny, but called out over his shoulder to the hallway. One of the Knights of Columbus poked his head in and Old Seamus told him to close the door to any visitors for now.

Johnny stepped over to the bed. "How are you, Patrick?" He touched the priest's foot. "I can't believe the way this all turned out. Who thought a cop would stoop so low."

From his chair, Old Seamus said "A cop?"

Johnny raised his eyebrows at Seamus. "Gallagher, from New York. He set the whole thing up. Killed Dermot for the key; must have kidnapped Junior somehow; found the guns and killed him, too." He turned back to Father O'Leary in the bed. "I still can't believe a cop would stoop so low as to shoot a priest just to frame Junior for it."

"John." Father O'Leary tried to sit up in the hospital bed. His brother, Old Seamus, stood to ease him. Johnny leaned in also and touched the priest's shoulder.

"John," the priest gasped, "you've got it all wrong, John." He leaned back into his pillow. "My God, John, you've got it desperately wrong." He closed his eyes and his head lolled sideways.

Johnny scrunched his brow at Seamus. "What —"

Seamus stared hard at Johnny. "John, Junior killed Dermot." He turned and looked back down at his brother. "And he shot Patrick." He touched his brother's shoulder. "He wanted the guns, John. Junior was selling them to the Arab." He stopped short and looked up at Johnny. "Why did you think the cop did it?"

"Boston PD said the gun was a match." Johnny pulled his shoulders back. His head spun at the possibility of such a dire mistake. He put his two hands up. "Hold on. This cop, he killed Junior: do I have that much right?"

Father O'Leary rolled his head back to center and opened his eyes. "Yes, John, he did; and it was an act of heroism. Captain Gallagher saved my life. Young Seamus shot me. And he killed Dermot, too; he admitted that in my presence just before he died."

"Junior?" Johnny stared wide-eyed at the priest. "Junior shot you?"

"Yes, John."

"Not the cop?"

"No, John." Father O'Leary looked from Johnny to Seamus and back. "You gentlemen have created a terrible and ominous situation."

Johnny pulled out his cell phone and began typing a text. The priest continued, "Whoever that other man was in the crypt with young Seamus is now in possession of at least half of the Guns of Antwerp."

Johnny hit 'send'. "So Junior double-crossed us all. He killed Dermot to get the key to the crypt and Gallagher busted him."

"So it would seem," Old Seamus deadpanned.

Johnny checked his phone. No response yet to his text. He sent another. He kept the phone in his hand, but maintained the conversation. "So all that's true, then? That old shipment of guns? The connection to the PLO?"

"So it would seem," Old Seamus said again, and eyeballed Johnny and his phone.

Father O'Leary pushed himself up in the bed. "Yes, John, it's all true. And the Boston PD now has half of the shipment."

"Yes," Old Seamus said. "And an apparent terrorist has the other half, John. What will you do about that?"

Johnny looked at them both. "Plenty. Plenty." He put his phone to his ear. "But I gotta take care of something else first." He stepped away from the bed.

"Something related, John?" Old Seamus asked.

Johnny held up a finger and walked to the bathroom. He stepped inside and closed the door behind him. His call was answered; he spoke first: "Why aren't I getting a goddamn response?"

His lieutenant, Pete Flynn, answered, "They're not picking up."

"Dammit, Pete, call off the hit, right fucking now. Do what you have to do. Now, Pete, now."

41

Against the advice of his handlers, Zafir pulled the stolen car into the parking lot. He might still need it. He didn't want to be overly dependent on the leaders at this mosque of the Islamic Society of Boston.

His uncles in Libya said these people swore their support, but still, he did not trust them. Moderates existed in their midst. He locked the car and walked around the building. There was no back door.

At the end of the parking lot, by the wrought iron fence surrounding the mosque, stood a small, wooden booth. The sign above it said there had been a coat drive for the coming winter. The man laboring at the booth looked up from sorting clothes. His eyes widened at the sight of Zafir and he whispered, "Khalifa." The man stood up straight and smiled as Zafir approached. Zafir addressed him. "This is to assist our people?"

The man nodded, "Yes, Sahid, we do much charitable work for the Muslim community, here."

Zafir pulled off his jacket and laid it on the man's booth. "Keep up the good work." The man bowed. "Thank you, Khalifa."

Zafir continued around the building onto Elmwood Street and then turned the corner onto the boulevard. He climbed the steps of the mosque and approached the main entrance.

Two men in security uniforms stood on either side of the revolving doors. Zafir stopped before them and addressed them with his eyes. One man did not smile, and turned away. The other offered a pleasantry and motioned to the entrance.

The doors came around and Zafir marched in through them like a man on a mission. He strode through the elegant lobby and headed straight for the elevator. He knew what floor he was going to. He did not acknowledge the receptionist, who appeared eager to greet him. He did not have the time nor the patience for such frivolous encounters.

The elevator ride was short. The mosque was large, but not tall. He strode past a workspace of cubicles without a word to the workers there and traversed the hall until he found what he was looking for: two large men sitting outside the Imam's office. He watched for recognition in their eyes. He sized them up in a flash. The one on the right was much older than the other, about the age of Zafir's father.

Zafir pointed at the man. "You knew my father, didn't you?" Zafir had never seen the man before in his life. "I remember you; you are a loyal soldier of jihad, are you not?"

The man stood and bowed. "It is an honor to see you once again, my young Khalifa."

Zafir did not bow in return. Instead, he took a step back and pointed at the office door. "You need to inform the Imam of my presence."

The man dropped his smile, but responded. He turned to the door, knocked, and stuck his head in. After a moment, he stepped back and motioned for Zafir to enter.

Though Zafir had never been in this particular building before, he had been in places of honor before, in a mosque. This office was familiar. Well-lit and professionally designed and furnished, it was a place for leaders to gather. Zafir reveled in the memory of how his father had been treated in mosques around the world in his day. Leaders of jihad had always held a place of honor in the religious communities. Zafir centered himself in the room. The Imam did not stand to greet him.

"The men who will assist you await in the basement." The Imam motioned to a man in a suit standing next to his desk. "This man will escort you."

Zafir stared hard at the Imam. The man in the suit walked up close and stood before him. Then the man sighed and tilted his head with a slight frown. "Come." The man walked for the office door.

Zafir continued to stare at the Imam. Others had responded to him in this manner in the recent past. He thought it might be his age: never before had a Khalifa been named before the age of thirty. He decided his response to this disrespect would come at a later time. He would not forget this, though. He turned and followed the suited man out of the office.

The elevator took them to the sub-level where they exited and found a small musty room with a bare metal table and three chairs. His escort left Zafir at the door.

Zafir did not recognize either of the two men seated at the table, but both came to their feet to greet him.

The man nearest him bowed to Zafir. "Khalifa, I am Kahil."

The other man, much younger, bowed and said, "I am Shata."

"Gentlemen," Zafir pulled out the remaining chair and motioned to the others, "please." They all sat.

"The mission has changed. I no longer possess an adequate number of handguns. However..." he paused and put his hands flat on the table. He realized the men of this cell needed to know only little more. He drew a deep breath and withdrew his hands from the table. "There is a key. That is what you will assist me with. We must recover this key."

"Zafir," the middle aged Kahil spoke, "we do not have handguns, either." He shrugged with his hands. "Recent events here in Boston have brought much scrutiny to our daily lives. Our people now are subject to being stopped and frisked by the Boston Police as often as other minority groups. What few guns we had have been disposed of."

"No bother." Zafir waved him off. "You have been trained?" He turned to look at the younger Shata and then back to Kahil.

Kahil answered, "Yes, Zafir, we are both well trained."

"Very well, then." Zafir stood. "This key is in the possession of either the criminal leader in the area or the elder of what remains of the Irish Republican Army."

The men glanced at each other first and then back to Zafir. Kahil spoke. "You have a manner of communicating with the IRA, yes? You have done so recently."

Zafir nodded. "That has been done. But there has been no response —as of yet." Zafir frowned. "There was bloodshed at our last contact." He put up his right hand. "Not by my hand, but I think this is why they hesitate. They lost one of their members, as did the criminal enterprise, though the lines between those two groups are not always clear."

The other man nodded down at the table. "The local criminal enterprise is easily recognizable, Zafir, but it may take us some time to ascertain who amongst them we shall communicate with to get the attention of their leader." He looked up. "I understand he is the surviving member of the enterprise that attended your last meeting, yes? A John

Dineen."

"Yes."

"Khalifa, if I may," Kahil continued, "how did you make contact with him the last time? This could save us time and effort if we knew where to begin."

"I didn't. The homeland contacted the IRA leadership; they brought the criminals to the table. I have no means of finding their leader." Zafir stood and began to pace around the table. "I must have this key." He looked from one man to the other. "The future of jihad in America depends upon it." He looked down at the floor and continued pacing.

Then the younger Shata spoke. "And where was the place of your last meeting with them?"

Zafir stopped pacing and looked Shata. A smile grew across his face. "Yes." He shook his finger at the young Fedayeen. "You are right, Shata, I do know where to begin. With the host of The Saints and Scholars."

42

Jimmy ended the call and watched Frank work. With both feet on the car's pedals, Frank's head spun like a tank turret. His left thumb worked the siren from the steering wheel. With his right foot steady on the gas pedal, he did a tap, tap, tap on the brakes with his left and a bwap, bwap, bwap on the siren. The car bucked like a bronco.

"Good on my side," Jimmy pitched in. Frank nailed it again. They'd have at least three more of these intersections to get through along Boston Post Road in the Bronx before they got to the highway.

Jimmy had just left a second message for Detective Ranaghan in Boston to let him know they were coming. Now he needed to call his own office, but decided not to distract Frank until they got off the side streets. They were staying off the interstate until they cleared the city limits. Rush hour. Frank muscled his way through another giant Boston Post Road intersection and Jimmy held on with both hands.

Frank glanced up in the mirror. "These freakin' intersections are like a half acre each." He turned back to the windshield. "You could put a four-bedroom colonial up in there."

Jimmy laughed and agreed. Then he smiled at the memory of a TrafficStat meeting he'd once survived. He turned to tell Frank about it, but saw his level of concentration and decided against it —Baychester Avenue was approaching. Tap, tap, tap —bwap, bwap, bwap.

Young Captain Gallagher had stood before all the Chiefs

of the Department in the cavernous Command and Control Center in One Police Plaza some years ago and had answered for every fatal vehicle accident in this command.

He had explained that New York City is a grid —for the most part, avenues generally run North-South and streets run East-West, forming normal, square intersections. Generally. But in this Bronx precinct, Boston Post Road went at an angle as it ran up from Manhattan and out of the city on a northeast track. Route 1 in America.

Every time Boston Post Road intersected with a major artery, blood was shed —literally. Jimmy nearly laughed out loud in the car remembering how he'd thrown his hands up at the podium and told the Chiefs that when the Bronx was designed and Boston Post Road was built, it wasn't his idea to pave over the hoof prints of the Pony Express.

They stayed on the side streets and paralleled I-95 till they were out of the city. They passed through Pelham Manor and, just before New Rochelle, merged onto the interstate and started making time. Jimmy picked up his phone and called the office.

"OCTU, Detective Dhakir."

"Hatim, Boston call yet?"

"Oh, hello, Captain. Uh, well, yes, sir, Boston did call; but not the detective you've been trying to reach. Their Intercity Correspondence people reached out just a short while ago. Apparently the priest, Father O'Leary, has come out of his coma, Captain. He confirms that the man you shot, his nephew, in fact shot that other character, Dermot Casey."

"Okay, good. So now they know the truth."

"Yes, Captain; in fact the priest is crediting you with saving his life, sir."

"Oh yeah? That's nice. Now maybe they'll stop breaking my balls and return my calls."

"Actually, Captain the sergeant I spoke with sounded almost... well, apologetic."

"Yeah, great. Now tell me about those two knuckleheads we pulled out of our Brooklyn basement with the crate of guns; you making any progress there?"

"I am doing all I can, Captain. So far, they have not asked for a lawyer. Apparently Zafir trained them well, I get the impression that they view him in some ethereal manner – that in their minds, he controls their destiny –but they do not appear to be part of any professional organization."

"That's interesting stuff, Hatim, but we need specifics: addresses, dates, times –something. Those two idiots you got there may be all we have to lead us to this supposed nuke. The FBI has the department convinced that no such weapon exists, despite what Shorotov says. You need to debrief them as well as you possibly can."

"Well, Captain, I can tell you that Zafir had expressed an interest in a rally to be held at City Hall the day after tomorrow."

"Tuesday? The day the UN General Assembly meets? That's a big day up on First Avenue. I'd be surprised if Zafir would ignore the biggest annual gathering of world leaders for some local, City Hall rally, Hatim."

"Yes, well, that is all I have elicited from our two prisoners, to this point. Apparently this rally is similar to the one that first brought Zafir to our attention. It is sponsored by Siban's Moderate Muslim group, the MMOA.

"The keynote is to be delivered by an historian and journalist. A man named Mohamed. Actually, Captain, you mentioned the UN: this Mohamed will be speaking there first in the morning and then going to the City Hall rally to give a speech in the afternoon. He is to draw the world's attention to the efforts in moderation by the Muslims of New York. 'A lesson in leadership'; that is his theme."

Jimmy paused and sat on that point. He glanced out the window at the passing landscape of tractor-trailers and guardrails on the interstate. After a moment, Hatim's voice came back over the car speakers.

"Captain, are you still there?"

"I'm here, Hatim." Jimmy took a moment. "Tell you what, have someone get all the particulars on the detail at the City Hall rally. Find out which Captain is running it, how many cops they'll have assigned there, and, if there was a 'pre-meet' with the event organizers, as there should have been, get me the minutes of that meeting, if they exist. Got that?"

"Yes, Captain."

"All right." Jimmy prepared to end the call, but thought of one more thing, "What's Donohue up to? He find anything yet?"

"Uh…" He could hear Hatim turning in his chair. "Captain," Hatim came back on the phone, "Sergeant Donohue is in one of those places where I believe it best not to disturb him. In fact, I don't think I could break his concentration very easily, at the moment."

Jimmy smiled. "Is the smoke coming out the top of his head, or out of his computer, this time?"

Hatim laughed. "Yes, sir. He is in that zone."

"Well, if, or, rather, when he comes up with something, have him get it to me right away."

"Of course, Captain."

"All right, Hatim, go get 'em. I'll be in touch." Jimmy

ended the call.

Half way across Connecticut, at exit 37, they hopped over to the Wilbur Cross Parkway to avoid the New Haven traffic. They paralleled I95 for thirty miles or so and grabbed I-91 just outside of Hartford to get up to I-84. Jimmy settled back. It would be another thirty miles of countryside until they reached the Mass Pike. After a while, the phone rang. Jimmy glanced at the caller ID: Boston PD. "Finally." He picked up. "Captain Gallagher here. How you doing, Detective Ranaghan."

"Not Ranaghan."

"Sheila?"

The woman on the phone cleared her throat. "Detective O'Neill."

"Hi, Sheila." Jimmy smiled over at Frank. Frank just shook his head and kept his eyes on the road. "So, you still looking to lock me up for homicide? I'll be right there, okay?"

"Okay –Jim." She pronounced his name with some contempt. "I guess you heard by now, the priest is awake."

"Yeah, thanks be to God, I guess, huh?"

"Yeah, I guess so. So what's up? You're heading up here? For what?"

"To see you, Sheila." Jimmy looked over at Frank again, grinning this time. Frank sighed and took his time checking all three mirrors.

"Next time Skype, Jim."

"Ha, ha, very good; Skype, okay. So anyway, my terrorist, Zafir: you seen him around lately?"

"No, should I?"

"Yeah, he's on his way up there. Or may already be there."

"Okay, what's he driving?"

"I got nothing on that, sorry. I actually have nothing beyond his physical description –but you have a copy of his photo, right?"

"Yeah, we have that."

"Well, I'm hoping you could help me with the rest. All I know is, he's looking for a key of some sort. We found the other crate; the one he got away from Boston College with. We recovered all fifty guns, but the other half of the crate was empty."

"So you recovered fifty and lost fifty. 'Cause that's what the crate up here had: two sections, each containing fifty handguns with ammo."

"Right; two sections. But the one he brought down to New York apparently had a special little surprise in it. Fifty guns with ammo in one half of the crate and a suitcase nuke in the other."

"Okay, Gallagher, stop pulling my leg. I don't have the time –"

"Sheila, no bullshit. I'm serious, my sources in –"

"Are there any responsible adults in the car with you? That can confirm this conversation for me?"

Jimmy looked over at Frank. Frank shrugged and looked away. "Frank." Jimmy opened his hands out. Then Frank sigh-laughed and spoke up: "Hey, Detective O'Neill, this is Detective Frank Ramirez; how've you been?"

"Hey, Frank. So what's up with this?"

"No, it's for real. This guy's got a nuclear device hidden somewhere in New York; we got it from a good source."

Then Jimmy cut in. "Our source is our source, though; the feds don't believe him. I wouldn't even bother contacting your Joint FBI Task Force; they would've been given the party line by now. It's a long story, but I believe my guy and, no one else does. But how can I take a chance like that, right? Besides, I like Zafir for a couple of shootings by now, anyway."

"A couple? I know about the UN thing; you mentioned that when you were up here last."

"Yeah." Jimmy paused and looked over at Frank. "Frank and I shot it out with a couple of Zafir's guys yesterday. He was there. I saw him, but I couldn't grab him."

"Oh, was that you? We got that on the news up here: quintuple killing –five dead. You guys all right?"

Jimmy paused and smirked over at Frank again. "Well, we stopped at a Taco Bell a few –"

Frank put arm his out across the car. "Don't. You know what? Just…" he emphasized his arm out again, "…just don't."

"What?" Sheila's voice came across the speakers.

"No, nothing. We're fine, thanks for asking. Apparently this Zafir guy wanted to show everyone just who he is. So he had two of his guys light up a couple of lookouts on a drug corner just as we pulled up looking for him.

"We took out his two guys, but not before they killed the lookouts. Then we turned to get Zafir, and the drug operation's enforcers came out. We had to take one of them out, and by the time we got back to it, Zafir was gone."

"Sucks."

"Yeah. But we did get a warrant later in the day and turned up his guns. And the info about the nuke and this key he needs. Apparently the bomb won't work without it."

"Okay, and he's heading back up here to look for his key. So it must have something to do with that meeting he had." She paused. They could hear her flipping through her notes.

"I'll call a meeting. We'll need to get with the people that were at that meeting."

"A meeting?" Jimmy waited. Getting no immediate answer, he continued. "You mean you're going to pull those people in for an interrogation, right?"

Another pause. "That's not how it works up here, Jim."

"Really."

"Suppose they don't want to come in? We have nothing to compel them, legally. Besides, we know them. Sometimes they help us…"

"And sometimes you help them?"

Another pause.

"Jim, this is Boston, we'll run this place, if you don't mind. Besides, the lines aren't always as bright as they seem. Look, I'll put something together and call you back; tell you where to come."

"It won't be at the station house?"

"No, Jim, it won't. Look, you need a freakin' gangster and an old retired terrorist to come to the table; both of whom are related to half the department and most of the politicians up here. There are ways to do this in Boston, and an interrogation isn't one of them. Let me guess, Mister New Yorker: you've never even heard of Jim Curley."

"Who?"

"Never mind, I'll explain later."

Frank smirked and whispered to Jimmy, "Terrorists retire?"

"What's that?" Sheila asked.

"Nothing." Jimmy answered. "So, okay, so who's coming to this little shindig?"

"Well, you tell me. Supposedly Old Man O'Leary was there along with Johnny Dineen, right?"

"Johnny Dineen," Jimmy said and paused.

After a moment, Shiela asked, "You still there, Jim?"

"Yeah, I'm here. Sheila, I guess you didn't know this up there, but Dineen put a hit out on my fiancé."

Another pause. A longer one this time.

"Sheila?" Jimmy leaned forward. "Tell me you didn't know that."

"For God's sake, of course I didn't know that. I don't dislike you that much, Gallagher. I'd have called you on that. It's just… okay, that makes a tiny bit of sense of now."

"How?"

"We had to straighten out some of Dineen's guys on something. We got to talking. They thought you shot the priest. Thought you were, like, the mastermind behind stealing the guns."

Jimmy sat up, eyebrows raised almost to the roof of the car. "They thought I shot the priest?"

"Yeah, they're not the smartest bunch of crooks."

Jimmy sat back. "Huh." He began nodding slowly. "Well, I won't say that makes sense now, but…" He sat up. "That prick put a hit out on my fiancé, Sheila. That makes him no good. I don't care what he thought."

"In your world, Jimmy, I understand that. But he may very well hold the key to all of this –literally, right? And we need to talk to him, nicely. Okay?"

"Sure. Sure, just tell me when and where."

"Fine. Where are you now; can you give me an ETA?"

Jimmy read the highway signs and switched on the car's GPS screen. "We should be getting on the Mass Pike from I-84 in about twenty minutes."

"Okay, meet me on the corner of Tremont Street and Temple Place, alongside the park. I'll be in touch."

43

Murray kept the match lit and puffed a few more times. Once the cigar glowed to his satisfaction, he turned to Rocket John. "Want one?" Rocket just scowled and shook his head. Murray looked up at the sky. "Beautiful day."

He walked a circle around the two men hanging upside down from the tree just inside the gate of Rocket's place. He got back around next to Rocket and blew on the end of the cigar. Need to make sure it burns evenly, especially when you first light it.

"So." Murray inspected Rocket's squad of Vietnam Vets. "Not a single shot fired, eh?" A few of the old-time vets smiled and nodded, M-16s at their sides. "Nice." Murray looked at the end of the cigar and blew on it again. "I knew I could count on you guys." He put the cigar in his mouth.

Rocket stepped over and handed Murray two cell phones. "They had these with them. Prepaids."

"So they were on their way out when you grabbed them." Murray took the phones.

"Yeah." Rocket said. "It would have been much worse for them if they kept coming, but when they checked their phones and began to retreat, we didn't want to let them get away." Rocket looked up at the tree branch. "So we sprang the trap as they retreated."

"All right." Murray took a deep drag and blew it out slowly. "Looks like the hit was called off —for some reason. Hand 'em over to Lieutenant Moroney here in the Orangetown PD; I'm sure he'd appreciate a couple of gun collars."

Murray stepped over to the boulder gate and examined the two handguns Rocket's guys had confiscated. A 9mm and a .38: not much firepower; definitely amateurs.

"Geez." Murray picked up the .38 and weighed it in his hand. "You guys were over-matched the moment you left Boston." He turned to the captives. "You know that?" He poked one of them. Then he stepped back and sniffed. He visually searched the ground around them. "Why does it stink so bad right here, Rocket?"

The squad all laughed. Rocket nodded to two of them. "Pull the planks." The men secured their weapons and knelt down next to the hanging men. They cleared away some brush and slid a series of connected planks of lumber out from beneath the men. The smell got instantly worse.

Murray stepped back. "Geez, Rocket, what the hell is that?"

"Cesspool from the Legion Hall." Rocket took a few steps back. "Due to be pumped out in a few weeks; damn near full. We can take the top off the tank and cut these guys loose if you want." The whole squad laughed.

The two gagged and swinging men swiveled and tried to do the impossible sit-up. Murray laughed. "Let me talk to the Captain first; we'll see what he wants us to do with them."

44

The body couldn't move. Dead bodies don't do that. All it could do was lie there on the concrete of the alleyway in which it was dumped. It bled. And though it couldn't speak, it could communicate, if the observer knew how to listen.

The footsteps came around again in a complete circle. Now they squatted. Not knelt: squatted. Apparently the footsteps didn't want to mar the crime scene.

"It's definitely not a robbery, Mike." The body gave its first signal.

"How so?"

"Watch and wallet are intact." The squatting footsteps again pulled on the pants pocket of the body and twisted the wrist.

"So what, then?"

The squatter stood. "I don't know; passion, maybe."

The other voice expressed doubt. "I don't think so, George: not enough stab wounds. A slit throat looks more like a hit; like professional, somehow."

"Yeah, but look at the fingers." The body communicated further. "Something happened there. Most of them are broken, fresh. Like torture, almost?"

"Maybe. But hey, what is a robbery but getting something from the victim, right? So if it's information they're getting, how is it different, huh?"

"Right. Well, the detectives can figure it all out. You notified them, right?"

"Yeah, they'll be here soon. We need to get the paperwork started, though. Did you get a name out of that wallet?"

"Yeah, hold on…

"Gaughan, Francis Gaughan."

"Why does that sound familiar?"

"Ever been to The Saint and Scholars? …business card says he's the host there"

The body had spoken.

45

Frank pulled over on the left at the corner of Temple Place. He threw the car in Park and Jimmy let out a deep breath. Since getting off the interstate, they'd navigated through block after block of narrow, crowded downtown streets.

But just before reaching Temple, Tremont Street stretched out to four lanes and a giant, beautiful park opened up on their right. Time to relax –almost, as far as driving went, anyway. But a road trip wasn't over until you could park the car.

Detective O'Neill said she had a place for them nearby that she'd show them when she got there. Jimmy needed to get out and stretch. Frank needed to stay with the car. But first they sat quietly together for a moment and took in their surroundings.

"Must be their version of Central Park." Jimmy looked to the right.

"Yeah, nice." Frank punched the button to turn the hazard lights on.

"I think I recognize some of this," Jimmy said. "From when I was a kid, vacationing with my parents." He opened the car door and watched for traffic. Tremont Street was a one-way. Jimmy got out, flipped the door closed, and walked around to the sidewalk.

He turned his back to the narrow little one-way Temple Place and looked out over the sweep of Tremont Street and the park beyond. He took a moment to enjoy the sights and sounds of the busy, yet homey, city.

It was very real and modern, but antique and early American at the same time. Majestic skyscrapers in the near distance stood back and supported colonial archetypes set amongst modern trappings.

It all had the look of miniatures in a child's dollhouse. Jimmy half expected to see some colonial guy stick his head out of an overlooking window with one of those three-point patriot hats and start waving an old-time lantern while talking on a cell phone. And all the people seemed to know just where they were going, too. Even the tourists with their maps didn't seem the least bit confused about their destinations.

A Boston unmarked car pulled up next to Frank, with Detective Ranaghan behind the wheel. Sheila O'Neill jumped out of the passenger's seat and made her way around the cars and onto the sidewalk. She wore a dark, slimming pantsuit. Her button down business-type blouse was well open at the top, and hinted at something wonderful beneath it. She wore heels, but moved like a woman in tennis shoes.

Frank waved at Jimmy and rolled off behind Ranaghan. Sheila joined Jimmy on the corner. "They're going to park the cars and meet us. We'll wait here. We need to show up together, otherwise you'd never get near this place."

"They're going to what?" Jimmy smiled at her. "Pahk the cahs?"

She squinted up at Jimmy and frowned. "Do you ever turn that off?"

Jimmy pursed his chin over at her. "Nice place you got here." He turned toward the park again and took in the landscape.

Sheila followed his gaze and nodded. "Yeah, Boston

Common."

Jimmy looked out across the manicured greens. "Nice view from here."

"Sure is. You can see a lot of Boston from right here."

"I remember walking the Freedom Trail with my parents when I was kid. I got a real kick out of the red painted footprints on the sidewalk."

Sheila smiled. "Funny." She pointed across the street. "It starts right there."

"The Freedom Trail?"

"Yeah. You see that entrance to the park right across from us? Now look down at the sidewalk. If you can see it from here, there's a narrow red line coming out of that gate? That's where it begins, right there."

"Ha. Awesome." Jimmy followed the line with his eyes until it wrapped right back into the park at the next entrance. Then he turned and took in the landscape again.

He pointed across to the far side of the park. "And what is that big gold dome out there? It's in almost every picture of Boston I ever see. Like postcards and everything."

"State House. Beautiful, isn't it?"

"Iconic," Jimmy nodded. "I like how it sits up over the Common."

"Yeah, I guess that was the point. That high spot it sits on is called Beacon Hill. Believe it or not, that's actually the 'new' state house —even though it was built in 1798. The original one is over by the bay." She thumbed to the east. "By Fanueil Hall, that one was built in 1713. It's still standing."

Jimmy looked at Sheila and nodded his admiration. Over her shoulder, he noticed another striking fixture of the Boston landscape: a slim brick church with a three-tier spire narrowing to a point like an arrow toward the sky. Tall, but dwarfed by its modern backdrop.

Sheila followed his gaze and looked over her shoulder. She turned to the east. "Park Street Church." She took her hands out of her pockets and crossed her arms below her breasts. "Imagine? That was the tallest building in the country for its first fifty years. Up until about 1840-something."

She uncrossed her arms and put them out in front of her. She squared her fingers like the frame of a photograph. "When Boston was first Boston, that was the sign to travelers that they'd arrived here. It was the first thing they saw." She turned back to Jimmy and smiled. "Cool, huh?"

"Yeah, nice." Jimmy brought his gaze back to Sheila. Her green eyes arrested all his attention. He just stared into them until they themselves began smiling back. His every instinct directed him to reach out and gently caress her cheek. He caught himself. Instincts. The downfall of man. Sometimes he wondered if it was immature to be so easily smitten, or was it just natural and okay as long you didn't act on it? He drew a deep breath and looked away.

"So." Sheila looked down and toed nothing in particular on the sidewalk. "How's your fiancé?"

"Yeah." Jimmy put his hands in his pockets. "She's good, now. Now that these idiots know the truth."

"Right." Sheila looked down Temple Place. "Well, I hope you're over it, because we'll be meeting with the top idiot in a minute."

"I still don't get this whole 'meeting' thing and why we're not just pulling them in for an interrogation."

"Jimmy, there's a culture here. To get things done, you have to understand the history and, the mores, and operate within them. Cops and criminals, judges, politicians, crooks… the only difference in this town is the titles.

"People are people, and when there's a common cause, titles and positions don't matter —especially in Boston. Look," she took a step in closer to Jimmy, "it would take you a lifetime to figure out who's who up here, and you still wouldn't get anywhere.

"Or," she put her hands out at her sides, "you could just follow my lead and let it happen."

"Okay, fine." Jimmy looked down the one-way street. "So where are we meeting? Not the Saints and Scholars, I see. Why not?"

"Neutral ground."

"But that's where they both met the last time."

Sheila patted Jimmy's forearm. "Neutral for us, Jim."

Frank and Detective Ranaghan appeared at the opposite end of the narrow street. Ranaghan waved. Sheila nudged Jimmy and began walking.

"So where are we going?" Jimmy asked.

"Jim Curley's." Sheila nodded down the block to a black and white neon sign fashioned as a top hat, overhanging a restaurant on their right.

"Jim Curley, that's the name you mentioned on the phone before. What kind of place is it? Who's Jim Curley; you know him?"

"Ha, no; nobody knows him —not anymore." She smiled. "Jim Curley was the Mayor of Boston and the head of the Irish mob —for generations, right up until modern times."

"That can't be true." Jimmy stopped walking.

"For real." Sheila turned to him. "He was the four-time Mayor of Boston from like nineteen-oh-something up until just 1950."

"That's nearly fifty years."

"Yeah; he won, he lost, he won, he lost; like that. In fact," she turned to keep walking, "the guy actually won an election while he was in prison, once. Prison was just like city hall for Ole Jim Curley: he was in, he was out, he was in, he was out."

"You have got to be kidding. You're telling me this Jim Curley guy ran the police department —as mayor, and ran the mob, all at the same time? Right up until the fifties?"

"Yup. Even went on to become Governor of Massachusetts, at one point. Like I told you, Jimbo, that's how it goes in Boston. Now, c'mon."

They approached the front of the restaurant. It wasn't until they got close that Jimmy noticed at least four potentially suspicious people hanging around out front. Jimmy stopped. "Whoa, Sheila, hold on."

She stopped and turned back to Jimmy again. "It's fine. They're with us. Well…" she looked over her shoulder at the two detectives and two mob goons in front of Jim Curley's, "…mostly us." She looked back at Jimmy. "Look, we need to meet at a place where decision makers can do business and not be bothered, right? Some place public, but not too private, right?" She pulled on his elbow. "Seriously, don't worry about it. Just trust me: it's a Jim Curley thing."

Frank and Ranaghan joined them at the door. Ranaghan opened it and they all filed in. The first thing Jimmy noticed was the noise, followed immediately by how crowded it was. They barely fit inside.

The door lazed closed behind Jimmy on its hydraulics and he had to push up against Sheila's back to fit inside. The place was narrow and long. Although both walls were a certain kind of red brick and the place had a definite old-school look about it, there wasn't much to it beyond a row of tables on the right wall and a full-length bar along the left. Diners filled every seat. Drinkers filled every square foot of floor space. Jimmy leaned down to Sheila's ear. "We're going to have a meeting here? What, after closing time?"

She smiled up over her shoulder at Jimmy. "Relax, just follow along."

They made their way through the crowd and Jimmy noticed a few more people that looked like they belonged with the other four outside. He put his hand on Sheila's shoulder. "More security?"

"Yeah," she nodded. "From all sides, though. It's fine, we're all on the same team with this." They got to the back wall of the place and stopped.

Sheila turned to Jimmy. "You say we have a Middle Eastern terrorist in town hunting for a key that operates a nuke. Everybody's on the same page." She glanced up and down the place, at the obvious bodyguards from all sides casually mixing in with the crowd; the IRA in their trim, tailored suits; the PD in their rumpled, well-worn suits; and Dineen's men in jeans.

"And everybody's on edge." She turned and looked Jimmy in the eye. "Look, I believe you. You told me this was serious, and I believe you. Because of that, everybody up here believes you."

Jimmy pondered her for a moment. Then he spoke purposely, under the rumble of the crowded bar: "In other words, you're connected up here."

Sheila squinted and turned an ear toward him. "What's that?"

"Nothing."

For the next two minutes, they all stood around, twisting

in the crowd. Jimmy looked at the bar. "Should I get us some drinks or something?" Sheila ignored the question. She was focused on the back wall of the place.

Jimmy followed her eyes. Ranaghan seemed to have the lead, at the moment. Jimmy watched Ranaghan sidle up to a dark oak door on the back brick wall. It opened. Two very large young men in tuxedos stepped into Jim Curley's place from an apparent back room. They exchanged quiet words with Ranaghan. They eyeballed Jimmy, Frank, and Sheila, and then stepped out of the way. Ranaghan nodded to the group and Jimmy made his way through the crowd to the back door.

They stepped into a stylish dining room of low lights and soft leather. Deep, decorative solid wood panels and plush carpet surrounded them. The door closed behind Jimmy and the rumble of the bar dissipated. Soft jazz wafted from hidden speakers.

There was plenty of room to get comfortable. The tables in what appeared to be a reservations-only steak house were brought together in the middle of the dining room to form a conference table set for ten. There were five men seated at the table. They all stood except for an elderly gentleman seated at the head of the table.

Jimmy saw the resemblance to Father O'Leary immediately and realized this must be the old IRA guy, Seamus O'Leary. A middle-aged man stood up from the table and stepped around behind the old man's chair. The other three men came around the table to greet the new arrivals.

Ranaghan and Sheila walked into the room and shook hands with two of the men. The third seemed to be an assistant to the man on the left and stood just behind him.

After greeting the two main players, Ranaghan and Sheila stepped off to either side and formed an impromptu reception line between them and Jimmy.

Frank hung back and Jimmy stepped up. Sheila was on his right, Ranaghan on the left.

Sheila put her left palm out toward Jimmy and spoke to the two men. "Gentlemen, this is Captain Gallagher." She then turned and looked at Jimmy with her hand now splayed at the man on the right. "Jimmy, this is Chief Mulholland, Commander of the Homicide Unit here in Boston." Jimmy shook the man's hand. Then Sheila turned her palm to the man on the left. "And this is Johnny Dineen."

Jimmy stood still. He did not offer his hand. He just stared hard. Other than the soft jazz, he could hear a pin drop. The man behind Dineen began to step around him. Dineen put his arm up and prevented the man from moving forward. He stared back at Jimmy.

"Captain." He didn't smile, he didn't nod, he didn't gesture at all. He just said it again: "Captain." Getting no response, he sighed and looked at the floor. "Believe me when I tell you, I know how you feel right now." He looked back up at Jimmy. "All I can do is offer my most sincere apologies for a very, very stupid mistake on my part." He put his hand out to shake. "I truly am sorry."

Jimmy looked at Dineen's hand. Then he looked up at the man, "Yeah, and lucky, too."

Dineen looked away. Then he turned right back. "Tell me, Captain: those young kids you killed out in Brooklyn yesterday, they had families?" Dineen crossed his hands in front of his crotch. He looked at Sheila first, then Chief Mulholland, then turned back to Jimmy. "I thought I read that in the papers somewhere: one of 'em had a couple of kids or something?" He tilted his head at Jimmy. "That right?"

Jimmy half smiled. "Yeah, I guess it cuts both ways. It's all in the perspective, right?"

Dineen opened his hands. "That's all I'm saying."

"Sure." Jimmy nodded. "Except that I had the balls to look each one of those guys in the eye when I shot them; didn't go after their girlfriends." He tilted his head. "Do I got that right?" He tilted his head further. "Johnny?"

Dineen pursed his lips and looked at the floor again. "Look." he turned his gaze back up at Jimmy. "I apologized. Sincerely." He tossed his hands up. "What more can a man do?"

Chief Mulholland stepped in. "Jimmy —may I call you Jimmy?" He put his hand on Jimmy's shoulder.

"Sure, Chief."

"Thank you." He looked Jimmy up and down. "Every man in this room has great respect for you, Jim, that's the truth." He stepped back. "But what I need to know right now is: will we be able to work together here today?" Chief Mulholland put his hands in his pockets. "We have pressing concerns, do we not?"

Jimmy nodded, "We do."

With raised eyebrows, Dineen put his hand out again. Jimmy shook it. Then they heard a loud rapping on the table behind them. Jimmy looked across to find Old Seamus O'Leary waiting for them with his walking stick poised.

"Come now, gentlemen," the old man spoke, "we don't have all day." Everyone separated and fanned out to take a seat. Jimmy walked around and addressed Old Seamus: "My best wishes to your brother." Jimmy held out his hand. "I understand he's feeling better."

"Thank you, young man." Seamus shook Jimmy's hand. "He credits you with saving his life, you know. I can't tell you how indebted we all feel to you, son. Anything we can do. Please." Seamus motioned for Jimmy to sit.

Jimmy walked around the table and took a seat between Sheila and Frank. Dineen, Ranaghan, and Mulholland sat opposite him. Two men remained standing, one behind Dineen and one behind Seamus. Second seats.

"Captain," Chief Mulholland began, "I understand, from conversations with Detective O'Neill, that you have reason to believe this possible nuclear device is not being transported into our jurisdiction. Is that right?"

"Yes, we believe it's being safeguarded somewhere in Brooklyn. I have my people doing all they can to find it, as we speak."

"Okay." The Chief folded his hands on the table in front of him. He stared at his hands for a moment, then turned again to Jimmy. "But you can't give assurances on that." It wasn't a question.

"No." Jimmy sat back. "I have an informant who has proven himself reliable, but he's getting that information second-hand."

"Okay." The Chief withdrew his hands from the table. "And you believe this target," Mulholland motioned to Ranaghan who pulled a copy of Zafir's photo from inside his suit jacket. The Chief took the picture and continued. "You believe he's up here looking for a key that is necessary to operate this device."

"Right."

The beeper on Chief Mulholland's belt, along with Ranaghan's and Sheila's, all went off at once. Mulholland pulled back the flap on his suit and, without pulling the beeper off, glanced down at it.

"I didn't know anyone still used those things." Jimmy said.

Mulholland smiled up at him. "For specific job-related matters." Then he turned to Ranaghan. "Brian? Look into this?"

"Yes sir." Ranaghan stood, pulled out his cell phone, and withdrew from the table.

Mulholland returned his attention to them. He looked squarely at Dineen and then to Old Seamus. "Gentlemen, about this key?"

Dineen nodded ever so slightly and stared at O'Leary. Old Seamus nodded once at Dineen. Johnny leaned in, elbows on the table. "I have the key." He looked at each person at the table. "I just have one need," he looked at Jimmy, "if it can be done."

Jimmy scrunched his brow and asked 'what?' with his face.

"My guys," Dineen said. "Think you could cut them loose? Good men are hard to find." He mustered a laugh.

Jimmy didn't return the laugh. He drew a deep breath and reached for his phone. "Put the key on the table and I'll make the call."

"I don't have it with me."

The table collectively threw up its hands. Mulholland spoke. "What the fuck, John?"

"Relax, it's in a safe place."

Mulholland shook his head. "All your security is here; how safe could it be?"

"It's back at The Mayo, in a safe place. Don't worry," he motioned out toward the restaurant, "they're not all my guys. Besides, I have one guy near the key, but it's in a very safe place. This Zafir guy'll never find it. And, what does he know from The Mayo Inn, anyway? All he knows is The Saints and Scholars; he wouldn't know to come to The Mayo."

Detective Ranaghan came back to the table and stood next to his chief. Mulholland looked up. Ranaghan hushed, "Homicide nearby. Looks like Sheila and I will have to run out."

"Tell me more." Mulholland pushed his seat back.

Ranaghan bent down and put his hands on his knees. "Victim had his throat slashed and a few fingers broken. Looks like they may have tortured him for information. We'll know more when we get over there."

"Name? Anything?"

"Yeah, I forget the name, but he was the host at The Saints and Scholars. Galligan? Grayson? Something."

"Gaughan." Jimmy slapped the table. "Francis Gaughan. Is that the name?"

Ranaghan looked at Jimmy. "Yeah. Yeah that is the name."

Jimmy looked over at Dineen. "Zafir knows about The Mayo Inn, now." Jimmy looked over at Mulholland. "I interviewed Gaughan at The Saints and Scholars; asked him if he'd seen Dineen in there. He confirmed that for me," Jimmy looked back at Johnny, "that you and your guys come from The Mayo Inn. Gaughan knew all about it." Jimmy stood. He pointed at Ranaghan's beeper. "Zafir's your guy on that." Everyone stood.

"Yeah," Ranaghan said, "him or his guys."

Mulholland pointed at Sheila. "Get on the air. Have the nearest radio cars converge on The Mayo Inn." He pushed out his chair. "Let's go."

"You need not fear death today. I will not grant you the glory of dying for something you believe in." Zafir drove his knee deeper into the man's stomach. "But you will suffer greatly until you open the safe."

"Go fuck yourself." The man coughed. He tried to spit up at Zafir, but failed miserably. Zafir smiled and knelt down harder. After initially breaking three of the man's fingers, he realized more would be necessary. This was no little host. He had already severed two of the man's fingers, but still had not gained compliance. Time was becoming a factor.

He looked over his shoulder at the door to this back office. Kahil still had his back to the room, peering out into the bar. Still safe, for now. Though Zafir knew that if someone were to try and enter from the street, Shata, who was keeping watch inside the front door, would have to slit their throats and add their bodies to the three already stuffed behind the bar.

When they had first arrived at The Mayo Inn, they circled the block and conducted the necessary reconnaissance. They found that the back door of the bar led to a parking lot that adjoined the parking lot of a small Credit Union building on the corner. That parking lot was empty and led to a side street. Perfect. Zafir had left the driver in the car and he, Shata, and Kahil had hopped the fence from the Credit Union parking lot into the back lot of The Mayo Inn.

Zafir had stayed at the back door while Shata and Kahil

entered the front, posing as customers. Within moments, Shata and Kahil had slit the throats of the two patrons and the bartender. Then they found the manager in the back office, secured him, and opened the back door for Zafir.

"Enough." Zafir stood. The man immediately curled up and cradled his left hand. "You will begin to lose limbs, now." Zafir picked up his bloody cleaver from the desk. "Then we shall move on to genitalia." He raised the cleaver and stood on the man's shoulder, pinning him back to the floor.

"Wait." The man trembled. "Just –just, wait." He put his good hand up. "It's not there." He coughed. "The key is not in the safe. It's in another place." He waved.

"You lie." Zafir knelt on the man again and pinned his left arm to the floor. He raised the cleaver.

"I'm not lying. It's not here. He has another place. I swear." The man tried to squirm, and Zafir pushed in harder with his knee. "There's a place. I'll show you. It has a vault."

Zafir stood. "Where is this vault?"

"Next door. At the Credit Union." The man gasped and tried to sit up. "No one is supposed to know he owns the Credit Union; ain't legal for him." He nursed his left hand again and looked up. "I swear to God, it's in there. I can take you; it's just across the back lot. Let me show you."

Zafir stepped back and held the cleaver inches from the man's face. "If you are lying to me, you will lose your eyes first; then your extremities, one by one."

The man shuffled to his feet. "I swear to God, I'm not lying." He stumbled to the back door and opened it –with his right hand. He stuck his head out and looked both ways. He turned back and looked at Zafir. "It's fine, no one's out there. There never is, it's quiet back here. Plus, it's a Sunday.

The Credit Union building is closed." He nodded and pulled the door open all the way. He motioned for Zafir to step through it.

"Go," Zafir said, and pushed the man out into the parking lot. He turned to Kahil. "Alert Shata. Then monitor my movements from this door." He stepped out into the back parking lot. "When I have the key, I will signal for you and Shata to join me at the car. Make haste." Zafir stepped out into the parking lot.

The man led Zafir across the small, empty lot to the short chain-link fence separating them from the Credit Union parking lot and the side street beyond.

Zafir's car and driver were backed up to the fence. Zafir made eye contact with the driver in the rear view mirror and signaled to him. They approached the fence and the man, still cradling his left hand, hesitated. He stepped up to the fence, but couldn't climb. The man turned to Zafir. "We could walk around," he nodded his head to the main street. Zafir did not respond. Instead, he squatted and put his shoulder under the man's rump and, all in one motion, threw him over the fence —head first.

The man reached out for the fence, even with his bloody hand, and desperately tried to break his fall. Zafir hopped over the fence in one swift movement and dragged the man to his feet. The man screamed once. Zafir turned and kicked him in the groin. The man fell to the ground. Zafir leaned in close to the man's ear and whispered. "Do not scream again." The man nodded. Zafir again dragged him to his feet. They progressed the twenty feet to the back door of the Members Only Credit Union and the man produced a key. They entered.

Ranaghan and Frank left the New York car in the lot and brought the Boston unmarked around. Jimmy and Sheila jumped in the back. Old Seamus and his bodyguard begged off and Mulholland allowed Dineen in his unmarked car with him as long as he left his muscle behind.

After a wild ride of lights and sirens heading south through downtown Boston, they turned off Gallivan Boulevard and onto Adams Street. They pulled up in front of The Mayo Inn just as the first marked radio car arrived.

Mulholland jumped out and took command. "Brian, Sheila, go around back." He pointed down the fence line along the left of the bar. He directed the two uniform cops to stay with him to approach the front door. Then he turned to Jimmy and Frank. "Guys, if there's fireworks here, I don't want to have to explain to your Mayor and mine how you two got involved." He paused and waited for a reaction. Jimmy just stared at him. Mulholland took a step toward Jimmy.

"Captain Gallagher, get on the other side of that fence. Now. That's an order." He pointed to the parking lot of the Credit Union next door. "Now, Jimmy."

Frank pulled on Jimmy's elbow and they both backed up. Mulholland looked past Jimmy and Frank to see Dineen waving himself off and backing into the parking lot. "All right, stay back, we'll keep you informed." Mulholland joined the two uniform cops and tactically approached the front door of The Mayo Inn.

Jimmy turned to Frank. "You watch their backs up here.

I'm gonna follow the fence to the back and watch out for those two." Frank hesitated. Jimmy noticed.

"Don't worry, I'll stay on this side of the fence. Just keep an eye on them, that's all. You up here, me in the back. We'll keep our distance."

Jimmy looked behind himself first, but there was no sign of Dineen. Then he walked casually along the fence to the back of the parking lot. He drew even with the back door of The Mayo and watched Sheila and her partner take up spots on either side of the door. Sheila and Ranaghan had their guns drawn and leaned in close, apparently listening.

Jimmy leaned on the fence and watched. Then shouting came from around the front. He couldn't see anything, but could hear Mulholland's voice. Then shots.

Jimmy watched Ranaghan and Sheila react. Ranaghan stepped out and positioned himself square to the door and reared back.

More shots fired around front. Ranaghan let loose with his right foot and crashed in the rear door. It nearly flew off its hinges. Shots immediately came from within.

Ranaghan hit the deck. Sheila knelt next to the door and, leading with her weapon, flashed her head in and out of the doorway in a split second. She pulled her head back but not her gun. She let two rounds go in through the door.

Jimmy grabbed the fence to hop over it. He thought about Mulholland's warning but chose to ignore it. He put his weight on his right hand to hurdle the fence, but it slipped off. Grease? He looked at the fence. Then at his hand. Blood. What the fuck? He noticed more blood on the floor by his feet.

He turned and looked across the parking lot. A trail, leading to the back door of that small brick building. He looked up. A Credit Union? He took a few steps. Even from twenty feet away he could see blood on the knob of the back door. Fresh. He turned back to The Mayo and realized he wasn't going to get anyone's attention there; they were in a gunfight, for God's sake.

He ran to the Credit Union door. He noticed a car in the parking lot. On a Sunday? The car was empty, though. He stepped right up to the office door. He turned the knob with his left hand, threw the door open, and pulled his Glock out with his right. The door slammed against the inside wall. Jimmy shouted,

"Police. Nobody move."

No response. Blood on the floor. He took a step in and let the door close behind him. The narrow hall ran only five feet to an open office on the right; no door. Beyond that, the hall ran past two more open rooms and then into a reception area in front. Jimmy could see straight out through the front door. "Police. Show yourself."

John Dineen appeared from the front cubicle and stepped halfway into the hall. "Jim, what's up, kid?" Only half of Dineen's torso was visible. The rest of him remained concealed by the wall. Dineen's gaze fell to the floor. Jimmy studied him. Something was wrong. Dineen shook, though it didn't appear to be of his own power.

Dineen jerked his eyes up to Jimmy. He looked defeated. "I always knew this day would come." He sighed. "Your terrorist guy has an axe to my head. Wants me to bullshit you into leaving –" Dineen fought off an invisible pull on his body from inside the room. He struggled to dive into the hall. Jimmy saw the meat cleaver slice from out of the room. Dineen dropped to the ground. The cleaver missed his head but cut a nasty slice through his shoulder.

Even though he couldn't see into the room, Jimmy let two rounds go through the sheet rock. He advanced. Dineen lay on the ground at his feet, moaning and bleeding. Jimmy stepped over him and pointed his Glock into the room. Stars burst into Jimmy's vision. Before he hit the ground, he turned to see Zafir's driver standing behind him with a tire iron in his hand. Jimmy fell on the opposite side of the doorway from Dineen. Zafir appeared with the meat cleaver in his hand. He stepped toward Jimmy and raised it over his head. Jimmy tried to raise his Glock, but his body wasn't ready yet to take commands from his mind.

Zafir suddenly doubled over. Jimmy saw Dineen's foot as it slammed into Zafir's crotch. Jimmy raised his Glock. Zafir leapt over Dineen and, in a flash, he and his driver disappeared out the back door.

"Motherfuckers." Dineen propped himself up against the hallway wall. He pulled his jaw in and tried to look at his shoulder. He gave up and sighed forward. He looked over at Jimmy. "You okay?"

Jimmy got as far as his hands and knees. "Not yet." He tried to shake his head, but that only brought more stars. He collapsed onto the wall. He felt the wet warmth of blood circling around the back of his neck. "Gimme a minute." He sat up against the wall. "Fuck." Jimmy rolled his head over toward Dineen. "He got away. I can't fuckin' believe it."

Dineen just stared back.

Jimmy asked, "Did he get the key?"

"Sorry, kid." He nodded to the front cube. "He killed my last lieutenant."

Jimmy looked over toward the room. "I'm sorry about that." Then he looked back at Dineen. "You did the right thing there by me. Twice. You saved my life, really."

"Yeah." Dineen nodded. Then he smiled on an afterthought. "So now we're good, right?"

Jimmy nodded. "Yeah." He rolled over and got to his hands and knees again. He mustered up a smile. "We're good."

Dineen raised an eyebrow at the sounds coming through the wall. Gunshots. Intermittent. "Geez, I hope they don't do too much damage over there." He fished out his cell phone.

"Is that all you care about?" Jimmy touched the back of his head.

"Actually, I realize we ain't getting help from next door; they're kinda busy at the moment. I'm calling 911 to get us an ambulance." Dineen perused his phone. He read something from its face and looked up. "Oh, uh, by the way; about my guys?"

Jimmy slid his hand off his neck and looked at it. Full of blood. Then he looked over at Johnny. "Oh, right, sure." He leaned sideways on the wall and reached for his cell phone. His head spun, but he scrolled through and hit dial. He went to put the phone up to his ear, but thought better of it. He hit 'speaker' and dropped it on his lap. The call was answered.

"Hey, kid."

"Rocket. How we doin?"

"We're doin' just fine, kid, how are you?"

"I've been better, John. Listen, those guys from Boston —long story but I want you to cut 'em loose."

"Oh, really?" Rocket John's sarcasm came through the speaker. Then he raised his voice and repeated Jimmy's words; "You want me to cut 'em loose."

"Yeah, John, it's a long story, but cut 'em loose."

Rocket laughed. "Oh no, Captain, I'm not questioning your decision, it's just... hang on a minute." They heard Rocket shouting in the background. Then he came back.

"Kid, I'm going to put you on speaker for a second." Again, a tumult of background voices. Then Rocket, again: "Go ahead, kid, repeat that order; say it again for me, would you?"

Jimmy looked over at Dineen, and they both puzzled at each other. Jimmy raised his voice to the speaker on his lap. "Cut those guys loose."

A roar of laughter came through the phone from what sounded like an entire squad. "You got it, kid," Rocket shouted out from the raucous background. "Cut 'em loose, boys." Rocket ended the call.

Again Jimmy and Dineen quizzed at each other. Jimmy shrugged. Dineen did too. "Thanks, Jim."

"Sure, no problem."

48

Security was tight at One Police Plaza. Siban knew that was an everyday affair and that it had nothing in particular to do with the meeting he was here to attend, but still, it unnerved him. After passing through the security kiosk on the plaza, he was issued a visitor's pass and now walked the last thirty feet to the main entrance. Though it was still autumn in New York, winter whispered in on a cool breeze.

Initially, Siban hesitated at representing the fledgling Moderate Muslims of America at this meeting; but in the end he decided it was the right thing to do. Most others were afraid, at this point. Afraid of Zafir, to be sure, but also fearful in general. This was a fairly new tack.

Though efforts had been made recently at the very highest levels of American government, not much success could be claimed. The White House's Countering Violent Extremism program did not produce the results a lot of us were hopeful for, he thought. Even the leader of that movement, Mohamed from Texas, had resigned himself to the fact that the program had collapsed towards the end of last year.

This movement needed to come from the ground up. Grassroots. The Muslim community still struggled to become mainstream and shake the suspicions of terrorism. Siban knew it would take time; perhaps an entire generation, and he also knew how difficult it would be. A narrow path was outlined before him.

He needed to convince his people that they could condemn the violence of jihad while still supporting their

Muslim world and its traditions. His people would follow him. Him and men like Mohamed, who flew up from Texas to speak at the UN General Assembly on the day of the City Hall rally.

Mohamed had also promised to join Siban and the MMOA at City Hall after his UN speech. But, Siban knew, the masses of their people would not readily abandon their idols of jihad. Old ideas die hard. All peoples, at one time or another, proudly whisper and wink at their connections to counter-heroes. He needed to provide better heroes.

He arrived at the revolving doors of One Police Plaza and took his turn scooting through. He presented his ID and visitor's pass at the small rotunda and was directed through another magnetometer. Once inside the lobby, he presented his invitation letter for the pre-meet for tomorrow's City Hall event. A detective directed him to the Community Affairs office on the ninth floor.

After an arduous and crowded elevator ride, he arrived at the outer office of the Deputy Commissioner of Community Affairs. He presented the invitation letter to the receptionist and took in his surroundings.

The office space ran straight back from the receptionist's desk. What appeared to be the office of the Deputy Commissioner herself was straight back at the end of the hall. Along the left side of the hall were three glass-walled conference rooms; two of which were currently in use. At the top of the hall, directly behind the receptionist, was a small waiting area with two couches and a coffee table.

The woman flapped Siban's letter back at him, motioned to the waiting area, and told him to take a seat.

After at least a half an hour, one of the meetings in the glass-walled room broke up. A stream of professionals exchanged farewells as they made their way out of the office. Some appeared to be police officials in business attire, some not. The last one out, a uniformed captain, stopped at the receptionist's desk. After a short conversation with her, the captain turned and approached Siban.

He was a youthful-looking, middle-aged African-American man. Siban stood and shook his hand. Then he began to step around the table, expecting to be brought into one of the empty conference rooms. The captain smiled and sat down on the far couch. Siban remained standing. He looked down the hall and back to the captain. "Won't your Counterterrorism people be joining us?"

The captain kept smiling, but shook his head. "They just left." He motioned to the outer entrance. "Please," he waved at the couch, "have a seat."

Siban hesitated, but sat. The captain perused a clipboard. "I see you have a permit issued for the corner of Broadway and Chambers Street for a two-hour rally tomorrow from noon to two p.m?"

Siban didn't respond right away. He stared at the captain. Then he surveyed another group of professionals making their way in, greeting one another, and heading for a back cubicle.

"Captain." Siban returned his attention to the man. He looked down at the captain's clipboard. "Yes." He looked back up at him. "Yes, that is all technically correct. Though that is not what we applied for. Restrictions were put in place by your office. We wanted to rally in front of the Tweed Courthouse. Plus, there may be a march of supporters coming down from the UN. And, we expect to be there more than two hours."

"Yes, I see all that." The captain flipped down a page or

two on his clipboard. "But you realize we can't accommodate those wishes. We don't allow protests in front of Tweed. Nor –"

"This is not a protest." Siban cut him off. "This is a rally. And the Tweed Courthouse holds a good deal of symbolism for our cause. We strive to assimilate in a manner similar to those who built that edifice."

"Sorry, poor choice of words." The captain flipped the pages back down. "I understand your premise." He laid the clipboard down on the coffee table.

"On behalf of The Department, I can say that we're very pleased by your efforts and wish you the best of luck going forward. But Tweed is off-limits. You can have the corner of Broadway, which is only a couple of hundred feet down from the Courthouse.

"You can take the whole corner as long as you don't spill into the street. We need to keep vehicular traffic flowing through there. And, if there is a march of supporters joining you, they will have to come down Broadway; that is our preferred route."

The captain sat back on the couch. "Tomorrow's a big day for us, it being opening day of the UN General Assembly uptown. Our resources will be stretched pretty thin up there as it is. I'm sorry we couldn't do more. But we rarely issue a permit that allows for everything that was requested on your application. I hope you can understand." The captain stood. Siban did not.

"Captain." Siban sat back and crossed his legs. "I don't think you realize the importance of this event. Of what we are trying to accomplish."

The captain sighed. "We do. Believe me, we do. And I don't mean to convey any disrespect to your efforts, Imam;

we just don't have the resources necessary to allow your event to be any bigger." He put one hand in his pocket. "If it were any other day, maybe..." He allowed his voice to trail off.

Siban stood. "Captain, I know that your department is aware of the fact that there is a madman loose in this city. A radical jihadist who is responsible for a number of deaths already. He –"

The captain raised his hand. "Imam. I've been briefed by our Intelligence people as well as our Counterterrorism investigators." He waved behind him to the outer entrance. "As you saw, we're in close contact on every event we permit." He put his hand out toward Siban and motioned for him to step out of the sitting area.

"I'm sorry, Imam, but every concern you could voice right now has been hashed out in depth. Whatever threat may exist to the safety of your event has been assessed, and appropriate measures have been put in place."

"The threat has been assessed." Siban did not follow the captain's urgings toward the exit. "And you don't think it merits more than nominal security?"

The captain looked at his watch again. Then he glanced down the inner hallway. The empty glass-walled room was now full, apparently awaiting his presence.

"Imam, your permit has been issued. Appropriate security measures have been assigned." He stepped in closer and put his hand on Siban's shoulder. "Our investigators know all about this Zafir. Steps are being taken to ascertain his movements. I'm told that whatever threat he actually does represent is well in hand." He patted Siban's upper arm. "No worries, sir." He glanced at his watch again. "I'm sorry, but I have to move on. Good luck." He stepped away.

49

Nora Zimmerman took one last look around. She laughed to herself about how, at her age, every time she went on vacation, she never knew if she'd actually be coming back. Though she and Morty took such great care of themselves all the way toward their nineties, life was day to day at this stage. She fondled the flowers on the dining table, knowing they would be dead by the time she got back from Florida next week. Then she shuffled into the kitchen and called to her husband. "Mort?" She didn't wait for an answer. "The car is downstairs, they just rang up. Time to go." She heard his muffled response from the bedroom. After over sixty years of marriage, they'd learned to communicate with grunts and bumps.

While she waited, Nora shuffled over and took in the great skyline of lower Manhattan through the kitchen window. Though they initially tried to buy a different condo, down on the fifteenth floor that faced west, this eastern view from their eighteenth floor unit was still magnificent.

She looked down toward the street. Through the window she enjoyed the sights of City Hall and The Tweed Courthouse right below her. She felt slightly dizzy looking down. Eighteen floors was very high. But she always loved the view —and not just of the important landmarks directly beneath them. This was the terminus of the canyon of heroes, one of the most famous thoroughfares in all the world. But her tired old eyes didn't notice that the window lock had been left in the open position.

Morty appeared from the bedroom. "We have

everything?"

"Morty, we've been packing for two days; of course we have everything."

"Okay, Okay." He gave her his usual backhand wave. "I'm just asking." He surveyed the kitchen and dining area. "Those flowers are going to die, why did you even buy them?"

"Oh, I know." She smiled at the vase. "I didn't actually buy them, Mort. That lovely delivery boy, Nagreb, brought them by. A going away present." She turned back to her husband. "Wasn't that thoughtful? He's such a lovely young man."

"Yes he is, he's very helpful." Another backhand. "Now let's go, the car is waiting."

"Oh you..." Nora followed Morty out the door.

50

Zafir overcame the temptation to reveal more than he should. Pride was a difficult thing to contain. But he would hold fast to his training. And to the truth. Nagreb had proven himself a loyal soldier and had done good work on this mission, but still Zafir would not divulge all. Not yet.

"Khalifa." Nagreb did not look at him, but kept his hands between his knees and his gaze on the floor. "I do not mean to question you, but the eyes of the world will be on the United Nations tomorrow; not City Hall." Now Nagreb looked up at him. "I know it will be difficult to bring our weapon close to the United Nations with so much security, but there are those among us who will sacrifice their lives to do so."

Zafir smiled. He stepped closer and dropped his hand on Nagreb's shoulder. "No worries, my friend." He shook him. "You will see. There is great significance in my plan. The sins of The Great Satan will, tomorrow, come full circle. And the world will take notice, I promise you that."

Zafir stepped over to the work table set up in the middle of the main room of the Brooklyn apartment. He examined each piece of equipment laid out thereon. He fingered the cross bow and checked with Nagreb one more time: "Your marksmanship is without question, yes?"

"Yes, Zafir, I have practiced hundreds of times. I will hit the mark that Shalit presents tomorrow on the opposite roof, I promise you."

"And the tensile strength of the fishing line and steel cable that will follow it, these have been tested?"

"Over and over, Khalifa, they will not fail." Nagreb stood and joined him at the table. Zafir watched as he picked up one end of the 300-foot coiled fishing line, the opposite end of which was properly fastened to an arrow yet to be mounted on the crossbow. "This is the latest technology in the industry. It is so strong, we hardly need to string the steel cable after it."

Zafir stared at Nagreb. "But we will take no chances. There may be contingencies."

Nagreb nodded, "Of course."

Zafir continued his inventory. In the center of the table sat the suitcase; next to it, the key. Zafir picked up the key and couldn't help but smile as he fondled it. He weighed it in his hand and looked over at Nagreb.

Being in possession of this key was, in itself, a great accomplishment. He said nothing to Nagreb and laid the key back down on the table. He reached to the top of the suitcase and pulled on the new steel eyelet they had attached just an hour ago. Big enough for the quarter-inch steel cable to pass through, small enough not to interfere with the function of the device. Zafir nodded his satisfaction.

"Khalifa," Nagreb leaned on the table, "why do we need to suspend the weapon in such a manner? I understand there will be much security on the street and that we can't just walk it into the crowd. But why don't we just drop it out the window instead of risking these overhead lines being discovered?"

Zafir decided to be patient with Nagreb. "Maximum exposure. Not physically, but maximum exposure for the psyche. It is fear we wish to instill beyond just death. They must know, first, what we have accomplished —I want them to see it coming; for the world to feel the terror as it is about to occur; but also, they must understand where it comes from. Specifically. They must know which building and exactly which floor."

Nagreb only responded with a quizzical look.

"More will be revealed my friend, in due time." Zafir stepped over to the window of the small Brooklyn apartment. He noticed the sun dropping low in the western sky.

"Soon we will depart." He turned back to Nagreb. "Everyone else will be in place? Shalit has his equipment and is assured access to the roof of The Evening Sun Building?"

"Yes, Sahib."

"And the Zimmermans?"

Nagreb pulled a key ring from his pocket. "They have left for their vacation. I have complete access to their apartment." He put the keys back in his pocket. "The doorman goes home at midnight; we shall have no problems getting set tonight. When the sun rises tomorrow, all will be in place."

"Yes." Zafir turned away from Nagreb and walked across the room. "Almost all." He removed from his pocket another disposable, prepaid cell phone; the fifth such device he had purchased in the last two weeks. He made his final contact with the leaders in the homeland. They, too, utilized similar phones, and so their exact locations were never known —not even to Zafir. The call lasted the full two-minute limit that had long ago been established for such contacts.

Not knowing the members of the assassination cell who would carry out tomorrow's sniper attack worried Zafir. He had much confidence in his handlers at home and understood that one local cell should never know the identity of another, but he had a hard time putting his trust in a sniper he had never met; someone whose skills were not known to him.

But he trusted the network. His handlers in the homeland had shown great ability and resourcefulness. After years of study and some infiltration, they confirmed that the route Mohamed would take from the UN to City Hall would include the famous avenue called Broadway — the Canyon of Heroes.

And their knowledge of the personal habits of Mohamed and his wife, Sultana Aisha al-Wahid, was extensive. Zafir knew her, too. She was, at one time, a dedicated jihadist, but was now a turncoat, just like the rest of these moderates. So they knew her. And could predict her response with much confidence.

Zafir ended the call with some trepidation. But the network trusted Zafir to this point, and so he would return that trust. And now the final pieces were in place.

He came back to Nagreb. "It is time, then. Get the camera. I will make my statement." He lifted his chin and stretched his neck left and right and prepared to speak to the world.

51

At seven o'clock Tuesday morning, Jimmy opened the door to OCTU's suite of offices on the eleventh floor of 51 Chambers Street. He found Kevin Clark already hunched over a workstation in the bullpen, his ever-present mug of coffee steaming next to him.

Clark turned his back to the computer and rotated his chair toward Jimmy. "You're up early." Clark stood and looked up at Jimmy's head. "How are you feeling?"

Jimmy rubbed the back of his head. "Couple of stitches, I'm fine."

Clark put his hands on his hips and shook his head, "There is no way you can tell me the doctors didn't diagnose a concussion. You really shouldn't be here."

Jimmy smiled. "Kevin, I'm sure you've had your share of concussions." He patted his lieutenant on the upper arm. "What's the treatment? Huh? Take it easy, right? So, here," Jimmy grabbed a chair and spun it in underneath himself, "I'll take it easy." He sat.

Then he noticed Sergeant Donohue, head down on a desk, sound asleep. "Now, if you should be lecturing anybody about not being here..." he pointed at Jack.

Clark looked at Jack and sighed. "You know, since he's asleep and can't hear me, I'll say it now: that kid is unstoppable. He researches things like I've never seen."

Kevin sat back down in his chair, next to Jimmy. "You know, while you were up in Boston, he checked all the transportation videos again. When he came up with nothing and his eyes were about to fall out of his big head, he started on cars stolen from Brooklyn during the week surrounding the day we did the warrant."

Clark turned his chair to face Jimmy directly. "Do you know how many cars get stolen in this city in a week?" Clark didn't wait for an answer. "On average, over a hundred and fifty. That's nearly twenty-five a day." He looked back at Jack. "Kid scoured through every single one of those reports." He turned back to Jimmy. "You know he found it, right?"

Jimmy shook his head. "Found what?"

"The car Zafir stole and drove to Boston. He put every possible plate on the air up there. Had their patrol people look out for them. Sure enough," he looked back at Jack, "they found it. Though it was too late to help in the hunt – by the time they found it, you were already on your way back."

Clark stretched, yawned, and picked up his coffee mug. "But at least we have confirmation that Zafir's involved with that big mosque up there –they found the car in their parking lot."

Jimmy gripped the armrests of his chair. He was about to reel off a list of tasks based on that info when Clark put up his hand.

"We're all over it. Boston PD's been sitting on the place around the clock, since. They got eyes on their train and bus stations, the airport, everything. In fact, for the time being, they've got detectives responding to every report of a stolen car."

Clark smirked. "They only get 4 or 5 a day up there for the whole city; not like here."

Jack stirred, apparently from the sound of their voices. "Yeah." Jimmy watched Jack wake. "He's a student of the game."

Clark raised his eyebrows and nodded. "Well said Captain: that he is."

Jack pushed his head up off the desk. He looked blankly, first at Clark and then at Jimmy. He closed his eyes and then opened them wide, stretching the skin on his face over his teeth. He drew a deep breath and put his hands on the arms of his chair.

"Captain." He turned to his desk and pushed around the few sheets there. He turned back to Jimmy. "Captain."

"Hold on." Jimmy held up his hand. "Go take a tall drink of water, first. Then go to the bathroom and come back and pour yourself some coffee. Then we'll talk."

Jack stood. "Yes sir." He rubbed his chest and stomach. "Yes sir." He turned for the door. The office suite had no restroom; they had to go out in the hall and turn halfway to the elevators. Jack opened the door to the hall and Hatim stepped in. Jack could only nod and walk around him.

"Captain," Hatim spoke with concern, "I thought you were injured, sir." Hatim glanced around at the back of Jimmy's head at the small bandage covering a medically shaved bald spot. "Captain, you have a head injury. Shouldn't you be taking some sick leave, sir?"

Jimmy smiled. "Thanks for your concern, Hatim; you're as bad as Clark." He reached up and shook Hatim's extended hand. Then he pointed to the coffee cup in Hatim's other hand. "Finish your coffee and then get me the minutes of that pre-meet I asked you for —regarding today's rally down the block at City Hall."

Hatim stood up straight, almost at attention. "I regret to inform you, Captain, but there are no minutes. I looked into it as directly as possible, sir, but there are no minutes because there was no pre-meeting."

Jimmy frowned. "Who's got the detail?" he asked and pulled out his cell phone.

"I have that information, it's in my office." Hatim put his coffee down and walked into his cubicle-sized room off the bullpen.

Jimmy didn't wait. He made another call. Siban answered on the first ring.

"Good morning, Captain."

"Good morning to you, Siban. Tell me, what time are you guys kicking off over there today?"

"It is planned for noon, but I will be there before eleven, myself."

"Great, I'll meet you over there." Jimmy switched hands with the phone. "Siban, I'm curious about the permit process: who did you meet with from Community Affairs; what did they have to say?"

"Ahh, some Captain; I don't remember his name. He had not much to say. This rally has been given what appears to me to be the minimum of attention."

"So there was no pre-meet with whatever uniformed Captain from patrol that is running the detail?"

"No. We were told that the barricades and personnel will be in place when we arrive, and we will be guided at that time."

"Okay. So how many people are you expecting?"

"It is difficult to estimate. Although support has been pledged from MPAC, The Muslim Public Affairs Council in Washington, most of their leadership will be at the UN this morning. In fact, there is an important appearance and speech to be made there just before our rally; after which our attendance should increase somewhat."

"Clarify that for me?"

"Yes, of course. There is a speaker from Texas; a man who has made great strides in bringing Muslim culture and communities into the mainstream in that state. In the recent past he has been associated with extremists, but now he has turned toward the middle. He is a great hope for the moderates. His speech at the UN General Assembly today is much anticipated."

"He's addressing the General Assembly this morning? So which country is he representing?"

"None. He is American. I know it is out of the ordinary for such a figure to address the UN during the opening week but, again, he is the face of moderation in the American-Muslim world and possibly, depending on how this morning unfolds, beyond. So when he is finished at the UN, his plan is to join us here at City Hall."

"I see. I'll make sure the uniforms running the detail down here are aware of that. So I'll see you in a couple of hours, then." Jimmy and Siban ended their call.

Hatim came into the bullpen and read off a sheet of paper he held in his hand: "Lieutenant Miller has the detail, sir. There will be one lieutenant, two sergeants, and sixteen police officers assigned."

"One lieutenant." Jimmy stood up. "Sixteen cops? No captain. This is bullshit." He pulled out his cell phone again. He called the Department's Operations Unit over in One Police Plaza.

"Yeah, Captain Gallagher here, get me —" Jimmy nodded. "Thank you, I appreciate that, Detective. I'm okay, just a couple of stitches. Yeah, right. Yes, okay. Now listen, I need to talk to Captain Raleigh; can you get him on the phone for me please."

Jimmy sat back down and waited. He put the phone on speaker and dropped it in his lap. After a minute, Captain Raleigh came on the line. "Ken, how've you been, pal; it's Jimmy Gallagher."

"Jim. How's the head, old friend?"

"It's fine. Hard as ever."

"Good to know. So what's up?"

"My detail this morning at City Hall: you're selling it short; what's the problem?"

"There's no problem, Jim, we're focused on the UN today; you know that. I've only got but so many resources to spread around, you know?"

"Yeah, sure, I know, but sixteen cops and no captain? That's not going to cut it. I'm expecting hundreds down here. This is bigger than I think you guys realize."

"No, we realize what it is. We've got you down there, so we've got nothing to worry about, right?"

"Don't blow smoke at me, Kenny, this guy I'm tracking is real. I –"

"Jimmy, no shit: we know he's real, and we know you are, too; it's just that..." Raleigh hesitated.

"Talk to me, Ken."

"All right, you want the company line, or you want the truth?"

"Talk to me."

"Your guy's real, we know that; but we also know something you don't."

"Really? What's that?"

"He doesn't have a fucking nuke, Jimmy. All he's got, from what we can see, is a set of balls. The truth from the very top down on this is: wherever this Zafir guy is and whatever he tries to pull, and, Jimmy I'm not bullshitting you here, the feeling is that you can handle him. You've come face to face with this guy what, twice already? It's only a matter of time until you nail him. The job's got bigger fish to fry today, and they're leaving this thing in your hands."

"Geez, Ken, when did you become a bureaucrat?"

"What are you talking about?"

"The way you put that, to complain now would be to put myself down. Where did you learn that kind of bullshit? I must say, it was well-crafted and right off the top of your head, too. Impressive."

"Look, Jimmy, just because you never had designs on becoming a chief doesn't mean you get to break my balls. I'm trying to play both ends, here. I wasn't supposed to tell you any of that. Bottom line is, you're on your own, and the job's not worried about it. Got it?"

"I got it, Ken. But look, you know what?" Jimmy stood and stepped over to the open door of his office. He looked out the window at the Boss Tweed Courthouse and City Hall beyond. "I've got an entire perimeter of notable buildings down here; places that need to be protected. And not just City Hall. There's Tweed, The Woolworth Building, The Evening Sun Building. Think about it, Ken: the site of this rally is surrounded by skyscrapers and historic sites.

"What are you thinking, Jim? Your guy is going to drop a suitcase nuke off a fucking building this morning? C'mon."

"Fuckin' Ken. I tell you what: any further insight into what my terrorist has up his sleeve, be sure to keep me in the loop with it, okay?"

"Sure, no problem, pal. Listen, you stay safe down there today, alright?"

"Whoa, whoa, hold on. You gotta give me something

here, Ken. Give me a sniper or two, something; maybe one of the War Wagons."

"The Wagons are off limits, Jim. All five of those armored trucks have very definite itineraries for the day; they're spoken for."

"Alright, give me a sniper, then. No; two –give me two snipers."

"Fuckin' Jimmy, you're making this really hard on me."

"Come on, Ken, for old times' sake." Jimmy knew he needed to pressure his old friend. He decided to hit him where it hurt, where any old street cop would feel it. "Try and remember what it was like to be a real cop."

"You know what, Jimmy, fuck you. Why don't you do this: take a minute and pretend you're sitting behind this fucking desk right here. Now look over your fucking shoulder and tell me what you see, alright? I've got every fucking chief in the building climbing up my ass looking for resources in every imaginable fucking spot in Manhattan today."

"Ken, Ken, I take it back. You're a real cop; you always have been. I know you. I'm sorry. I didn't mean that. I just need something, here. Whatever you can do, I'd appreciate it. I'm sorry."

"Alright. Alright, I'll call over to Special Ops and see what I can do, but no promises." They hung up.

Jimmy looked up and realized the leadership of his unit stood before him in a semi-circle. Sergeant Donohue had returned and held a fresh cup of coffee. Jimmy pointed at him. "Feeling better?"

"I'm ready to go, boss."

"Okay, well," Jimmy pointed toward the back offices, "you and your detectives have some leg work to do, yes?"

"Yes sir." Jack held up his coffee. "We have surveillance on Zafir's haunts in Brooklyn and, we're going over any and all summonses and arrests in the area in the last forty-eight hours: all crime reports, relevant phone records, all –"

"Okay, okay." Jimmy held up his hand. "Kevin?" he turned to Clark.

"I'm taking Hatim and going over to the detail with you."

"Okay." Jimmy stepped back over to his office and looked through it again and out the windows over Chambers Street. "Alright, someone put on another pot of coffee and we'll walk over to the detail in an hour." He went into his office and closed the door.

52

Zafir looked out the eighteenth floor window of 270 Broadway. He opened the window and tugged on the micro-thin steel cable. Secure. He smiled. The crossbow worked well, as did the fluorocarbon fishing line that Nagreb had fired across the street to the roof of the Evening Sun Building at two o'clock this morning. Zafir remained at the windowsill and looked over his shoulder at Nagreb. That young man had seemed to enjoy spending the night here in such luxury. Zafir had made a mental note of that.

He watched Nagreb disassemble the fishing rod he had used to string the cable back across the Canyon of Heroes. Once he had shot the arrow with the fishing line attached across the void, Shalit had secured it on the opposite roof. Then Shalit untied the arrow and replaced it with the end of the micro-thin steel cable which he had coiled and waiting atop the Evening Sun Building.

Then all Nagreb had to do was reel it back in. Initially, when just the fluorocarbon fishing line stretched between the two buildings, it was entirely invisible from the street. Though now the thicker cable could be seen if one concentrated and knew exactly where to look, it was still virtually invisible from below.

Zafir had studied the mechanics of the famous tight rope walker, Philipe Petit, who had also started with fishing line on a cross-bow and ended with a much larger cable between the twin towers of The World Trade Center some forty years ago.

Ironic. Touching, almost, that he was now using

information related to those towers. Zafir smiled broadly and turned back to the window. Touching, but not nearly as meaningful as this building; this very apartment he now occupied. In a few hours, when the weapon was attached to the cable and slid out above the crowd gathered below, they would all realize the significance. And it would shock the world into acknowledging the sins of the Great Satan.

Shalit had attached a clip at a precise point along the cable so when the suitcase rolled out the window and flew down from its eighteenth floor height toward the seventh floor height across the street, it would stop and be suspended exactly above today's rally. And the world would be watching. And they would know immediately what the suitcase was.

Maximum exposure. That is one of the tenets of a most profitable mission. The deaths that were to occur today were only part of the mission. Beyond just these deaths, the greatest amount of terror possible must be infused into the culture. The media would play their part, albeit unwittingly, but they would help spread the fear.

Zafir withdrew the flash drive from his pocket. The video he had made last night would soon be posted to every available social network site and sent to the world's media outlets. That would get their attention.

And then the deaths would come. His own too, maybe. But he was prepared for that. He turned again to look at Nagreb. He wasn't so sure about that young man's willingness along those lines. Maybe he would have to kill Nagreb himself, just to be sure. He pocketed the flash drive. It was not yet time for broadcasting. He turned to the window again and looked down at the gathering below.

After a moment, a broad smile came across his face.

Well, well, my old friend Captain Gallagher. Maybe I should have had my sniper stationed here with me instead of up town. He stopped smiling. *No matter, Captain Gallagher, you will die soon with the rest of them.*

53

At a quarter of eleven Jimmy came out of his office and marshaled his squad. Clark and Hatim came with him. Donohue stayed in the office on the computer with the remainder of the unit. They got down to Chambers Street and walked the three hundred feet to the corner of Broadway.

The police barricades formed a pen on the southeast corner. It was still an hour before the scheduled start of the rally, but at least a hundred people milled about inside the pen. Some unfurled banners. Others attached posters to the outside of the barricades and such. Jimmy found Siban in the middle of the small crowd, and waved.

"Good morning." Jimmy extended his hand across the barrier.

"Good morning." Siban reached over from his side and the two men shook hands.

"Good turn out so far, for an hour beforehand." Jimmy surveyed the crowd.

Siban sighed. "Captain, if I realized the level of attention that would be on Mohamed's speech at the UN this morning, I may have abandoned these efforts here. MPAC is in attendance up there. Our fledgling MMOA is the only organization that will be present at this rally. It's a matter of local efforts having less priority than those of a larger scale. As I have said, Mohamed's speech is much anticipated. Of all the problems in the world today that the General Assembly will contemplate, peace among Muslims is the top concern. The eyes of the world will be on Mohamed and those groups outside the UN this morning."

Jimmy looked around the area and frowned. "So why did Zafir express interest in this gathering?" Siban only shrugged. Jimmy looked him up and down. "Maybe it's you. You don't think he knows you gave us the location of those guns, do you?"

"No. You staged that very well. I have interacted with his followers since; they do not suspect me of that."

Jimmy nodded. "Well, just in case." He turned to the street side of the barricades and did a visual search for Lieutenant Clark. Finding him, he motioned for Kevin to join them.

Kevin arrived and handed Jimmy a flyer. "This what you're looking for?"

Jimmy looked at the flyer and smiled. "You're a mind reader, Clark."

Kevin responded with his usual weary smirk. "Spoke to Lieutenant Miller. All his guys have one of those." He pointed to the picture of Zafir on the wanted poster in Jimmy's hand. "They've been told he's armed and dangerous." He looked at Siban. "We got you covered out here this morning."

Siban nodded his thanks to Kevin. Jimmy folded the flyer and put it in his jacket pocket. Kevin walked off and continued surveying the area. Jimmy turned to Siban.

"If not you, then what? Why here? Especially when so many people calling for moderation in the Muslim struggle are up at the UN." Jimmy again turned and checked the surrounding area.

Across the street to the north stood the old Evening Sun Building, its hundred-year-old giant ornate clock commanding the corner of Broadway and Chambers. *Not much of a target,* though, Jimmy thought. Behind him and three hundred feet to the east stood Boss Tweed.

Then Jimmy turned in a circle and took note of the grandiose architecture of the famous Woolworth building. He looked the grand old landmark up and down but couldn't think why that would be a target of any significance.

"Maybe since some of the groups from the UN will be joining us later?" Siban offered. "At least, they promised to."

Jimmy frowned and shook his head. "They're not all coming down here, though, right?"

"Only MPAC has committed to join us here, and even they have only promised a few members of their leadership panel. Their followers may or may not come. And the other groups have not responded to my requests.

"But I did speak with Mohamed himself. He expressed to me his understanding that all politics is local. That grass roots is where any meaningful and lasting effort begins. He is completely committed to joining us today. And his wife, well, she is more determined than him. Some say she is his true motivator, and she is a friend of mine. I have known her for years. They will be here, of that I am certain."

"Okay, well, we'll keep our eyes out for anything out of the ordinary. Meanwhile, let me check on something." He pulled out his cell phone. Siban gestured that he'd be in the vicinity and waded into the growing crowd. Jimmy's call was answered.

"Jack, listen, do some research on my exact location. According to one of his minions that we collared out in Brooklyn, Zafir has zeroed in on this little rally to make his statement." Again, Jimmy looked up and down the cavern of Chambers Street. From the Municipal Arch at the foot of the Brooklyn Bridge in the east all the way across to the wide open Hudson River to the west, he couldn't imagine anything of particular significance to a terrorist. "Tell me why."

"You're not far from Ground Zero down there, Captain."

Jimmy looked over his shoulder to the south. "Nah, I doubt that, Jack, you can't even see that site from here. That has to be at least a half mile away."

"Not as the crow flies," Jack responded.

Jimmy shook his head. "Maybe that is it, Jack but I don't think so. I'm thinking something more immediate. Look, we have a guy who, we believe, has a suitcase nuke and his attention is on this rally while the rest of the world is up at the UN. Why here, Jack? Find that out for me; it's what you do, right?"

"Yes sir." Jimmy heard the determination in Sergeant Donohue's voice. "I'm on it, sir."

54

Murray guided his teams over the radio. Their mark left the UN building just as this Mohamed cat began his speech. Murray watched the Malaysian Minister of Foreign Affairs cross First Avenue on an angle to the north. He didn't like that the Minister chose to walk. Murray had a bulletproof limo waiting for him but, with the weather being what it was, the man chose to walk. Pain in the ass. "Team Three, you got a visual?"

"That's affirmative boss, we got him."

"Alright, he's yours up until he enters the residence." Murray let the Minister disappear into Forty-Fourth Street, knowing he had two sets of competent eyes on him. "Let me know when he turns in."

"Ten-four."

Murray turned to his driver, Dan Hearn. "Head back up to the main entrance. Things look to be getting interesting up there." Hearn put the SUV in gear and rolled out up First Avenue.

Media trucks with satellite dishes on the roof lined the street in front of the United Nations and all the attendant reporters gathered at the main gate.

A crowd of Muslim demonstrators from moderate groups —Murray couldn't remember their names —seemed to grow with every minute. Then the crowd itself crushed in past the reporters and surrounded the gate. Murray had Hearn pull up adjacent to the excitement. He rolled his window down and listened.

A uniformed cop approached on foot with an

aggravated look on his face. No body but the press was supposed to be parked along here. Murray reached for his ID, but didn't need to pull it out. When the kid got within five feet of the SUV, he recognized Murray and waved as he turned away.

Not only did Murray have clearance to be in the area as part of his assignment as a private eye guarding the Malaysian Minister, but just about every cop in New York knew who he was.

Murray grunted his wallet back into his pants pocket and then grabbed the Daily News off the console. He flipped it open and scanned the Page One story. Then he looked out the car window at the growing chaos of press and demonstrators.

"So this guy, Mohamed; after he gives this supposedly rousing speech," he turned to Hearn, "plans to hoof it down to that rally at City Hall; the one Jimmy's working."

"He's walking down there?" Hearn responded.

"Yeah." Murray tossed the newspaper back on the console and pointed at it. "Says there, he wants to make some kind of procession out of it."

Hearn shook his head. "That's like, freakin' three miles or something."

Murray laughed and looked up at the clear sky. "Yeah, well, he's got the weather for it. The article says he wants to raise awareness and support from all New Yorkers and then stand in support of a local group. Must mean that guy that Jimmy's been dealing with."

"Sounds like a security nightmare, marching halfway across Manhattan. Glad we ain't watchin' him."

Murray nodded but said nothing. He got on the cell phone and called Mister Gallagher, the boss, Jimmy's father.

After a few minutes on the phone, he hung up and turned to Hearn. "No one's got him."

"What?"

"This Mohamed guy is not a head of state, so no government resources are guarding him. And he says he's broke. He either can't or won't spring for private security." Murray shook his head. "Fucking deadbeat. Raise awareness my ass; he's probably turning it into a procession so the NYPD will have to follow along, for traffic if for no other reason. I'm sure he knows that the department would never let a large group like that take to the streets without pinning a detail on them."

A news reporter, microphone up, backed into Murray's large rear view mirror. She turned and stared at him. Murray said nothing. She pulled the mic down and spoke to Murray with obvious sarcasm: "You want to be in the shot?"

"Turn the other way, sister," Murray smirked. She did. The crowd burgeoned past the sidewalk and into the street. Soon the SUV was surrounded by hundreds of people, turning into thousands.

Hearn grabbed the gear shifter. "Should I get us out of here?"

"No, hold on," Murray answered. "I want to hear this." He put his arm on the open windowsill. The sarcastic reporter raised her mic and signaled her cameraman; as did a few other reporters on the edge of the crowd. The noise level was high, but the reporter had a good set of lungs. Murray leaned out a bit to hear the report.

After a brief introduction of who she was, where she was and what this was all about, she continued with some commentary:

"Never before has the General Assembly responded to

a speech with such enthusiasm. Leaders from around the globe cheered loudly for Mohamed as his words astounded the world. They were strong enough for those who believe Islam to be the one true religion on Earth, but harmonious enough for the rest of the world to have hope.

"He laid out an actual plan for peace. A lasting, believable peace that could change the face of the world today. He spoke with such passion that you couldn't help but believe it would be possible –that a page was turned here today; a page in history that we have all been waiting and hoping for. Frank, Sue; back to you." She continued to stare at the camera until the light went off. Then she lowered the mic and pulled out a pack of cigarettes.

Murray pulled out a lighter and called to her: "Hey, Miss, here, let me give you a light." She stepped over to the SUV. "So you were in there?" Murray asked. "You heard the speech?"

"No, they gave it to us on a live feed." She bowed her head and stuck her cigarette into Murray's flame. Then she pulled up and exhaled. "I gotta tell ya, cynical as I can be, it was good. This guy's for real."

"Great, that's great. So now he's marching downtown?"

"Supposed to, that's –" Her attention was pulled back to the gate. "Here he comes." She dropped the cigarette and shouted at her cameraman: "Here he comes." She pushed her way into the crowd. Mohamed appeared on the sidewalk and his forward progress pushed the crowd further out into the street.

Within seconds the crowd enveloped the SUV. Dan Hearn threw his hands up and then just laid them on his thighs. "Ain't a fucking hope of moving this car now, boss."

"Relax," Murray said. "Let it ride. They'll mill past us and then we can follow alongside."

"Am I getting overtime for this?" Hearn smirked.

Murray deadpanned over at him. "Jimmy's on the other side of this. Besides, our mark is in for the day; we got time."

"Whatever." Hearn waited for the crowd to drift past them and then reached for the gear shifter.

Hearn pulled out slow and Murray put the news radio on. Captains and chiefs from the NYPD flowed out onto the Avenue alongside and behind the crowd of thousands of people, including news reporters and their cameramen.

Murray kept his window down and watched as a detail of uniformed escorts was peeled off the UN contingent and assigned to corral the marchers onto the sidewalk and keep traffic flowing.

A lieutenant led the effort, but made little progress as more and more people flowed out from the gate of the UN and joined the procession. The news on the radio finally cycled around to the march. Murray listened to the broadcaster describe how, after the most stirring call for peace many people had ever heard, a great number of dignitaries gave Mohamed a standing ovation. At the end, Mohamed apparently called for anyone who believed in his words to follow him. Thus, the impromptu swarm out onto the street.

It was described that mostly diplomats and secretaries joined him, but even some world leaders and heads of state stirred from their places. Though most did not leave the Assembly, they visibly encouraged their staffers to do so.

The head of the march had already disappeared south on First Avenue, though the back end was still just clearing Forty-Second Street. Murray waited until the crowd cleared the Avenue and then directed Hearn to drive around to

Second Avenue and shadow their progress. First Avenue runs one way north so they couldn't stay right next to them.

Murray turned down the news radio and turned up the police scanner mounted under the dash. By the time the SUV rolled south on Second Avenue, Murray heard that the march had made a right turn across Thirty-Seventh Street, passing the entrance to the Queens-Midtown Tunnel. Hearn hurried the SUV down Second Avenue and pulled up just short of Thirty-Seventh Street. "Good timing," Murray pointed. "Here they come."

Murray and Hearn watched as Mohamed, with his wife at his side, led the procession through a left hand turn and marched south on Second Avenue. By the time they passed and the crowd control platoon re-opened Second Avenue to traffic, the lead marchers had already approached Thirty-Fourth Street.

The cops had their hands full trying to keep the marchers penned in. They gave up trying to restrict them to just the sidewalk and gave them the entire right lane of traffic. Hearn sidled the SUV up alongside the detail. They found the lieutenant toward the front. "Hey, Lou," Murray called out; but the lieutenant was in the middle of making radio transmissions:

"Captain, I need more people." The lieutenant looked up and down the line of marchers stretching now from Thirty-Second Street all the way back up to Thirty-Seventh.

The lieutenant continued talking into his radio: "I've got at least three, maybe four thousand people out here, and growing. They're picking people up along the way, too, Captain. Must be a 'Twitter' thing or something, but people are coming out of their buildings and storefronts and such and joining in with them.

"It's getting out of control and I need more help. I need at least another squad of one and eight and, I dunno, maybe a couple of horses or something? I'm going to lose the Avenue soon if you don't." The lieutenant held the radio next to his ear and waited for the response. "Ten-four, Lieutenant, continue to update us with your exact location."

Hearn kept the SUV apace and by now the lieutenant had noticed Murray rolling alongside him.

"What's up, Murray?"

"Got your hands full here, eh?"

"Yeah, you ain't kidding,"

 "So what's the plan?"

"Isolate and contain." The lieutenant turned back in at the burgeoning crowd and spread his arms wide to either side, coaxing a few stragglers back into the barely contained line of march. Without breaking stride, he turned back to Murray. "We got 'em up to City Hall; apparently there's a detail in place down there that'll take them."

"Ha," Murray laughed and held up his cell phone. "I was just talking with Captain Gallagher a little while ago. You know they only have one, two, and sixteen down there?"

"One, two, and sixteen?" The lieutenant looked up and down at the still growing demonstration. "Shit, that ain't enough."

"So you're doing traffic control. What about security?"

The lieutenant laughed. "Murray, we have no intel on this guy. We don't even know who his friends are, let alone his enemies. There has been no pre-meet, no briefing, and we don't even know what route he's taking. How could we have security? We don't even know which way he's going to turn next. We have no teams sweeping the route in front of him; no snipers, nothing. There is no security."

By now they had passed within a block of Bellevue Hospital and horns blared behind them as traffic snarled on Second Avenue. The lieutenant looked out beyond Murray's ride. Then he turned directly back to him. "Murray, do me a favor, huh?" The lieutenant motioned to the lane of traffic tied up behind the SUV. "You're not helping here, pal."

"Gotcha." Murray motioned for Hearn to pull out. They drove out well ahead of the mess and pulled up on the far side of Second Avenue, just before the next major intersection.

A moment later, a loud roar of engines came from out of Fourteenth Street on their left. An entire squad of huge, NYPD Harley Davidson motorcycles, seven in all, rolled out into the intersection and shut it down momentarily.

Behind the Harleys, two NYPD vans full of uniformed cops pulled to the curb. Once the motorcycles had complete control of the traffic, the foot cops jumped out in formation. Within seconds they'd unfurled a bright orange mesh barrier, the words NYPD emblazoned across every five-foot stretch.

The marchers arrived and the disorder control team very deftly split the vehicular traffic from the marchers. They sent the cars south on Second Avenue and physically forced the march to turn right on Fourteenth Street.

"Outstanding," Murray said from inside the SUV. "Dictate the route." He nodded. "Right out of the playbook. Nicely done." He nudged Hearn and pointed south on Second Avenue. "Go down one block, make a right, and go across to Broadway, just below Union Square. That'll be the next turn."

Hearn threw it in gear. "Yeah, Broadway, right. The Canyon of Heroes."

Murray nodded. "Yup, that route's been secured so many times, the disorder control people have their spots picked out for them. It's old hat by now."

As the march plodded west along Fourteenth Street to Union Square, Hearn shadowed it along Thirteenth. He made the left on Broadway and dropped south for a few blocks, pulling over in front of Grace Church.

Murray turned up the scanner and opened the car door. "Keep me posted." He stepped out into the street and stretched. Traffic was light on this lower part of Broadway –for now, he thought. The light was in his favor and he walked out to the middle of the roadway. He finished a satisfying yawn and gazed up at the gothic grandeur of Grace Church, still standing since, what, eighteen forty-something, he pondered.

Murray looked north. No sign of the march yet. He admired the canyon of Broadway as it ran at him, arrow straight, all the way from Midtown Manhattan down through Union Square Park. The tip of the Empire State Building loomed in the distance just above the greenery.

Murray turned to the south where Broadway again ran in a perfectly straight line all the way down to The Battery at the tip of Manhattan. Broadway made its one and only turn right where Murray stood at Tenth Street with Grace Church at the vortex.

Amazing, he thought. He could look south and have a clear view of The Woolworth Building, at one time the tallest building in the world; and then look to the north and see the spire of The Empire State Building: two icons separated by a distance of three miles, planted on the most crowded island on Earth, and yet visible through the most striking man-made canyon a pair of eyes had ever seen. I love New York.

The light changed. Murray stepped back toward the SUV and around to the sidewalk. Broadway ran one way southbound, so the SUV was at the left curb, with Hearn's window open to the sidewalk.

Dan pointed to the scanner under the dash. "They're approaching Broadway now. Sounds like The Disorder Control Unit is setting up at the corner of Fourteenth and Broadway to turn them south, just like you said."

Murray looked north. Sure enough, the bright orange mesh barrier became visible four blocks up. "Yeah, I see it." Then Murray turned his attention to the passing traffic.

Within a moment, an unmarked radio car crept up with two sets of eyes scanning every inch. They slowed at the sight of the SUV and looked closely. Murray smirked, waiting for the driver's eyes to meet his. Intel Detective, Bronx guy, can't remember his name. Murray kept smiling until the detective's eyes met his. When they did, he recognized Murray right away. They nodded to each other and the unmarked rolled on, continuing its survey of the route.

Murray turned back north to see the intersection at Fourteenth Street fill with bodies. "They've lost it." He stepped closer to Hearn's window and peered up the avenue. "They're going to end up giving them the whole roadway if they don't tighten it up."

"Small wonder." Dan scrolled around on an iPad. "Someone just created a Facebook group, and..." He fingered the screen some more, "...you wouldn't believe the number of tweets going out about this march."

"From who?"

"NYU. Some student group." Hearn looked up. "You

know we're practically 'on-campus' right here."

Murray surveyed the storefronts and building entrances in the immediate vicinity. He realized the Main NYU Bookstore was just three blocks to his left.

The side streets suddenly flowed with people, mostly students. Hundreds of people poured onto the sidewalks from the streets to the south: Astor Place, Waverly Place, Washington Place. Then thousands.

"Shit," Murray laughed. "Intel has it all regarding structures, utilities, facilities —you name it." He looked at Hearn and his iPad. "But on local culture, not so much."

"Yeah," Hearn smirked. "If they'd ever ask the local sector cops, maybe they'd know something." He looked up at the crowd growing around them. "There's over ten thousand kids that live right here in these dorms. Twenty thousand, total when you count the commuter students."

The head of the march approached. Murray could hardly see this Mohamed guy through the crowd. Beyond his wife at his side and his few closest operatives, a small cluster of Community Affairs detectives in light blue windbreakers obscured him.

Murray watched the communication flow from the Community Affairs detectives right next to Mohamed's people out to the uniform lieutenant who relayed info and intel to the chiefs at headquarters over the radio and then from the lieutenant to the intel detectives on the fringe of the march.

"What a mess," Murray remarked.

"Should I get this thing out of here?" Hearn reached for the gear shifter.

"No, let it pass, we'll be fine."

The demonstration now filled the entire street and

marked radio cars began appearing at the forward intersections, closing cross-town traffic as the marchers flowed through. Once the procession passed their location, those radio cars would then speed around the blocks and re-appear three blocks in front of the march. Leap frog.

A brand new, sparkling clean radio car pulled up to the corner of Tenth Street. A uniformed captain emerged with two more lieutenants. Murray watched as the leaders used hand signals to muster out a platoon of cops that had pulled up behind them in vans.

"Looks like this is finally getting the attention it deserves," Murray said.

Hearn looked up at Murray. "Yeah, it's the top story on the news radio right now."

Mohamed and his wife now walked even with Murray in front of Grace Church. Murray got a good look and noticed that the man held up a book in each hand. Murray focused in and realized that one was a Bible and the other, the Koran. He also noticed that Mohamed's wife was strikingly beautiful.

"Wow," Hearn said from inside the SUV. "She's some looker."

"Yeah," Murray said. "Reminds me of the Queen of Jordan, the most beautiful woman in the world."

Hearn did a quick Google search on the iPad. "Sultana Aisha al-Wahid."

Then, above all the sounds of the city, a sharp but distant crack pierced the air. Murray instinctively fell flat on the sidewalk. He knew the sound of a high-powered rifle when he heard it. Hearing just one shot, he peeled himself off the ground and moved as far as the cover of the SUV. He peered in to find Hearn laid out across the front seat. Dan looked up. "Sniper?"

Murray poked his head up over the windowsill. "Fuckin' eh." He stood up straight and looked out into the street. "Christ, they nailed him. Mohamed's been fuckin' assassinated."

The stillness of shock held the moment frozen in time. The Sultana stood motionless, blood splattered across her shoulder and onto her face, her eyes wide, her jaw slack. Mohamed lay dead at her feet. The Community Affairs detectives and some others in her immediate vicinity lay flat on the street, calling for her to join them and get out of harm's way. Murray watched real-time creep back into her eyes. Shock was not replaced, however, by fear. Instead of taking cover, the woman reached down to her husband's hands and removed the books.

The rifle shot's echo subsided through the canyon and the realization of what had just occurred spread throughout the throng of thousands. The invisible surge of panic emanated from the epicenter. Like sprinters in a starting block, thousands of people turned to escape the danger. But Sultana did not. Murray watched her stand up tall and raise the two books above her head. Tears streamed down her face, and she began to march. She went forward down Broadway, Bible and Koran held high.

In place of panic, inspiration, nearly visible, gushed through the crowd. The inward crush of people toward the Sultana was nearly unstoppable. The uniform cops in the immediate vicinity were torn between their duties of maintaining a crime scene and their own human awe of this magnificent woman.

Municipal resources now mobilized into lower Manhattan on a grand scale. Within seconds, Murray heard the roar of an Aviation Unit over head. Three blocks down, the howl of air brakes on two separate War Wagons filled the Avenue. A phalanx of uniform cops filled the street one block down, moving building to building like a blue wall. No mesh this time –Hats and Bats.

In formation, the uniform cops split down the middle – left face, right face, and the barrier of blue became a reception line along the edges of the street. The Sultana led tens of thousands of people through the gauntlet and on to City Hall –before the eyes of the world.

55

Jimmy bit his tongue. Chiefs and Indians and every imaginable resource poured into the City Hall area and all he wanted to do was scream, 'I fucking told you so.' He turned to Clark. "Get Jack on the phone."

Once news of the assassination came over the air, they had to give up on restricting the demonstrators on Chambers Street to just the sidewalk. Not only did people swarm out of the surrounding office buildings and residences, but now actual heads of state and world leaders from the UN General Assembly began showing up in droves.

Limousines and satellite-adorned press vans flooded in from the east and south. Jimmy heard from a newly-arrived pair of Intel Detectives that word in the General Assembly was: if you were in favor of a lasting peace, now you had to show it by coming down here. Jimmy shook his head. He asked the Intel guys if they ever got snipers put in place down here; but they didn't know: "Gotta call special ops for that, Captain." The march approached from the north. Clark handed the phone to Jimmy. Jimmy shouted into it: "Jack. Anything?"

"I don't know, Captain. Maybe it's the long-abandoned, secret subway station directly beneath you? Do you know about that?"

"I know about it. But, hold on." He turned to his lieutenant. "Kevin, do we know if there is a Transit contingent in place regarding the City Hall subway station?" He pointed to the ground, referring to the historic but hidden iconic cavern below them.

Clark frowned. "Is that all he could come up with? Of course Transit is down there, they always are. Hold on." Kevin turned and rose up on his tiptoes. He looked across the lawn between The Tweed Courthouse and the City Hall Rotunda at the normally locked subway grates hidden in the landscaping. Seeing two Emergency Service Teams armed with machine guns, and ballistic helmets in place, he turned back to Jimmy. "Yeah, it's covered."

"No, Jack, that's not it. Keep looking." He hung up and gave the phone back to Clark. Chief Shea showed up. In his usual manner, the Chief of Detectives remained calm under the mounting pressure.

"Hey, Jim, I didn't get a chance to congratulate you the last time we spoke. I understand you're engaged to be married; that's great." Shea put his hand out to shake Jimmy's.

Not taken aback, Jimmy shook his hand. The Chief had a propensity for lightening things up in the midst of battle, ensuring that those around him felt some of his confidence. "Yes, Chief; thank you, sir."

"Have you made honeymoon plans?" As they chatted, Chief Shea was constantly battered with handwritten notes and gestures from his ever-present entourage of detectives, but didn't miss a beat, speaking with Jimmy.

"My bride and I went to Hawaii. I highly recommend it." The crowd crushed in further and forced them toward the foot of the small stage set up on the corner of Broadway and Chambers.

"Uh, no sir, we haven't made those plans yet, sir. But —"

"You'll love it." The Chief glanced at a text message, responded with one letter, and continued. "Brush up on your Japanese if you go, Jim. Everywhere we went in Hawaii, there were more Japanese tourists than anything... streets signs are all written in both English and Japanese. Did you know that? Interesting, isn't it?"

Jimmy just looked at him. He marveled at how the man had his eye on every little detail and his finger on the pulse of the action, and yet could shoot the breeze like this. It actually did relax Jimmy a bit, though. "That is pretty interesting, Chief." Then he smiled. "Did you visit Pearl Harbor?"

Chief Shea smiled. He responded as if the small talk was a reverie even for him.

"Ha, funny you ask that, Jim. Yes we did. And we didn't see any Japanese tourists at the Pearl Harbor Memorial." He put his hand on Jimmy's upper arm and looked him directly in the eye. "How you doing?"

Jimmy frowned. "He's here, Chief, I can feel it. But I just don't know where or why. It's frustrating."

"I know. Well, hang in there. We're putting everything we have on the table here; hopefully he'll show himself and we'll defeat him." He patted Jimmy on the back and walked off.

Jimmy made his way through the crowd to the far side of the street. The small stage on the corner had been cleared of anyone but Siban and a few chosen event organizers.

Now the crowd crushed in around it. The Sultana arrived at Chambers Street. She stopped in front of the stage and Siban came down the two steps to greet her. He bowed deeply before her.

For a brief moment, with hundreds of thousands of people already in place and tens of thousands more filing in behind Sultana Aisha al-Wahid, there was complete silence.

The blood across her face and shoulder had not yet fully dried. She remained stoic and climbed the steps, aided by Siban, still holding the books. The crowd pressed in.

Helicopters, both police and press, hovered high overhead. Horses, motorcycles, and platoon after platoon of cops filed up from lower Broadway and across the City Hall lawn from the foot of the Brooklyn Bridge. The crowd burgeoned out. It seemed that not even the buildings could contain them.

The huge buildings were standing tall, occupying their place in history, and witnessing more being made. Jimmy looked across at the Evening Sun Clock, then over at the majestic Tweed Courthouse. Every bit of history spoken for, marked out, and celebrated. He caught a glimpse of Chief Shea over by the stage. He thought about their conversation. He looked out again at all the historic markers before him. Then it hit him.

"Oh, my God. The Manhattan Project." He pulled out his cell phone and got Jack on the line. "Jack. The Manhattan Project. Tell me why they called it that."

"Called what that?"

"Jesus Christ, Jack, even you don't know that? The development of the atom bombs we dropped on Japan! The project was headquartered somewhere in the area; that's why it became known as The Manhattan Project. Find out exactly why. And where. I'm staying on the line. Work fast, Jack."

Jimmy held the phone to his ear and turned in every direction. He took in every nearby address. Directly across from him was 275 Broadway. The building he stood in front of, converted to condominiums years ago, was 270 Broadway. He scanned and scanned, waiting for Jack.

Of course, there would be no monument, he realized: that's a page in our history we're not particularly proud of. He put himself in the mind of Zafir. *You son of a bitch. That's it, isn't it. You've got a fucking nuke and you want to set it off right here where we designed and developed them into existence. You son of a bitch.*

"Jack, hurry, what the fuck do you have on this?"

"Okay, okay, I'm getting things loaded up. You're right, Captain. It was called the Manhattan Pr-"

"Get me a fucking address, Jack."

"Yes sir, yes sir... There were numerous sites throughout the world, but in New York... -let's see, uh, Columbia University, Syracuse, uh... Okay, I got it. 270 Broadway, that's where the U.S. Army Corps of Engineers were headquartered. They quarterbacked the entire proj-"

"What floor, Jack?"

"Oh, uh... Eighteen."

56

Zafir looked out the eighteenth floor window of 270 Broadway and watched the world gather at his feet. He felt a tingle in his spine. He turned to Nagreb. "Send it now." Then he pulled on his gloves –just in case.

Nagreb obeyed and Zafir watched him send the video to all manner of social media –YouTube, Facebook, Twitter, and the like –and now to all the major news outlets around the world. It may take a few moments, he realized, but he would know when. He watched the crowd below and anticipated their reaction. Heads would rise first; then he would act.

He ran through the video again, frame by frame, in his mind. Two days ago, he'd had Nagreb film the opening shot from down on Chambers Street. Zafir himself had done the voiceover.

The film focused in on the eighteenth floor of this building and Zafir condemned the United States of America and its allies for the evil they had introduced to mankind here in this very place. Then it cut to himself, in Nagreb's Brooklyn apartment last night. He showed them the suitcase weapon. He opened it, explained how it would function, and showed them the key. He didn't bother explaining how he'd gotten the key: that was not material to today's action. He simply needed them to recognize what was happening at the moment when he would release the suitcase out onto the cable. They needed to know. He wanted them to see it coming and to understand why.

He stood at the window fingering the cable strung

through the steel eyelet bolted to the top of the suitcase. Then the crowd stirred and the attention of many moved upward to the building. He watched the information spread through the crowd to those even without the electronic devices necessary to receive the news.

It moved like a wave until every face below him looked up. He opened the window fully, the silence of the apartment suddenly infiltrated by the crowd's noise from below. He slid the suitcase out onto the windowsill. He knew that once he inserted the key and turned it, detonation would occur after ten seconds. He positioned the key for insertion. A sudden loud crash came from behind him. He turned to look. Panic knifed into his very soul at the sight of Captain Gallagher bursting through the apartment door and sprinting across the room toward him.

"No." Zafir raised his left hand toward Gallagher and the suitcase slid out onto the wire. Zafir watched it slide down toward the crowd, the key still in his hand. He felt Gallagher's hands on him. His misfortune overwhelmed him —but also motivated him like never before in his life. Without turning to look at Gallagher, he raised his left leg and kicked the man in the groin with all his strength. Then he jumped out the window.

57

Jimmy couldn't believe his eyes. The guy jumped out the fucking window –eighteen floors up. He rushed over and stuck his head out and looked down. But Zafir wasn't splattered on the sidewalk like Jimmy expected; he was sliding down a cable in pursuit of the nuke. "Oh, shit." Jimmy, like everyone else on Earth, had seen the two-minute video. Jack had sent it to Jimmy's iPhone and he'd watched it on his run up the eighteen flights. He understood exactly what was happening. He could actually see Zafir holding the key in his mouth so he could grab the cable with two hands.

Jimmy watched Zafir slide toward the atom bomb. "Shit." Jimmy realized he had no choice. "This is gonna hurt." He climbed out the window, grabbed ahold of the cable, and slid out after him.

"S-1 to Special Ops base, I have acquired the target. Ready for the go-ahead."

"Special Ops base to S-1, are there civilians in your background?"

Detective Sergeant Anthony Acosta, the NYPD's most proficient sniper, took his eye out of the scope for just a second. From the roof of 51 Chambers Street, he watched Zafir dangling from the cable and struggling to insert the key into the suitcase.

From the high angle of Acosta's sniper perch fifteen floors up, thousands of people were directly below Zafir. "That is affirmative, base; civilians are in my line of fire, below the target." Acosta responded knowing that even if he hit the target, his high-powered rifle round could possibly go right through the man and take out someone in the crowd below. "S-1 standing by for orders." He put his eye back on the scope.

The voice of the Chief of Detectives came over the air: "Fire." Jim Shea called the shot. He weighed the pros and cons for no more than a split second. Take out one civilian —maybe, or possibly lose them all… no brainer.

Sergeant Acosta put his eye back on the scope. He let out one last breath. When all the air was removed from his lungs, he willed his heart to slow nearly to a stop. No breath, no pulse. He began his smooth trigger pull. He could feel the firing pin about to release when something blurred in his crosshairs. "What the –" He pulled his head up off the scope. Then he smiled broadly. "Captain Gallagher, you goddamn lunatic."

After the first two seconds on the cable, Jimmy realized what a fucking mistake this was. The skin ripped off his hands and he threw his feet up onto the cable in front of him to share the weight. Now the leather on his shoes began burning from the friction.

He tried to remove one hand from the cable and hook his forearm around it, hoping his jacket would protect his skin, but he nearly fell to his death. He repositioned his grip over and over, but the cable now cut nearly to the bone. He couldn't see Zafir clearly; his own legs were in the way. But when he hit him, he felt it. He crashed into Zafir about three-quarters of the way down the wire.

His hands were useless. He began kicking Zafir without even looking at him. He glanced downward for a microsecond. Mistake. He was still at least a hundred feet in the air. One false move and he was dead. He kicked and kicked for all he was worth. His downward slide stopped; he was able to get his forearms around the cable. He dropped his legs and got a good look at Zafir. The kicking had helped. Zafir had put the key back in his mouth, but now reached for it with one gloved hand.

The noise from above and below was deafening. Ambulance and fire truck sirens blared in while choppers dropped as low as they dared from above. Hundreds of thousands of people screamed, trampled, and shouted. Jimmy took a deep breath and let loose with the strongest kick he could muster. It worked. Zafir cringed so badly, he lost his grip. He plummeted out of sight immediately. Not a second later Jimmy heard an awful splat. The sound of the crowd's reaction was even worse.

Then his arms began to slip. He tried to get his feet up on the cable again. He just didn't have the strength; not after what he'd just been through from Boston to this very moment. He tried to re-grip with his arms, but could barely raise his weight at all.

The sounds of an FDNY ladder truck came from below. His left arm slid off completely. He tried grabbing the cable with his left hand, but the hand wouldn't obey. The top half, from the knuckles up, was nearly severed off. Jimmy looked down again. *I may not make it,* he realized. The incredibly loud blare of the ladder truck drowned out all other sounds. His right arm began to slip. He desperately tried to kick his legs up over the cable again; but to no avail. He heard a voice in the near distance.

The fire truck, against all industry standards and safety regulations, had begun raising its ladder before the truck came to a stop. When it had finally blared through the crowd and pulled up underneath, the man in the bucket came close. But Jimmy was about to fall now, and he knew it. The voice called for him to stop kicking: −"I'm coming for you."

Jimmy relaxed his legs and let them drop. The dead weight made it worse. His arms slipped off. He fell. But right into the bucket. He lay there on the floor of the container for a moment, stunned.

Above the incredibly loud blare of the ladder truck below, little else could be heard. Then the siren stopped. And Jimmy noticed that the crowd of hundreds of thousands of people below, with the eyes of the world focused through hundreds of live news cameras amongst them, fell completely silent.

He tried to grasp the side of the bucket to pull himself up, but his hands were useless. The fireman reached down and helped him up. Jimmy stood and looked out over the rail of the bucket.

A seismic roar came up from the crowd. They cheered so loud, it nearly shook the surrounding skyscrapers. Jimmy looked at the fireman to thank him. When their eyes met, Jimmy smiled broadly but shook his head. "Oh, no."

John Wilson smiled back. "There you go again, just hangin' around."

Father O'Leary looked up at a bright autumn sky. A brief wind blew through and colorful leaves fluttered out from the tall surrounding trees. The leaves wafted all around him and he smiled. He brought his gaze back down to the gathering before him. As a Jesuit priest, Patrick O'Leary had performed hundreds —nay, thousands —of wedding ceremonies; but none quite like this.

Jessica's mother didn't insist that a Rabbi be present for the wedding, Jimmy did. As Father O'Leary understood it, Mrs. Shore only hinted at it, and that was all Jimmy needed to turn this into an interfaith ceremony. Jessica was only Jewish on her father's side, and the elder Mr. Shore had passed away some years ago. 'But still," is what Jimmy had said.

Father O'Leary smiled again and looked back up at the sky. He stood at the tree line of Rocket's place, his back to Lake Tappan, now visible through the colorful but vanishing leaves. A white-ribboned trellis stood between him and the scores of attendees, all seated in white folding chairs awaiting the bride's appearance.

Just past the trellis, Jimmy stood alone, grinning nervously. Father O'Leary turned to the man on his left. Rabbi Kass, one of the NYPD's Department Chaplains, held an old and tattered Bible and smiled out at the attendees. Then Father O'Leary turned to the man on his right. Imam Siban smiled at him and held the Koran with both hands.

The Catholic priest saw it now, more clearly than ever.

The struggles. And the parallels with the history of his own people and his own faith. He put his hand on Siban's shoulder and smiled. He prayed, as he knew Siban did, that his people could find a similar solution —that the supporters of Islamic extremism would have their own Omagh moment one day. Siban smiled back. Father O'Leary let his hand slip off and thought: *one day, with God's help.*

And so it would be —a tri-faith ceremony. And, Father O'Leary realized, it was an honor to be a part of it.

Through the colorful swirling leaves and from the bright blue sky came the shrill call of the bagpipes. The NYPD Emerald Society Pipe and Drum Corps rounded the house and marched up the aisle. Amazing Grace. How sweet the sound. The pipers finished their tribute and marched off down the side aisles and there she was, at the back of the aisle: the beautiful bride.

In keeping with the environs of Rocket's place and her own earthy style, Jessie wore a simple off-the-shoulder white dress, tailored to appear frayed at the edges. She wore sandals. For a headpiece, her sister's two daughters, seven and nine, had sat with her all morning and made a beautiful crown of flowers, branches, and ribbons.

Her hair was tied back under it and fell forward over her left shoulder in a thick French braid. She held a bouquet of white roses and, Father O'Leary thought, couldn't have been more beautiful.

Next to her, Murray Elfman stood tall and firm with the diminutive Jessie's hand resting inside his bent forearm.

The band, off at the far corner of the property, stirred up the wedding march and Murray walked Jessica up the aisle.

Jimmy waited patiently to kiss the bride while the clerics

performed a unique and beautiful ceremony. When the holy men were done, Jimmy turned to Jessica. They stared deeply into one another's eyes until a tear welled up and slid down Jessie's cheek.

Jimmy lost it. He nearly cried like a baby. And he didn't just kiss her; he swept her up off her feet and twirled her around under the trellis. The crowd roared and the band let loose.

There was dancing, cocktails, and some good old time rock and roll. Hors d'oeuvres floated by on tuxedo-ed waitstaff trays, and dinner would be served in another hour. Jimmy and Jess moved from table to table and spent a few minutes at each.

Eventually, Jessie's two nieces, one on each hand, pulled her away to come sit with Grandma. Jimmy settled in at Kevin Clark's table with Jack, Hatim, and Siban and their guests. Jimmy had met Mrs. Clark a number of times and the two of them, with Kevin, fell into conversation. Mrs. Clark commented on how pretty young Jack Donohue's date was. Kevin smirked, as usual. "I don't know how he has time for a girlfriend."

"Well, maybe if you didn't let him work all those hours..." Mrs. Clark showed where Kevin got his facial expressions.

Murray blustered over. He dropped a huge paw on Clark's shoulder. "When are you going to pack it in and actually work for a living? We could use an old war horse like you at the firm."

Clark shook his head. "The day I pack it in is the last day I go to work —for anyone. When I'm done, I'm done." He looked at his wife. "We're out of here."

Murray looked at Mrs. Clark. She smiled up at him from

her seat. "Georgia, I've got family."

Jimmy stood with Murray. Together they surveyed the crowded reception. Friends, family, and cohorts mingled, danced, and drank together as the band played on.

"C'mon," Jimmy nudged Murray, "let's go say hello to the old man." They made their way across the field to Mister Gallagher's table. They bumped into Rocket along the way.

"Geez, Jimmy," Murray said while looking Rocket up and down. "How'd you get him to put on a tie?"

Jimmy laughed. "Wasn't easy."

Rocket glared at Murray with a look that launched a thousand deaths. Murray returned the gesture until they both slid softly into knowing grins. Rocket turned to Jimmy with a most sincere smile. "Nice work out there, kid; proud of you."

"Thanks, John." Jimmy looked around at the reception. "For everything."

"Love ya, kid." Rocket patted him on the shoulder and walked on.

Mister Gallagher, retired Captain and long-time CEO, stood as Jimmy approached his table. "Hey, Pops." Jimmy walked around to his father's side. Joseph Gallagher pulled a pair of cigars from inside his suit jacket. He gave one to Jimmy and pulled out a lighter. After lighting his own cigar, he lit Jimmy's cigar for him. They puffed them until they glowed and sighed back to the table. Everyone smiled up at them and Jimmy nodded to Johnny Dineen. "Hey, John, how are you feeling?"

Dineen touched his sling. "I'm getting there, kiddo; how about you?"

"I'll be all right," Jimmy held up his hands, "soon enough." Then he looked at Mike Kelly, his father's old-time friend from the west side, sitting next to Dineen. Still looking at Kelly and Dineen, he said to his father, "Now there's an unholy alliance." Everyone laughed.

"You know, Jim," Joseph Gallagher put his hand on Jimmy's shoulder, "the ends of justice, much like politics and religion, can make for strange bedfellows."

"Don't I know it," Jimmy nodded.

His father turned to him and spoke privately: "So what's next for you, Jim?"

Jimmy looked quizzically at his father. "Hawaii."

"That's not what I meant, son."

Jimmy grinned. "No, I know." He took a deep breath and looked out across the lake. "I'm not sure."

Joseph Gallagher gestured to Jimmy's bandaged hands, "You know, you could probably get a disability pension based on that injury. You nearly lost both your hands."

Jimmy looked down at the bandages. "Yeah, I suppose."

"There's plenty of work out there for a man like you."

Jimmy looked at his father. "Yeah, I don't know."

"Well, Jim, I might be retiring from the business myself, one of these days." He looked around at the table before them. "And then who's going to watch Murray?"

Jimmy laughed, "Ha. Now that's a job you couldn't pay me enough to do."

"Right; no one can do that job, actually." They puffed their cigars another moment and the old man hugged his son across the shoulders. "We've made much headway into the marketplace. Now, after this case, there'll be many more contracts for us.. Let me know."

Jimmy nodded. "I will, Dad, I will." They pulled up chairs and re-joined the table of family and friends.

THE GUNS OF ANTWERP
NYPD Takes Boston
is the second book in the Jimmy Gallagher series.

Please turn the page for a preview of the first in the series,
HEAD ON
NYPD Dies Hard

1

The unmarked car—no lights, no sirens—joined the rush hour traffic gathering along Lexington Avenue. Alone in the back seat, Jimmy tossed his notes up front and turned sideways for a better look. He knew he shouldn't stop–his promotion interview at One Police Plaza was a half hour away and this is exactly how he'd gotten jammed up the last time.

He slid across the back seat, closer to the driver's side window. Only 39 years old but nearing his twentieth year with the NYPD, Jimmy was never good at making these kinds of decisions. He let his instincts guide him. And his instincts as a street cop were never wrong–ever—but they often ran contrary to his political survival. And in that arena, he had no instincts. He had tried to learn; he listened to his father and even got a formal education at John Jay College, attending day and night for ten years; but the street called louder at moments like this.

The light at Eighty-Sixth Street turned green and the unmarked again began to crawl forward. The scrum of commuters that just came up out of the subway and onto the sidewalk actually outpaced the car as they approached the corner. Jimmy slid his hand onto the door handle and studied his subject. He watched with the eyes of a man who had been on patrol his whole life. As a child with an absentee, then-drunken father, living in a rotten neighborhood, he learned to spot the ones with 'bad' on their minds.

The group of commuters reached the corner and sifted off in different directions—now he was convinced of what he saw. But still, the thought of pissing off the Police Commissioner lingered. His resurrection was nearly complete. After some of the wild shit he'd pulled over the years, today he would be interviewed for a high-level counterterrorism job. And, as he'd been told numerous times, he should consider himself lucky to have even made Captain three years ago. But Jimmy just couldn't drive by possible bad guys. Even his father, sober these last thirty years and a respected, retired Captain himself, told him he should learn when to put the blinders on. Jimmy smirked, remembering his answer to that: "I don't own a set, sorry."

It made him think of his first interaction with the police when he was eight years old. He'd never forget the fear that shot straight into his heart through his mother's hand as they were being mugged. And then a moment later when a big man in a blue uniform turned the corner and those muggers ran off, the injection of relief at the sight of this hero. But the muggers only ran across to the other side of The Concourse. They saw the cop wasn't chasing them. They stopped and taunted. Then came that lazy shrug. 'Look, it was a bad neighborhood; there were worse things going on, blah, blah.' Jimmy would never forget that taunting, or the fear, or his own anger. But mostly, he never forgot that lazy shrug.

Without taking his eyes off the street, he reached around the front seat and tapped his driver on the shoulder. "Frankie, make a left." All thoughts of career and promotion had fled.

One hour earlier

From the inside, Ibrahim unlocked the two deadbolts on the apartment door but didn't open it. He turned back and gently placed his hand on the young man's shoulder. He wanted to look Masul in the eye one last time and say goodbye. After these months of living together, Ibrahim had fallen into the trap of seeing the humanity in these young men. Ibrahim himself was only thirty-three years old and the five fedayeen in his charge were just ten to fifteen years younger. But their hearts and minds were far less developed. Ibrahim firmed his grip on Masul's shoulder and peered into the eyes of his charge. Nothing there. Ibrahim frowned grimly and opened the door of apartment 3C. He tousled the youngster's hair and watched him turn out into the hallway.

Ibrahim closed the door behind the suicide bomber. It would only take a few minutes for the fedayeen to go upstairs to apartment 4C and have his bomb vest filled with explosives. The detonators were already set. Ibrahim figured he may as well wait here by the door rather than go back into the living room and deal with the two escorts. His four remaining fedayeen were asleep in the back bedrooms. No sense in waking those young men, their time would come soon enough.

He leaned his forehead against the door and closed his eyes to hear better. He would miss young Masul's docile spirit. Shame. Ibrahim could hear the two escort soldiers chatting quietly behind him in the living room, waiting. The two vicious killers had arrived during the night at different times.

The sharp click of a lock opening in the hall made

Ibrahim's heart jump. He pulled his head off the door and looked out through the peephole. Then he relaxed. The old woman across the hall in apartment 3B was going out for groceries again. He watched her struggle to the stairs, pulling her empty cart behind her. She would peruse the shops of their Brooklyn neighborhood and be back in one hour—she always was—and that cart would be full of provisions. America. Ibrahim had been casually hailed by her and other residents of the building at the local markets. Since he remained clean-shaven and polite, none had given him more than a passing salutation. His status remained safe.

Ibrahim closed the peephole and leaned his forehead back against the door. He was tired. He realized his motivation was slipping, too. His once-burning desire to murder the enemy glowed less brightly now. When he joined Fateh in his native Afghanistan, that twelve-year-old Ibrahim wanted nothing more than to fight and kill Americans. That young boy had watched the aunt and uncle who'd raised him die a violent and horrible death during an American air strike. He and his cousins Jaouni and Leila, who'd lost their parents in that strike, then went into training together. Jaouni and Leila tested high on the academic assessments and so were sent to Iran to become educated. Ibrahim had only spoken to Leila since, but he and Jaouni each managed conjoining cells in the network and saw each other often.

He sensed a few beads of sweat forming at his hairline. He lifted his forehead off the door and wiped it with the back of his forearm. He stood up straight and confirmed for himself that his devotion to Islam had not wavered. However, the more he read the Koran lately, the more confusing it all became.

He stuffed his hands down into his jeans pockets and leaned his shoulder on the door. He consoled himself with the thought that once he completed his part in launching today's mission, there were only four more fedayeen left for him to take care of. He sighed. In three days their escorts, too, would arrive. And then it would be finished. He held onto the promise that if he completed this current mission with no mistakes, he would be allowed to go and live a private and productive life anywhere he wished. Three more days.

Finally, footsteps descended the stairs from above. Masul was returning from the armory apartment. Ibrahim turned back to the living room and signaled for the escort team to come forward. He glanced down at the sneakers of the first escort. Though shorter than most, the man stepped up to Ibrahim, squatted, and jumped nearly to the ceiling to show his physical ability to run. Then he squatted again and tugged on his laces to show that his sneakers were properly tied.

The second escort was taller. He smoothed his hands over the front of his windbreaker to show no visible bulge. Then he smiled at Ibrahim and lifted the front of his jacket. A large, semi-automatic handgun sat neatly tucked inside his slim waistband. Ibrahim nodded only with his eyelids and turned to the door.

They were ready. Ibrahim opened the door and the runner, followed by the fighter, went out into the third floor hallway. Ibrahim watched as each escort patted his young fedayeen on the back. He observed them engage in their training and go single file down the stairs with the runner in the lead, followed by the glassy-eyed bomber, the keen fighter disappearing last from the landing.

Ibrahim stepped back inside the apartment and closed the

door. It was quiet beyond a soft snore coming from the back bedroom. Ibrahim thought he would go into the living room and watch some American television; take his mind off things. But instead he just stood there in the hallway, leaning on the door. He couldn't get his mind away from all the innocent people that were about to die. Except, of course, for the target himself: he was not innocent, but many others would die, too. Ibrahim continued standing alone in the quiet hallway and a shiver ran down his spine.

2

In the bustle of commuters Jimmy noticed some condescending frowns attempting a cover of patience with their slower counterparts. Then he noticed that all those New York scowls had the same targets.

That group of three morphing through the crowd were slowing everyone down and were pretending not to be together. They stole glances at one other, ensuring they moved in the same direction—all Arabs. Jimmy watched the disconnected group make their way to the corner of Eighty-Sixth Street. One of them looked like 'special needs' or something. Interesting trio. Jimmy almost forgot he was in uniform and had to back away a little from the car window.

"Go ahead, Frank, make the left in front of these pedestrians."

Jimmy saw his driver, Detective Frank Ramirez, look up at him in the rear view mirror. "No problem, Captain, but don't you have some place to be?"

"Yeah, well," Jimmy glanced back out the side window. "We have to check these guys out—might be nothing, but let's at least talk to them." Jimmy looked out the front windshield, then back at the three. They seemed to be crossing south also, same as the car, but with a left, easterly angle.

"Go ahead, make the left." Jimmy watched the stream of pedestrians clear the crosswalk as Ramirez waited to turn. The timing looked to be just about right. Sure enough, Jimmy got a good look as the trio passed right in front of the car.

Jimmy checked Ramirez' eyes in the mirror.

"You see what I see?"

The trio continued to satellite each other and angled for the bus stop on Eighty-Sixth Street. One of them, the one with the windbreaker, looked over his shoulder and directly into the car. Ramirez looked away and mumbled, "I don't know you, you don't know me–yeah." Frankie said, "They're up to something."

"Pull in the bus stop."

Ramirez weaved the unmarked through the remaining strands of pedestrians and pulled ahead to the curb in the open bus stop. He threw the car in Park. "Okay, how do you want to play it?"

"I like it head on." Jimmy pushed open the passenger side door.

"Yeah." Ramirez pushed open his door. "You always do."

Jimmy got out and stepped onto the curb. He found himself at the front of a line of passengers waiting for the next crosstown bus. The queue lined the curb back toward the corner of Lexington and Jimmy noticed two of his three new friends tail off together around the back of the line and onto the sidewalk.

The shortest of the three, a wiry little fella, broke away from the other two and walked along the curb line right toward Jimmy.

Jimmy stood fast. Through the crowd of commuters, he kept the other two in his peripheral vision and addressed the little one: "What's up there, cool guy?"

"What?" The man stopped about four feet from Jimmy and threw his arms up. "You want something from me?" the man said in decent but heavily accented English. "What's the problem, Officer?"

Jimmy didn't advance toward him. With Ramirez closing in behind the little guy from around the radio car, Jimmy kept his radar on the other two, who'd advanced almost parallel to him, now. They were in single file close to the building line; the spacey-looking one in front 'eagle eyes' in the windbreaker bringing up the rear. Jimmy turned back to the loudmouth at the curb. He called to Ramirez: "Talk to this guy, Frank, I'll be right back."

Jimmy slid sideways to his left and was about to cut the other two off when eagle eyes pulled on the shoulder of his cohort from behind and turned him around. For the second it took the space cadet to respond and walk in the other direction, Mister Windbreaker stood perfectly still and stared hard at Jimmy.

Jimmy knew a bad guy when he saw one, and this guy was the real deal. Jimmy took a quick glance down at the man's waist, looking for the telltale bulge of a weapon. Seeing none, he closed the distance.

Just then the little loudmouth from the curb broke away from Ramirez and ran, screaming, right at Jimmy.

Like a fighter pilot watching out all windows Jimmy angled himself to keep both parties in sight. The little scrapper sprinted directly at him and Jimmy raised his right fist, ready to ram it down into the crazed little man. At the last second, the runner reversed and lunged back toward the curb. He ran to the unmarked, whipped open the front door, dove across the seat, and within moments pulled the gear shifter down and was screeching out into Eighty-Sixth Street traffic.

Ramirez ran out into the street behind the car. Jimmy could see two things in Frankie's eyes: one, the department didn't care how hectic the situation: you lost a car, that was your ass. And the other: Frankie thought he could catch up to the radio car before it broke through the traffic at the next intersection.

Then Jimmy remembered his other two friends and turned to see them hustling back towards Lexington Avenue. A bus approached. Jimmy turned back to Ramirez and just before he lost sight of him, he yelled: "Leave it, Frank; come with me."

The bus suddenly filled the space between them. Jimmy spun off after the other two, who were now down by the end of the line. Jimmy ran toward them. Windbreaker turned around and again pulled the other guy with him.

It looked to Jimmy like the tough guy would use his pal as a shield, but he instead pushed the kid into the crowd of passengers and shouted something to him in a foreign language that Jimmy didn't understand.

Jimmy went right past the strange one and up to the windbreaker. Almost within arm's reach, Jimmy was surprised when the guy lifted the front of his jacket and pulled out a handgun. Jimmy couldn't believe he had missed that bulge. Now he was faced with one of those moments: should he back up and draw his own gun, or close in and try and take this guy's gun away from him?

Again, no decision: just instinct. Jimmy jumped at the guy and grabbed his gun hand just as it came up toward him. Jimmy wrapped both his hands around the gun and tried to wrest it away. Didn't work. Windbreaker was stronger than he looked.

Jimmy gripped the gun with both hands as hard as he could and tried to twist the barrel toward the man. Jimmy felt a little panic when he realized that the guy had only been using one hand, to this point. Windbreaker brought his other hand into the mix now, on top of Jimmy's two hands. Eight the old horse.

Still holding onto the gun, Jimmy burst forward and drove his shoulder into the man's chest, but it was like hitting a fucking wall. Jimmy took a half step back and concentrated all his energy on twisting the gun out of the guy's hand. They stood there, arm's length apart, and wrestled for their lives. Jimmy felt he was losing. The twisting mash of hands and steel turned in toward Jimmy.

The man stopped trying to pull away. Instead, he stepped in towards Jimmy. He pushed the gun in hard at him. Then he suddenly jerked the gun back toward himself. It broke free.

The man lowered the barrel and Jimmy heard the loudest goddamn gunshot his ears had ever endured. The accompanying flash of light nearly blinded him, but he kept his focus and watched the right side of Mister Windbreaker's head blow off onto the sidewalk.

Jimmy dropped to one knee and caught his breath. Looking up from under his brow he said, "Thanks, Frank."

"No problem, boss." Detective Frank Ramirez smiled at Jimmy and holstered his weapon. "I guess it was my turn to watch you today."

Jimmy exhaled an exhausted laugh and stood. "Yeah? So where'd you park the car?"

Frankie tilted his head and deadpanned.

Then Jimmy turned quickly to the bus. "Where's the

other guy? There were three of them." Jimmy looked around and saw the effect of the gunshot on the crowd. The New Yorkers picked their spots and went for cover. Some tried to push their way onto the steps of the bus.

Jimmy and Frank walked around to the front of the bus. Frank scanned the sidewalk and transmitted on the radio, calling for back up and giving directions on the stolen police car.

Together they backed out into the street and Jimmy made wide waves at the bus driver, signaling him not to pull out.

Ramirez turned back from the sidewalk and shook his head—no luck there. Jimmy nodded and together they stepped toward the bus door.

Before the sound came, Jimmy flinched. It seemed that the back of the bus just lifted off the ground by itself. Then Jimmy's eyes flashed blind for a second and his ears seemed to explode inside his head. The percussion lifted him off his feet and tossed him back on the asphalt a good five feet.

Jimmy landed on his butt with his legs flat out in front of him and his palms on the ground on either side. The explosion from inside the back of the bus actually lifted the rear of the twenty-five-thousand pound vehicle about ten feet in the air. The nose of the bus hardly moved, and so for a moment it looked like a wingless plane crashing into the street in front of him.

The burst of light, the percussion, and the incredible sound put him on the verge of shock. He had been here before. He felt his senses drawing back to within. All his outward abilities—sight, hearing, even touch—began to recede rapidly into his core. It was like his mind pulling its hand away from an open flame.

All he had control over at the moment were his thoughts. He first tried to focus his vision. The large windshield of the bus was gone and the driver was draped out over the front of the bus, dead. Jimmy blinked and dragged his legs up underneath himself. He tried to stand.

A sudden stillness hung in the air. In the abrupt silence, he glided toward the bus, his eardrums swollen shut. Slowly his senses crept back to the fore. The reality before him demanded he not succumb to the peace of shock. He had work to do.

He floated toward the sidewalk and the moans began. They always started low at first, and built slowly into screams. Then, like a deadly gas permeating the air, chaos always came next. 'Chaos, the enemy, musn't let that take hold.' He came to completely.

Faces began appearing in shattered shop doorways. Curious, frightened groups formed at either end of the street. Sirens. He turned to look for Ramirez. The detective wandered on the sidewalk, his mind not having fully returned.

"Frank."

Ramirez hesitated and then turned to Jimmy, as if awakened from a dream. "Captain?" The detective stood straight. "Sir, what… what do we-"

"Give me your radio, detective." Jimmy held his hand out and spoke as he would to a man threatening to jump from a ledge. Shock was a dangerous condition, even for an experienced professional. You had to take people out of it gently. Jimmy took command of the radio and began directing the responding resources of the NYPD.

The crowd thickened. Jimmy spoke again into the radio:

"Central, I need the Task Force up here for crowd control–forthwith, please."

"Affirmative, Captain. Task Force enroute," the dispatcher responded. "Captain, do you want a Level Four Mobilization at your location?"

"Negative, Central. Level Three will be sufficient for now; leave the outer borough cars at home."

"Car Three to Central," the radio squawked. "Level Four. Repeat, Level Four Mobilization. Mobilization Point is Eighty-Sixth Street and Lexington Avenue. Be advised, I am in command of the situation. Chief of Department Gates, over."

Jimmy sneered at the radio as if it had malfunctioned. *Chief Gates, you asshole. You just made a major assessment without a conferral. A Level Four wasn't a terrible idea, but you never make a call like that without speaking to the commander at the scene.* Jimmy decided to wait until Gates arrived to discuss it, but for now the mobilization point had to change. He couldn't have a couple hundred cops swarm directly in on the focal point, looking for an assignment. That would only add to the chaos. The mobilization point had to be remote.

"Borough Captain to Central."

"Borough Captain, go."

"Central, inform the Chief that we've got a very large crime scene at Eighty-Sixth and Lex. We need to move the mobilization point over to Third Avenue." Jimmy held out the radio and waited for the Chief's reply.

"Car Three to Central."

"Go, Chief."

"Central, have the captain stay off the air. I'll be 10-84 in two minutes; will advise."

"Captain, read direct Central." Jimmy shook his head and slipped the radio into his back pocket. He turned to the few local sector cars that had already arrived. He directed them to escort the injured around the corner and get a roll of yellow crime scene tape from their car. The department-issued cell phone on Jimmy's gunbelt rang.

"Captain Gallagher."

"Captain, this is Detective Golden, Operations Unit. Stand by for the Police Commissioner."

Jimmy raised his eyebrows and turned in a complete circle with the phone to his ear. He quickly surveyed the bigger picture. His head pounded. That wonderful stillness that transitioned him from shock to operational was gone, now. A furious flurry of activity replaced it. Too much action with not enough direction. He needed help; lots of help.

"Jimmy, what do we have up there?" The Police Commissioner came on the line. Jimmy had enormous respect for Bill Pratt. Jimmy knew him as a man that had done just about every street job in the NYPD on his way up the ranks; and did them well. Unlike Gates who, Jimmy knew, spent his career in every office in One Police Plaza. Also, Pratt had, at one time, been partners with Jimmy's father, Joseph Gallagher.

"Boss, it's bad. We have at least twenty or so dead and many more injured; some seriously. But, it's contained. The affected area appears to not go beyond Eight-Six and Lex."

"I see we have a Level Four going up there?"

"I didn't call that, boss. I called a Level Three. I think we should leave the outer borough cars at home. What if Yankee Stadium or Coney Island is next?"

"Good call, Jimmy. But it's the day tour; we've got

massive amounts of people in the outer boroughs. A Level Four won't hurt, but I do like your assessment. Who called it, anyway? Let me speak to him; hand him the phone."

"Uh, Chief Gates isn't here yet, sir."

There was silence on the line. Jimmy knew that, on his way up the ranks, Pratt had actually authored the disorder control guidelines that said not to change a Mobilization Level without a personal observation. The phone stayed quiet for another second. If the Police Commissioner was going to berate the Chief of Department, he wouldn't do it through the Borough Captain–Pratt was above that.

"Tell Gates to call me on my cell when he arrives," Pratt grunted. "I'm leaving headquarters now. I'll be there in a few minutes."

"Yes sir." The line went dead.

Made in United States
North Haven, CT
21 May 2025